DEATH
AT THE DIOGENES CLUB

DEATH AT THE DIOGENES CLUB

A SHERLOCK HOLMES | LUCY JAMES STORY

BY ANNA ELLIOTT AND CHARLES VELEY

This is a work of fiction. Names, characters, organizations, places, events, and incidents are either products of the author's imagination or are used fictitiously.

Sherlock and Lucy series website: http://sherlockandlucy.com

Typesetting by FormattingExperts.com
Cover design by Todd A. Johnson

ISBN: 978-0-9991191-3-6

CHAPTER 1

Contrary to Doctor Watson's chronicles, the biggest drawback to Sherlock Holmes's character wasn't his use of cocaine, or smoking shag tobacco, or his—admittedly somewhat accurate—view of himself as vastly more intelligent than the entire rest of the human race.

No. I decided within a week of knowing him that the *real* trouble with Sherlock Holmes was that he had no switch to turn his mental powers off and on. Entering into conversation with him was like being a butterfly and *asking* to be skewered by an entomologist's pin; if you spoke to Sherlock Holmes, you placed yourself under the fierce lens of his scrutiny—inescapably.

It made him an excellent detective. As a father, however, it made him more than slightly maddening.

At the moment, he was fixing me with the keen gray gaze that felt as though it could penetrate clear to the back of my skull.

"I understand that you are seeing Constable Kelly tonight."

"*How?*" I demanded. "How can you possibly know that?"

We were standing in the sitting room of number 221A Baker Street, where I had been living for the past two months.

In fairness, it would probably have been easier to keep secrets from Holmes if I had not been living directly downstairs from his own address of 221B. But despite my best efforts, the thought of returning to the flat I kept in Exeter Street still made my skin crawl.

"No, wait, don't tell me." I let my eyes travel across the room. "While I haven't yet changed clothes, the boots I intend to wear are standing ready by the door, I've re-done my hair three times—which is far more trouble than I usually take with it—as evidenced by the scattering of hairpins on my dressing table. And the corner of the music I intend to give to Becky tonight is visible at the top of my handbag."

It was five o'clock on a September evening, which meant that my curtains were drawn against the fog that crawled through the London streets outside. The gas jets above the mantel were lighted, their glow patching Holmes's hawk-like countenance with shadow and throwing his sharp, intelligent features into relief.

He gave me a calm look. "While all those indicators are, now that you mention it, entirely true, in this case my knowledge stems from the telephone call I received earlier from young Miss Kelly. She wished to make sure that you would be coming to St. Giles tonight."

I blew out a breath, silently counting to ten inside my head.

It was not Holmes's fault that I had spent much of the past ten weeks alternately feeling as though my skin was stretched too tight with the effort of containing my frustration with life in general and then at other moments jumping at every noise and seeing an intruder lurking in every shadow.

Holmes was still watching me. "How is Constable Kelly faring?"

"He's ... fine."

If struggling to adjust to a life of having a badly damaged leg could be considered *fine*.

"He says that he's managing."

Holmes's expression didn't change, exactly. But the look in his gray eyes told me that he was no more convinced by Jack's statement than I had been.

"I will turn my attention to thinking what may be done for him."

"*Have* you any thoughts on what may be done for him?" Ordinarily, I would respect Jack's privacy too much to consult with Holmes about him, but at the moment I was willing to try anything.

Holmes's brow furrowed. He was wearing an elaborately patterned silk dressing gown over shirt and trousers, which I took to mean that he wasn't currently involved in any cases.

"My own sovereign remedy springs to mind." He spoke half to himself.

"I think Jack has troubles enough without your encouraging him to become addicted to cocaine."

"That was not the solution to which I was referring." Holmes was silent a moment as though pondering something, then turned his attention back to me. "And how are *you* faring?"

"Fine. Also fine."

Holmes's eyebrows rose slightly, but he didn't question my answer. He had no need to. I knew from looking in the mirror that I had faint purple shadows under my eyes; it wouldn't take a deductive mind like Holmes's to conclude that I hadn't been sleeping well.

Knowing him, he had probably deduced the subject of my recurring nightmare too, though at least he refrained from saying, *I told you so.*

He had warned me of the cost of taking part in his investigations, but I had refused to leave him to face the danger of tracking down a particularly vicious traitor to the crown alone.

And, really, nightmares were a small price to pay for the fact that my father was alive and unharmed.

"Hmmm." Holmes's eyes unfocused, his expression turning to the faintly bored look that meant his thoughts were following some complicated inner track. "I believe I might have heard of something that would suit ..."

Without another word, he turned and vanished back up the stairs.

I crossed to close the door behind him and then went into the bedroom to change.

The second disadvantage to having Holmes for a parent: Only now, after nearly two years' acquaintance, was I becoming even remotely skilled at guessing what he was thinking. And in this case, I had no idea at all.

* * *

The extra trouble I had taken with my hair was actually wasted since whenever I visited Becky and Jack I tucked it under a cloth newsboy's cap. I also wore boots, trousers, and a loose-fitting tweed overcoat so that I could pass for a boy somewhere in his teen years.

Becky and Jack's neighborhood of St. Giles was a warren of dirty, poverty-stricken streets and houses so decrepit that they looked as though a single push would send them falling over. Those same houses were also dens for criminals of all types: pickpockets, smash-and-grab men, prostitutes and their procurers ...

The street where Becky and Jack lived was too narrow to accommodate a carriage, so I had to walk the last block or two. I attracted less notice if I wore male attire and, in the event I had to defend myself, boots and trousers were also significantly more convenient for fighting than petticoats and corsets.

Tonight, a small girl with blond braids was waiting for me at the end of the road, with an enormous brown and white dog seated on the ground beside her.

There were a few other pedestrians about, but even the roughest-looking gave the pair of them a wide berth. Prince, Jack and Becky's mastiff, was an extremely effective deterrent against being assaulted or robbed.

"Becky!" My heart tried to jump up into my throat at the sight of her. "Is something wrong?"

Jack's wounds were healed—externally so, at any rate—and the danger of sepsis had passed. His life could well and truly be considered out of danger. But I couldn't prevent the unpleasant lurch of fear. Another memento of the days when we weren't sure whether Jack was going to live or die.

"Yes—I mean, no." Becky shook her head, looking up at me. "I mean, it's Jack. He's not sick or anything, but he's ..." She stopped, clearly searching for the right words. "He's all *wrong*."

"What do you mean?" I was fairly sure that I already knew the answer, but I didn't want to say it out loud, especially not to Jack's little sister.

Becky's shoulders were stiff. "He hates it. I know he does. He hates everything about not being able to walk properly anymore. But he never says so, and he never complains, never."

"It will take time, but he *is* getting better—" I started.

"*Pigswill!*" Becky interrupted. She looked up at me. In the greenish glare of the street lamps, I could see that there were tears standing in her blue eyes.

"Jack's never out of temper, he's never anything but calm—because he never *lets* himself be anything but calm," Becky went on. "It's like he's keeping himself locked up, tight. But he barely sleeps, and he does those exercises that Doctor Watson gave him so often that I'm afraid he'll hurt himself. I can hear him at night, when he thinks I've gone to bed. He almost never laughs anymore, either, and he won't talk to me, not really, not about anything important, and it's all *wrong*."

Becky stopped, swiping a hand angrily across her eyes.

I put an arm around her, and she leaned against me.

When Becky and I had first met—nearly a year ago now—she had been dressed up as a boy and running away from an enraged tavern owner because she had snuck in to secretly play his piano.

I had known on the spot that we were kindred spirits.

"I'm sorry," I told her now. "It *is* all wrong. The trouble is, I have no idea how to put it right again."

CHAPTER 2

"Try …" I scanned the front page of the newspaper, searching for as short an article as I could find. "Here, try this one."

I pointed to an article headline that read *Public Notice*.

We were sitting side by side at the Kellys' battered and scarred dining table. Becky and I had sung through her music lesson already, and now she was asleep in the inner room of the two rooms of rented lodgings that she and her brother shared. Prince was in the next room too, collapsed across the foot of Becky's bed.

"Public notice." Jack read slowly. "Please be advised that due to normal maintenance, the gas lamps on Pall Mall will be unlit from September 8 through September 16 so that said normal maintenance may be carried out. During the routine maintenance period—"

Jack stopped, and I studied his face, feeling the familiar tightening around my heart, an odd ache that was painful and yet I somehow wouldn't wish away.

It wasn't just that he was handsome—though he was, breath-catchingly so. Jack had almost gypsy coloring: very dark brown hair and eyes, with chiseled features and straight dark brows. He was broad-shouldered and lean, athletically strong in a hard-edged way.

At the moment, he was looking down at the paper with a slight frown between his brows.

"Is something wrong?" I asked.

"I was just thinking—using 'normal maintenance' that many times in one paragraph? It's like saying, *Pay no attention to the tiger at the breakfast table.* Not the kind of thing you'd say if everything actually is just normal routine."

He shook his head. "Never mind, it's probably not important."

He turned back to the newspaper, rubbing his eyes as though they were aching—not that he would have admitted it to me if they were—before going on.

"Pedestrians and carriage traffic should be advised to carry their own"—Jack hesitated for a second—"lamps."

I bit my tongue, stopping myself from correcting him by saying *light*. Except that *not* correcting him probably wasn't doing him any favors. That was the entire purpose of my being here, after all.

Nearly two months ago, Jack had stepped in front of a gun aimed at my father and had been shot twice in the process. The first bullet had struck his shoulder and luckily missed hitting the bone. He had nearly regained the full range of motion of his arm and his strength. But the second bullet had torn through the muscle of his right leg, damaging nerves, ripping tendons, and nearly costing Jack his life.

Now Jack was a beat constable who could no longer walk a beat, and he still had Becky to support.

The Metropolitan Police had strict rules about promotion through its ranks. Usually constables were older and more experienced than Jack before they were encouraged to apply for a promotion to the rank of sergeant. Jack was only twenty-three and had served in the London Metropolitan Police for just under three years.

But he had not only saved the life of Sherlock Holmes, he had also been wounded while foiling a plot to detonate a bomb at the Queen's Diamond Jubilee, assassinate His Royal Highness Prince Albert, and bring down the government.

Jack's superiors had informed him that he was eligible to take the exams to qualify for a sergeant's position. To pass the exams, though, he had to have fluent skills in reading, writing, arithmetic, and the study of English law.

Jack was one of the most quick-witted, observant, and intelligent men I'd ever met, but he had never been to school of any kind. His mother had abandoned him when he was younger than Becky, and he'd grown up alone and homeless on the London streets. It was amazing that he'd taught himself to read as much as he had.

"That wasn't right, was it?"

Jack's voice broke in on my thoughts.

I sighed. I might have known Jack would be able to tell if I tried to make this easier on him.

"No. It's *light. i-g-h* almost always says *i.*"

Jack nodded without speaking. The earlier fog had turned into rain that spattered against the windows and drummed on the roof over our heads.

Three months ago, he had radiated a kind of controlled energy and a competent self-assurance that said he was strong and quick to respond to any threat and that any criminal who crossed paths with him was extremely unwise.

Now Becky was right; the control was still there, but it was … *harder*, somehow, seeming to shut out everyone from coming too close.

Or maybe it was only me he wanted to shut out.

He went on reading slowly but steadily, in an all-but-expressionless tone, moving on to the article just below the notice about the lamps, which seemed to be about the ongoing conflict in northern India. "The two brigades which compose—"

I interrupted him in mid-sentence. "You hate this, don't you."

He looked up at me and, just for a second, a shadow of some unidentifiable expression flickered in his dark eyes. Then it vanished. "It doesn't matter whether I hate it or not. I've still got to learn it."

He looked back at the paper. "The rising of eighteen ninety-seven is the most successful attempt to date to combine the frontier tribes—"

Something seemed to snap inside me.

Three months ago, Jack and I had been … I wasn't entirely sure how to put a name to it, but there had been *something* between us.

He'd never spoken of it, but he had at least looked as though he loved me.

Now he never touched me, ever, not so much as by a brush of his hand. He was perfectly polite, but …

Usually I left extravagant literary metaphors to Watson, but it felt as though Jack looked at me and then firmly closed some invisible door between us.

When Jack had first been shot, I had been afraid he might blame me for it, since he would never have been drawn into the Jubilee affair if not for me. He didn't seem angry now. But then, he didn't seem *anything* now.

I was fairly sure he loathed having had to ask me for help with his reading, but he hadn't had much choice. The exams for promotion would be given in just over a month's time, and unless he passed them, he wouldn't have a way of keeping a roof over his and Becky's head.

Still, I couldn't escape the feeling that my visits here were just one more torturous duty for him to grit his teeth and endure.

"I have another idea." I pushed my chair back from the table and stood up.

Jack stopped reading and looked up, clearly startled.
Good.

It probably wasn't fair to be angry with him, after everything that he had been through. But I suddenly couldn't stand to sit here and be the object of his calm, controlled, impersonal *politeness* for a single second longer.

"I'm out of practice with sparring. Performing at the Savoy doesn't give me very many opportunities to train for hand-to-hand fighting."

Up until now, I had thought Sherlock Holmes was the master of the inexpressive look. After tonight, though, I might have to hand the title over to Jack. The look he gave me was completely level, scrubbed clean of even the faintest flicker of emotion.

"Are you forgetting I've got a crippled leg?"

"Uncle John gave you permission to exercise weeks ago." I raised my eyebrows. "Unless you're afraid that I'll beat you?"

Jack didn't move.

I shrugged. "I suppose I could always try one of the fight clubs in Limehouse. Or I could just walk into one of the beer halls down the road. I imagine I'd find *some* sort of practice in close-range fighting. There aren't exactly a shortage of bar room brawls in this neighborhood."

A muscle tightened in the side of Jack's cheek. "I know what you're trying to do."

I ignored him. "Of course, I won't have to do either of those things if you just get up out of that chair."

I watched as Jack pulled himself to his feet. Becky was right. He must have been doing the strength training exercises that Uncle John had given him practically tirelessly. He had always had a strong, hard-muscled form, but his shoulders were even broader now, tapering down to his narrow waist, flat stomach, and long legs.

He could stand on his injured leg—although not quite with his full weight. My heart cramped a little as I watched him limp a few steps away from the table and then turn.

"This isn't a good idea—" he started.

I didn't give him the chance to finish. I threw a punch directly at his face.

Even caught off-guard, Jack's reflexes were lightning-quick. He blocked me instinctively, catching hold of my hand and then stepping aside, using my momentum to knock me off balance.

The step he'd taken had thrown him off balance too, though.

He toppled over, pulling me with him, and we crashed onto the floor together, our legs tangled and Jack's body half on top of mine.

"God, Lucy, are you all right?" Jack sounded out of breath. "Did I hurt you?"

By some miracle, Becky hadn't woken up.

I shook my head, trying to get back the air that had been knocked out of my own lungs. "No."

Jack looked down at me. "Is this the part where I get to say that I told you this was a bad idea?"

He was smiling, though—the first genuine smile I'd seen from him since he'd come out of Uncle John's surgery. The light from the fire picked out the strong, hard angles of his face and shadowed the graceful curve of his mouth. Shivers slid down my spine and all along my arms.

"Are you sure about that?" My voice sounded a little unsteady. I raised one hand, lightly tracing the line of Jack's cheek.

Something sparked in his gaze. He shifted, leaning towards me—

A knock sounded on the front door.

Jack startled, rolling to his feet. Not as quickly as he would have done three months ago, but he *was* improving.

He steadied himself on the edge of the table, and a second later, I heard him open the door then say, "Mr. Holmes."

I squeezed my eyes shut, wondering whether it would be horribly unfilial to get up, shove my father back out into the street, and then slam the door in his face.

"Ah, Lucy." Holmes's voice broke in on me. "I was not sure whether I would find you still here."

I opened my eyes to find Holmes looking from me to Jack, his gray eyes taking in my position—still on the floor—and no doubt the rumpled state of Jack's clothing and my disordered hair, as well.

Jack cleared his throat. "There was nothing … that is, I hope you don't think …"

Holmes fixed him with a keen gaze. "Notice that I am shaking your hand, young man, rather than gifting you with a broken jaw—as I would if I supposed for a moment that you had been guilty of any sort of impropriety towards my daughter."

If it ever came to a fight between them, I wasn't actually sure who would win. They were equally matched in height, but Holmes was thinner, his tall frame more spare.

Jack, though, smiled briefly, accepting the handshake that Holmes offered. "Thank you, sir."

I stood up. "Have you been visiting Mycroft?"

Holmes carried a leather attaché case in one hand, stamped with an official-looking government seal like the ones I remembered seeing in my uncle's Whitehall offices.

He glanced down at the case, then set it on the table. The catch was loose, and I caught a glimpse of the papers inside: some sort of complicated-looking diagrams for what seemed to be mechanical parts.

"You infer correctly," Holmes said. "Mycroft wished to consult me over some recent unpleasantness at the Diogenes Club."

Unless the members of the Diogenes had conspired to bore each other to death, it was difficult to imagine what sort of unpleasantness might have cropped up. Mycroft's gentleman's club was a bastion of upper-class English breeding: upper lips were stiff, collars were starched, and all talking—except in the Strangers Room—was strictly prohibited.

Holmes swung the sodden overcoat from his shoulders, dropping it over the back of a chair before sitting down.

"That, however, is not the reason for my visit." He focused on Jack. "I have come with a proposition for you. There is a clinic, run by a man of Doctor Watson's acquaintance—a colleague—

that has had some significant success in aiding the recovery of people with injuries such as yours. I would be willing—"

Jack interrupted, his voice quiet, polite, but entirely firm. "Thank you, Mr. Holmes. But I can't pay for anything like that. And I don't want you to offer to help out of obligation. You don't owe me anything."

"You saved my life, Constable Kelly." Holmes fixed Jack with another of his hard stares. "The debt is there, whether you wish to acknowledge it or not. If not for your quick wits and ready action, I would not be here to make this offer to you tonight. However, if you are worried that I offer assistance out of some form of sentimentality or pity, let me assure you that I do not. I am not the man to offer pity where none is required. Nor— as many besides Lucy will tell you—do I allow sentiment to influence my decisions."

This was so patently true that even Jack couldn't argue. Expecting sentimentality from Holmes was like asking a shark to sing lullabies.

"Lucy." Holmes turned to me, flicking open the pocket watch he carried and consulting the time. "You are due at the Savoy tonight, are you not?"

I was. In fact, a glance at Holmes's watch told me that I had to leave now, practically this moment, if I was to avoid arriving late for tonight's performance. Still, I narrowed my eyes at Holmes.

"What are you up to?"

"I?" Holmes's brows rose. "Nothing at all, beyond what I have already mentioned. There is a cab in the street outside; I directed my driver to wait. He will bring you to the Strand, while Constable Kelly and I take a few moments to discuss the matter before us."

I nodded slowly. "Thank you."

Jack still hadn't spoken. Watching him, I couldn't at all tell whether he was likely to accept Holmes's offer.

"Tell Becky I said goodbye. I'll see you next week?"

Jack tipped his head in acknowledgement, looking up at me only briefly. "Thanks for the reading lesson. I'll see you then."

CHAPTER 3

I woke with a jolt, sitting bolt upright. My heart was pounding so hard it felt as though my ribs ought to be cracking. The white cotton of my nightdress was damp and clammy with sweat.

I sat for a moment, resting my forehead against my raised knees and trying to erase the dream from my mind. The dark, moisture-slick walls of the ice house, the feeling of iron shackles around my wrists—

I straightened. Light was creeping in around the edges of the bedroom curtains, which meant that at least it was morning.

The worst was when the nightmare struck in the middle of the night, leaving me to lie awake for hours, staring at the ceiling and not wanting to close my eyes.

Someone rapped on the flat's outer door, and I realized that was what had awakened me.

I allowed myself a silent curse and a fervent wish that I hadn't screamed or cried out in the middle of the nightmare.

The night of the Jubilee Ball, Mycroft had been drugged, tied up, and threatened … Holmes and Uncle John could both easily have been killed … Becky had been captured by one of the villains—

I shook my head fiercely. It seemed like weakness—worse, *self-indulgent* weakness—to let myself be terrified of nightmares about that night, when everyone else had just as much if not more reason to be haunted by the memory of that affair than I did.

The real trouble was that the nightmares were never about what had *actually* happened. It was the *could-have-happened* scenarios that came to life in monstrous form every night.

I caught up my dressing gown, slipping it on as I went to answer the knock.

"Lucy!" I had barely gotten the door open when Becky bounced inside, blond braids flying. She had recently lost her two front teeth, and it showed when she smiled. "Jack has gone to stay with a friend of Doctor Watson's who might be able to help him get better, and he left this morning, so I'm going to stay with you!"

She delivered the tumble of words in a single breath, beaming at me.

I hugged Becky automatically, still trying to blink away the last lingering remnants of the dream.

"That is good news."

It was. If Jack really was willing to accept Holmes's help— and if this colleague of Uncle John's really could do something to make his injuries heal faster—then that was quite probably the best news I had heard in the last two months.

Even if he hadn't bothered to tell me in person. Or say good-bye.

I worked at not letting the sting of that blossom into anger inside me.

Becky looked up at me, a slight frown marring her brows. "You don't mind having me here to stay, do you, Lucy?"

I shook my head. It wasn't fair to spoil Becky's happiness with my own wish that I'd actually gotten the chance to punch her maddening brother in the face the night before.

"Mind? Of course I don't mind. I'm delighted!" I manufactured an answering smile, which wasn't hard. I really did love having Becky to stay with me. "We're going to have a wonderful time."

Becky's face cleared. "Oh, good." She bounced on her toes again. "Hurry and get dressed then, and come to the kitchen. Mrs. Hudson promised to teach me how to bake scones."

* * *

An hour later, I was cleaning flour off my hands and watching as Mrs. Hudson pulled a tray from the oven.

"Ah, well." Mrs. Hudson's kindly, pink-cheeked face was carefully neutral as she inspected the pallid lumps of dough on the baking sheet. I'd somehow managed to make them turn out burned in some places and at the same time underdone in others. Possibly a new record.

"Perhaps if we served them with butter ..." Mrs. Hudson began.

"It's all right, Mrs. Hudson." I smiled at her. "We had to take cookery classes when I was at school. If it were humanly possible to set the kitchen on fire while slicing cucumber sandwiches, I'm sure I would have done it."

Becky giggled. The scones that she and Mrs. Hudson had made together were already resting on the kitchen table, steaming and golden in their perfection.

"We can feed them to Prince. He won't mind."

Holmes appeared in the kitchen doorway. He gave my scones a slightly startled look, then focused on Mrs. Hudson.

"Ah, Mrs. Hudson. I fear that I shall not be in for lunch today after all."

Holmes's housekeeper was used to my father's ways. She simply slid the cold veal pie she had intended to serve back into the icebox.

"Will you be back for supper, Mr. Holmes?"

Holmes made a vague gesture. "That remains to be seen."

Mrs. Hudson gave him a resigned look. "Just as you say, Mr. Holmes."

Becky was busy offering half-burned scones to Prince, who was lying in front of the big cast-iron cooking range. Holmes looked at her a moment, then raised his eyes to meet mine. He didn't speak, but he tilted his head just slightly towards the kitchen door.

I untied my apron. "I'll be back in a moment, Becky."

I followed Holmes through the doorway and into the hall, swinging the kitchen door shut behind me.

"What's happened?" I demanded. My first thought was that there was some bad news about Jack, since Holmes clearly didn't want to speak in front of Becky.

But his first words were, "The unpleasantness I mentioned at the Diogenes Club has taken a somewhat graver turn."

I tried not to let out a breath of relief. "Graver in what way?"

Holmes's face was grim, but there was an undercurrent of … not enjoyment, exactly, but at least satisfaction in his expression. He might dedicate his life to fighting criminal activity in London, but he also came alive at the news of a fresh challenge. That was simply how he was made.

"Murder."

CHAPTER 4

"Murder," I said. The word still somehow seemed entirely incompatible with everything I knew about the Diogenes. "Who has been killed?"

Holmes turned away from the carriage window. We were in a hansom cab, on our way across town to Mycroft's club on Waterloo Place.

Becky had been happy to stay behind at Baker Street, having extracted a promise from Mrs. Hudson to teach her how to make shortbread this afternoon—and a promise from me that I would tell her all the details of the mystery when I came home.

Holmes raised his voice to be heard over the creak of the carriage springs and the steady clop of the horse's hooves.

"The victim is one John Pettigrew, a retired general in the Indian Army. Which is odd, because ..."

Holmes's brows knitted together.

"Because?" I finally prompted.

Holmes gave a quick, impatient shake of his head. "It is immaterial. Matters have simply played out differently than I had anticipated, that is all."

"Had you met this General Pettigrew?" I asked. "Do you have any idea why someone should want him dead?"

Holmes leaned back in his seat. "As you know, the Diogenes Club's entire purpose is to provide a refuge for the most unsociable men in London. Some are shy, others misanthropic. General Pettigrew fell into the latter category. He was one of the club's oldest members and had a pervasive hatred of the world and humanity in general."

"He sounds a charming character."

"As you say. However, to answer your question, I do not know of any specific reason why someone should have wished him dead."

Holmes stopped as our cab drew up outside a handsome white stucco building, with bow windows and neoclassical columns framing the entrance.

"Are you sure that it's all right for me to come inside with you?" I asked, eyeing the large brass knocker on the front door. "As I recall, the Diogenes isn't exactly a bastion of progressivism when it comes to welcoming female visitors."

I had come to the club before while we were working on another case. The ban on talking had prevented anyone from outright demanding that I leave, but there had been an absolute thunderstorm of outraged newspaper rattling from the reading room as I passed through.

"Quite probably. However, Watson is seeing patients at his surgery this afternoon, and I believe you may have better success than I at questioning some of the maidservants and kitchen staff. For some reason, girls of that class seem to find me intimidating."

"No, really?"

Two years ago, I would have said that humor was as foreign to Holmes's nature as sentimentality. But now the briefest trace of a smile hovered at the edges of his mouth before vanishing.

I followed him out of the carriage. "I wanted to ask you, where exactly is this clinic that Uncle John recommended to Jack?"

Holmes was frowning again, eyeing the front door of the Diogenes in the manner of a general planning a military attack on an enemy stronghold. But he answered without hesitation.

"Bath."

"Bath," I repeated. That made a certain degree of sense; the city of Bath was filled with doctors who catered to the needs of those who came to take the supposedly medicinal waters. "So Jack must have caught the train from Paddington Station this morning?"

Holmes gave me an odd look. "The eight-fifteen, to be precise. Is there some purpose behind these quest—"

The door to the Diogenes opened, revealing a thin, narrow-faced man in a brown suit and bowler hat.

"Ah, Holmes," Inspector Lestrade said. "I thought you'd turn up sooner or later, given your connection."

"Is my brother on the premises?"

Holmes looked past Lestrade into the hall.

"No, he sends his regrets. He had an important meeting in Whitehall that he could not postpone."

Holmes nodded almost absently, which probably meant that he already knew of Mycroft's meeting and its importance.

"I doubt that there's much to interest you about the business," Lestrade went on. "Seems a clear-cut case, no mystery about it."

"I am delighted to hear you say so. Nothing gives me more assurance that the truth about this affair will prove to be quite the reverse."

Lestrade's sallow cheeks flushed. He looked for a moment as though he had taken a drink of sour milk. "I suppose you've heard Mrs. Mudge the charwoman's ridiculous story. But take it from me, there's nothing to it but hysterics and—"

"A hysterical charwoman?" Holmes's voice was calm, but he had gone still, his whole pose suddenly alert.

I had never been fox hunting, but I imagined that was how a trained hound might look at catching the fox's scent.

"I had not, in fact, heard anything of the sort. But I would be most interested to hear the tale the charwoman tells."

Inspector Lestrade's voice was sharp with exasperation. "There's nothing to it, I tell you. It's just … well … two weeks ago, the fool woman was cleaning out the fireplace grates in the bedrooms upstairs—the ones club members can stay in if they've come up to London from the country—and …"

Inspector Lestrade seemed to be having difficulty in getting the words out.

"Well, the woman claims she saw a ghost swoop out of the broom cupboard at her."

Lestrade paused, giving Holmes a wary look, as though expecting my father to break into derisive laughter.

Instead, Holmes's brows drew together. "Two weeks ago, you say?"

"Exactly. She's carrying on today, saying it was a warning of doom. But it can't have anything to do with today's business."

I looked up at the stolid, eminently respectable facade of the club building. "A ghost?"

Inspector Lestrade's face grew a shade ruddier as he looked at me and gave me a brief, stiff nod.

I had an ongoing bet with myself that one day the police inspector would come to accept and value my involvement in my father's detective cases. It did not appear that that day was going to be today, however.

"Probably saw a curtain flapping or some such. Just the usual female hysterics and nerves. *Women*."

I clamped my mouth shut before I could inquire whether Inspector Lestrade was married—and if he was single, add that I could with reasonable certainty guess *why*.

"As I was saying, Mr. Holmes," Lestrade went on, clearly making an effort to leave the question of ghosts behind. He led the way inside the Diogenes Club, stopping in a front hall that was thickly carpeted and paneled in dark wood. "It's a clear enough case. The general was poisoned, and we've already got the fellow who did it."

"Indeed, inspector? That is quick work. My congratulations."

Lestrade made an attempt to look modest. "It was nothing. This Mr. Teale—our culprit—was known to have quarreled with the deceased just yesterday. Had violent words with him right here in this club, and from what I heard, it nearly came to blows."

"Indeed?" Holmes said again. I had the impression that he was only half attending to what Lestrade said. He took a few steps down the hallway to an open door and peered inside. "This, I take it, is where the unfortunate General Pettigrew met his demise?"

Lestrade gave him a startled look. "How did you—"

Holmes made a quick, impatient gesture. "The members of the Diogenes Club are creatures of habit. As I recall, General

Pettigrew was invariably to be found seated at a desk in the writing room, engaged in his favorite pastime of writing vitriolic letters to the editor of the *London Times*, excoriating everything from the Prime Minister's most recent speeches in Parliament to the current fashions in men's evening dress. It requires no very great deductive leap to conclude that is where he was this morning, as well. Also, this room has plainly been cleared of all other club members, leading one to believe it the scene of the crime. Incidentally—" Holmes turned, pinning Lestrade with his gaze. "You have, I presume, kept all club members who were on the premises at the time of the general's death here?"

Lestrade nodded. "They're all in the common room, there." He indicated a doorway across the hall. "Not happy about it, but I said we'd try to get through the questioning as quick as we could. Shouldn't take long, since as I say, we've already got—"

"Indeed, yes, your chief suspect."

As Holmes spoke, I moved forward so that I, too, could peer into the room.

The writing room had been set up with several desks spaced around the room, all partially enclosed by heavy wooden screens that effectively turned each writing place into its own tiny room—presumably the better for club members to completely ignore each other's existence.

Like all the rest of the Diogenes, the room was dimly lit, the windows draped with heavy curtains, and the carpet thick enough that a circus performer on stilts could walk across it without disturbing the quiet with their footsteps.

I had been braced for the sight of a body, but there was none.

The only sign that anything out of the ordinary had occurred was a teacup that lay on the floor near one of the screened-off desks closest to the fireplace. The cup's handle was broken off, and most of the contents had soaked into the rug, leaving only a small puddle of what looked like black coffee inside.

"General Pettigrew's body was moved?" I asked Lestrade.

Lestrade grimaced, though whether with annoyance at the crime scene's having been disturbed or at me for having asked the question, I could not be sure.

"Yes, he was carried to one of the bedrooms upstairs. At first they thought he was just taken ill and needed a doctor summoned."

"At what point was it decided that something more sinister had occurred?"

"The men who'd moved him smelled bitter almonds on the body."

Holmes's brows climbed just a fraction. "Cyanide."

"I can take you to see the body now, if you'd like," Lestrade said. "It's still upstairs. Or maybe you'd like to talk to Mr. Teale—"

"I believe I shall postpone that pleasure for a few moments more," Holmes interrupted. "I would prefer to speak to the gentleman who occupied the desk there."

He indicated the mahogany desk and chair that sat across the room from the one with the broken teacup. "Lord Lansdowne, I believe?"

I stiffened involuntarily—then ordered myself to breathe. There was no reason to panic, just because fate appeared to have an extremely nasty sense of humor.

Inspector Lestrade gaped at Holmes a moment. "How did you—oh, I see. Creatures of habit. All right, Lord Lansdowne's here, and if you want to speak with him, I won't stop you. Doubt he'll be able to tell you much of anything, though."

"And I deeply appreciate your indulging my eccentricities." Holmes's voice was pleasant.

Inspector Lestrade gave him a sharp look, half puzzlement, half worry, but then he nodded—a little heavily, I thought. "I'll go and fetch his Lordship for you."

* * *

I shook my head. "Poor Inspector Lestrade."

Holmes had moved to study the placement of the broken teacup on the floor, but looked up to give me an inquiring glance.

"He's worked with you often enough to know your ways," I said. "I imagine at this very moment, he's picturing his beautifully constructed case against this Mr. Teale crumbling into a pile of rubble."

Holmes's shoulders twitched as he crouched down to sniff at the spilled liquid that had stained the rug. "Lestrade is a capable officer, and occasionally even intelligent. He is, however, prone to seize with misplaced optimism upon the easiest solution to a problem."

"Whereas you are never optimistic."

"My optimism is rarely *misguided*," Holmes said. He sniffed at the carpet again.

"Is the cyanide in the coffee?" I asked.

"That would be the obvious vehicle for delivering poison. However, the coffee in this cup at first inspection bears no trace of containing cyanide."

"Really?" I looked at him in surprise.

Holmes waved a hand. "The remains will have to be analyzed, of course." He drew a small glass vial from his pocket, picked up the cup, and tipped the remaining liquid into it.

I moved over to the desk, looking down at the surface without touching anything. There was a half-melted stick of sealing wax and a sheet of blotting paper with ink marks visible, but no letters.

"Maybe it was a slower-acting poison, then?" I said. "Something he ingested before arriving at the club? Or are we sure that he was poisoned at all? They could have imagined the bitter almonds smell."

Although Mycroft must have believed the general's death suspicious, otherwise we would not be here. And Mycroft Holmes was wrong about as infrequently as his brother.

"We shall have to go into all of that." Holmes spoke almost absently, though, his attention seemingly fixed on something else.

He turned to look at me. "Do you wish to remain for the interview with Lord Lansdowne?"

This was another moment when I wished that my father's observational powers could occasionally be turned off.

I would have sworn that I hadn't shown any signs of distress after the first mention of Lord Lansdowne's name. But then, that single start of surprise had probably been enough for Holmes.

"Of course," I said. "Why wouldn't I wish to stay?"

I doubted that Holmes was convinced, but at least he didn't argue. "Very good, then. I doubt the interview will last long in any case. As Inspector Lestrade said—"

He broke off as the door to the writing room opened, admitting both Lestrade and another, taller man.

Henry Petty-Fitzmaurice, 5th Marquess of Lansdowne, was in his early fifties, with dark hair sharply receding from a high, domed brow. His eyes were light and very intelligent, his face not handsome, but pleasant-looking all the same.

He was high up in Her Majesty's government, serving as Secretary for the Department of War and, from our past meetings, I knew him to be honorable, quick-witted, and courteous.

It was not his fault that I had been taken prisoner and nearly murdered on the grounds of his London house.

I concentrated on breathing, slow and deep from the bottom of my lungs. It was the same technique I'd used to combat stage fright when I was first starting out in the theater.

The method seemed to be far less effective at blocking out memories of being trapped in an ice house with a sadistic madman bent on killing me, but it was better than nothing.

"Miss James. A great pleasure to see you again."

Lord Lansdowne bowed over my hand before turning to Holmes. "I'm glad to see you, Mr. Holmes. Very glad. General Pettigrew was a good man."

"You knew him personally?"

"He was stationed in India during my time as viceroy there. A hard man, some would say an unlikeable one. But an honorable soldier. Scrupulous about following orders to the letter. One had only to give him a directive to know it would be carried out. He was instrumental in putting down a local rebellion in one of the hill states in 1890."

"You were seated there when he was struck down?" Holmes indicated the desk across from the dead man's.

"That's right, that is my customary table when I have letters to write and documents to review—as I did this morning."

Lord Lansdowne's official place of work was the War Office, also located on Pall Mall—close enough to be visible from the

Diogenes' front door, in fact. But I knew that when he wished to work without interruptions—or to consult Mycroft—Lansdowne used the club as a kind of secondary office.

"I was sitting there, just as you say, when he was taken ill," Lansdowne said now. "I thought at first it was some sort of apoplectic fit."

"Poison does not leap immediately to the average person's mind," Holmes murmured.

"Poison?" Lord Lansdowne gave him a keen look. "You are certain that is what killed him?"

I missed Holmes's reply.

I could manage the *actual* memories of what had happened the night of the Jubilee Ball. I had chosen this life, and the danger that went with it.

I had chosen to put myself in danger, the night of the ball. The entire scheme had been entirely my own idea.

Last night, though, I'd had the dream in which I was shot through the chest and lay on the ice house floor, feeling my life blood drain drop by drop.

Though even that dream was better than the nightmare in which Holmes and Watson arrived to free me, but then looked at me with pity in their eyes and said—

I dug my nails hard into my palms, focusing on the small points of pain.

Holmes was asking Lord Lansdowne to give him as exact an account as possible of the progression of events before the general's death.

"We had sat down at roughly the same time, the general and I." Lord Lansdowne frowned in an effort of remembrance. "The waiter came in to take our orders for coffee."

"Waiter?"

Lansdowne nodded. "Yes, new chap. Never seen him here before. He brought back two cups, gave one to me, one to Pettigrew. Pettigrew drank from it."

"He drank from it?" Holmes asked quickly. "You're certain?"

"Well." Lansdowne's brow furrowed again. "I wasn't watching him. But I recall hearing the clink of the cup and saucer, as though he had picked the cup up and put it down. I assume he must have drunk some."

"General Pettigrew was in the habit of writing letters here in the mornings," I said. It was an effort to keep my voice steady, but I managed. "But there are no letters on the desk now. Did he get up to mail them?"

Lord Lansdowne frowned. "I can't recall. I don't remember him doing so. But I may have been absorbed in my own work and not noticed."

Holmes opened his mouth, then seemed to change his mind, turning from Lord Lansdowne to me. "Lucy, perhaps you would be so good as to begin the interviews with our other witnesses? You might perhaps take your choice of the haunted charwoman or our chief suspect Mr. Teale to begin with."

I knew the real reason for Holmes's suggestion, of course. He was trying to help. Which was both touching and extremely annoying.

Not so annoying that I could bring myself to refuse the offer of escape, though. It made absolutely no logical sense, but it was as though the sight of Lord Lansdowne had driven a jolt of memory through me like a spike.

For a moment or two, I'd felt as though I had actually been transported straight back into my nightmare. I'd *seen* the windowless brick walls, felt the dank chill of air on my face and the cold, metallic bite of handcuffs around my wrists.

Inspector Lestrade opened his mouth as though to argue. Holmes fixed him with a quelling look.

"Miss James has my full authority to conduct interviews on my behalf. I have a few minor details about which I wish to consult Lord Lansdowne, but I will be along in a few moments."

Lestrade looked sullen. "It can't be the charwoman. Last I saw of her, she was still having hysterics in one of the bedrooms upstairs."

I nodded. "Mr. Teale it is, then."

Lestrade looked from me to my father, then shrugged with a resigned, "All right, come on, then."

I stood up, followed the inspector out of the room, and tried to leave all memories of imprisonment, torture—and knowing that even if I survived the night of the Jubilee Ball, Jack might not—behind.

CHAPTER 5

If Diogenes Club members ranged from the misanthropic to the simply shy, I thought at first glance that Mr. Teale likely fell into the latter category of unsociable gentlemen.

He was somewhere around thirty years of age, with a tall, slightly stoop-shouldered frame. His face was long, thin, and sensitive-looking, with blue eyes peering diffidently out at the world from under a thatch of untidy straw-blond hair.

And—not particularly surprisingly—he did not at all look like a man who had just committed a murder.

He blinked as I entered the room. "Who on earth are you?" He caught himself. "I beg your pardon. That sounded rude. What I mean is—"

"It's all right."

He was being held in a small cloakroom off the main entrance hall. Mr. Teale wasn't handcuffed, but there was small chance of his escaping. There were no windows, and a uniformed police constable was positioned at the door.

"My name is Lucy James," I said. "I'm assisting Mr. Holmes with the inquiries into General Pettigrew's death."

I didn't specify *which* Mr. Holmes, just in case my father decided that he wished to keep his name out of the affair. As a Diogenes Club member, though, Mr. Teale had to be acquainted with Mycroft.

Mr. Teale's eyes widened, which wasn't unusual. Most men were surprised by a young woman who assisted with murder investigations.

Except Jack.

I took that thought and shoved it firmly away, far to the back of my mind.

"And I'm Neville Teale." He leaned forward across the table, stammering slightly. "L-l-look here, do you think you could convince that police inspector that I didn't actually kill anyone?"

"I suppose that depends on whether you *did* actually kill anyone."

I smiled to soften the words, letting my gaze travel over him.

Since coming to London from America, I had learned that class distinctions were far more stratified—and sometimes far more subtle—here.

Mr. Teale's heather tweed suit and polished brown leather shoes were of extremely good quality—good, but not ostentatiously so, with the quietly refined look of old money rather than new. At a guess, he came from a family that had carved out their fortune several generations ago.

Certainly his hands were smooth, giving no indication that he had ever worked for a living.

Mr. Teale's look of earnest appeal deepened. "I *didn't* kill anyone. I promise you. I know I quarreled with General Pettigrew yesterday, but only because he insulted my wife."

"Your wife?"

"Yes. He said—" Mr. Teale's cheeks flushed. "Well, never mind what he said. It doesn't bear repeating. I told him he was a boor, and we had angry words. But that was all."

I studied him, wondering whether it would do any good to press him on what exactly the general had said about his wife. Probably not.

In addition to the Savile Row suit, Mr. Teale's tie pin was from Balliol College, Oxford. No Oxford-educated English gentleman would willingly repeat something like that to a near-stranger. At least, not while he was sober.

"Angry words in the Diogenes? Here that is practically equivalent to a capital crime."

"Don't I know it." A shy twist of a smile transformed Neville Teale's face, making him look younger and less solemn. "I had no less than five other members of the old guard tell me I was in danger of having my membership revoked."

"Did you see General Pettigrew this morning?" I asked.

"Yes." Mr. Teale's answer was prompt. "But I didn't speak to him. I didn't even go near him. The last thing I wanted was to have any more dealings with the man."

"What time did you arrive at the club?"

"I suppose—" Neville's face screwed up in an effort of remembrance. "I suppose it must have been somewhere around nine-fifteen or thereabouts?"

"And what did you do?"

"I looked into the writing room, saw that Pettigrew was in there at his usual desk, and took myself to a chair in the library instead." He indicated a pile of books on the floor beside him.

Apparently, Mr. Teale was interested in history. The uppermost book's title read *A History of James I.*

"Did anyone else see you there?"

"Yes. I spoke to no one, of course, as per the club rules. But there were at least half a dozen others there who must have seen me. I can give you their names."

"Did you leave the drawing room at all?"

"No. I sat reading my newspaper, up until I heard all the commotion in the reading room. Then I got up and went to see what had happened, along with everyone else. I saw them carrying Pettigrew upstairs."

I was silent a moment, watching the young man across from me.

Having a background in theater was, I had discovered, a fairly good foundation for work as a detective. Every day, I was surrounded by people who were acting a part on stage, trying to convince an audience that the part they were playing and the words they were speaking were real and true. Lying, in other words.

It made it much easier to tell when someone was acting—or lying—in real life.

At the moment, I couldn't detect any sign at all that Neville Teale was being untruthful in his answers to me.

"You didn't go into the kitchen at all?" I asked.

Holmes had thought the coffee benign, but until we knew that for certain, it seemed worthwhile to ask the question.

"The kitchen?" If Mr. Teale's astonishment wasn't genuine, he had missed his calling and in fact *ought* to be a performer on some London stage. "Good heavens, no. I've never set foot in the kitchen in all my years as a club member."

Mr. Teale raised a good point, actually. I doubted that any of the gentlemen belonging to the Diogenes Club had ever set foot inside the kitchen or other service areas. If they did, they would attract more notice than a zebra in the middle of Waterloo station.

"You didn't actually go into the writing room?"

"No."

The door opened behind me, and I glanced around to see Holmes in the doorway, along with Inspector Lestrade.

"Well?" Holmes gave me a look of inquiry.

"Unless Mr. Teale is a secret medium and summoned a ghost to administer poison to the general by unknown means, I do not see how he can be the guilty party."

It wasn't quite that easy, of course. Until we knew for certain how General Pettigrew had been killed, we couldn't entirely rule out anyone from our list of possible suspects. But Mr. Teale seemed a long shot, at best.

Holmes inclined his head. Inspector Lestrade looked sour.

Neville Teale cleared his throat. "If that's the case, do you think you might let me go? Or at least let me telephone to my wife? Suzette was expecting me home to lunch, and she'll be worried if I'm late."

Holmes's gaze rested on Mr. Teale. "I think a phone call might reasonably be permitted, Inspector."

Lestrade's scowl deepened. "Just don't try anything funny," he growled at Mr. Teale.

Holmes turned to me. "That settled, I believe the time has come for us to have a look at the dead man's body."

I had been bracing myself for him to say that we needed to speak to Lord Lansdowne again. There was probably something wrong with the fact that my heart rate slowed and my muscles relaxed at the thought of communing with a dead man instead.

I stood up. "Of course."

* * *

"I have sent for Watson to join us here as soon as he is able," Holmes said as we ascended the stairs. "He will likely be able to tell us more about how the general met his end. But until he arrives, we may at least—"

Holmes stopped abruptly as we reached the head of the stairs. The first door on the left, Inspector Lestrade had told us, was where General Pettigrew had been carried and then subsequently died. Now, like Holmes, I could see that there was no policeman on guard outside, and the door was partially ajar.

I gave Holmes a look of silent inquiry. Instead of answering, he stepped forward, moving with a light, almost cat-like tread, and flung the door open.

I leaped up the last few steps to join him, biting off a curse under my breath. I couldn't object to Holmes risking his own safety, as often as I had done the same. But in this case, I strongly suspected my father had rushed to enter first so that any attack would fall on him rather than me.

No attack came, though.

The room stood in near-total darkness, the lights all extinguished and the curtains drawn. I had a brief look at the shrouded figure on the bed, a white sheet pulled up to cover the face. Then my attention was caught by a flutter of movement deeper in the room.

I caught my breath, shock moving inch by inch down my spine.

A man's spectral face, pale and glowing with a faint greenish light, hung suspended in the air. It wavered, hovered an instant, then vanished with a crack and a flash of near-blinding light.

I stood momentarily frozen, locked in place, with Holmes statue-still beside me.

Someone hiccupped in the hallway behind us.

I whirled to see an elderly woman—I assumed she was the charwoman, from the evidence of her grimy hands and soiled apron—who had come to peer over Holmes's and my shoulders into the dead man's room.

To judge by her breath, she had been shoring herself up with medicinal doses of brandy. Now she dipped her chin with the ponderous, solemn air of the deeply intoxicated.

"Told them I seen a ghost." Her voice was slurred. "*Now* maybe someone'll believe me."

CHAPTER 6

Holmes gave a muttered oath and sprang forward, towards the place the ghostly apparition had vanished. He flung open the curtains, which let in a stream of sunlight, but nothing more. No hidden figures crouching behind the thick velvet draperies.

There was nowhere at all that an intruder could hide, that I could see.

Apart from the heavy four-poster bed, the room contained only a small bedside table, a chair, and a chest of drawers, too narrow to serve as a hiding place.

Muttering under his breath, Holmes crossed to the bed, yanking aside the sheet that covered the motionless form on top of the mattress.

Beside me, the charwoman gave a shrill scream of protest, and Holmes shot me a look—part irritation, part appeal.

"It's all right." I drew the older woman with me back out into the hall, turning her so that her back was to the bedroom door and the dead man.

Over her shoulder, I could see the figure on the bed.

He was somewhere around sixty years of age, with a tall, barrel-chested frame that had begun to go to fat. His hair was gray and thinning, his face flabby, with a ruddy tone to the skin. The skin around his eyes was puffy, and overall his face had a surly, discontented look, with deep grooves running from his nose to the corners of his downturned mouth.

He was also unquestionably dead, though I saw Holmes—ever the skeptic—reach to feel for the pulse in his neck.

The charwoman was still screaming. A startled-looking police constable's face appeared at the head of the stairs, followed immediately by Inspector Lestrade.

"It was his ghost!" The charwoman's voice rose to a shriek. "A murder victim's spirit never rests easy! He's come back to punish us all!"

More police had joined Lestrade on the stairs. Lestrade bounded up the last steps, starting to join Holmes inside the bedroom.

"Mr. Holmes, what's going—"

"Halt!" Holmes flung up an arm, his voice a sharp bark. "No one is to enter this room. Do I make myself clear?"

The charwoman's screeches were reaching an even higher pitch, oscillating back and forth like a siren.

Holmes ground his teeth. "Lucy—"

I put a hand on the old woman's arm and spoke soothingly. "It's all right."

The charwoman jumped, looked at me blearily, then moaned, "We're all doomed!"

But at least she had stopped screaming.

"I'm sure that's not true. Here, come along and sit down."
I drew her a little further down the hall to a window alcove
where there was a small, upholstered bench.

Lestrade and the other officers were crowded at the door of
the bedroom, though they were obeying Holmes's orders about
not coming in to trample any evidence.

My mind was still racing, replaying the sight of the ghostly
face over and over again, trying on and then discarding one
explanation after another for what we had just seen. I would
have liked the chance to search the room along with Holmes.
But then, it was unlikely I would be able to notice anything that
Holmes himself wouldn't find as well.

"Besides," I said. "I thought you saw the ghost first two weeks
ago? So it couldn't have been the general's spirit, can it?"

The elderly woman collapsed heavily onto the bench beside
me. "Ah, well. Maybe it was a premonition. A haaaarbinger of
doom." She raised her head and fixed me with a drink-glazed
stare. "My old grandmother had the second-sight, you know."

"What is your name?" I asked.

She looked at me, hiccupped, then wiped her mouth on the
back of her hand. "Mrs. Mudge."

"And where did you first see the ghost?" I asked.

"In th' b-brrooom cupboard." Mrs. Mudge's eyes were half-
closed, and she made a vague gesture with one hand. "I haven't
been near it since. Been keeping my brooms and rags and such
down on the first floor. Couldn't pay me enough to go near th'
place again."

She slumped back.

"Mrs. Mudge?"

The only answer was a drunken snore. Plainly there was no more to be got out of her until she had slept it off—if then.

I stood up and went back down the hall, where I found Holmes just coming out of the bedroom.

A glance at my father's face was enough to tell me he had found no logical explanation for the apparition. His cheeks were lightly flushed with anger, white dents of temper at the edges of his thin mouth. Sherlock Holmes did not appreciate being outwitted—still less made to think he might have seen a spirit manifestation.

He turned to Lestrade, his voice short. "May I suggest that you order your men back to their assigned places. And conduct a headcount of everyone—both club members and servants—who ought currently to be on the premises?"

"But Mr. Holmes—"

Holmes cut him off. "The most logical explanation for what we have just witnessed is that it was intended for a distraction." He glared at the ring of uniformed police assembled outside the room. "A distraction that has apparently succeeded only too well!"

Lestrade gulped air visibly as the meaning of my father's words registered. "Yes, Mr. Holmes." He turned to his constables, his sallow face flushing. "You heard what he said—get back downstairs and count heads! If there's so much as a mouse missing from the pantry, I want to know about it."

I waited until they had gone thundering back down the stairs before asking Holmes, "Anything?"

"Nothing whatsoever. No hooks or wires, no paint or motion picture projectors that could have produced the ghostly face." Holmes shook his head. "The window was open perhaps an inch at the top, but that is the only route either into or out of the room."

"Obviously not large enough for anyone to have escaped that way, though."

"Obviously. And yet—" My father's annoyance had started to pass, and now his face had a keen, intensely focused look. He was silent, then asked, "What of our inebriated charwoman? Had she anything of value to add?"

"She's not what I'd call the most reliable witness—"

I stopped at the sight of Lestrade, who was racing back up the stairs. The inspector's sharp-featured face had gone from ruddy with frustration to strained and pale.

"Yes?" Holmes barked.

Lestrade looked as though he were entertaining a wish that the ground would open and swallow him whole. "You asked for a headcount, Mr. Holmes—"

"Get to the point of whatever bad news you are about to deliver, Lestrade. Who is missing?"

Lestrade took a shallow, gasping breath. "Well, Mr. Holmes, the fact is that Royce—he's the waiter who delivered the general's coffee—is gone."

CHAPTER 7

I reached the green baize door that led through the back hallway and into the club's kitchen area and paused, the back of my neck prickling. The servants—the remaining servants—were all still grouped together in the club library, under police guard, as were the club members. Holmes, myself, Lestrade, and his other officers were searching the club, which I thought was slightly like searching the empty barn after the horses have been stolen out of it, but which had to be done, just on the off chance that the missing waiter was still somewhere on the premises.

So far we had found absolutely no one, either ghostly or mortal. Now, though, I would have sworn I heard a slight sound coming from inside the kitchen.

I inched forward, eased the door open silently ... and caught sight of a red-haired man just about to go out through the back door.

He was on the slender side, but tall—and if he had just committed murder, he would be extremely motivated to get away. Which made taking him by surprise my safest bet.

I stepped quickly forward, seized hold of his wrist, and twisted his arm quickly up and behind his back in a move I'd learned from an elderly wrestling instructor back in America.

"You can stay still, or you can get yourself a broken arm," I said. "Your choice."

"I'm sorry!" The man raised his free hand in the air in a gesture of surrender, making no move to fight back or struggle. "But I think—that is, you may have mistaken me for someone else."

"What are you doing trying to sneak out of here?"

"I wasn't sneaking, I—" The man paused, twisting his head awkwardly in an effort to look at me over his shoulder.

He was somewhere in his middle twenties, with a pleasant, square-jawed face and blue eyes. "Would you be Miss James?"

Surprise made me almost lose my grip on his arm. "How do you know that?"

"Lord Lansdowne mentioned you—my employer. That's why I'm here. Lord Lansdowne has an important meeting with the War Office to attend, and there's a crush of police carriages and newspaper reporters outside the front entrance. He asked me to come and look to see whether he might more easily be able to exit through the back of the club in order to reach his meeting without delay."

I studied his face, debating whether I believed him. "Would that be the same meeting that Mr. Mycroft Holmes has gone off to attend?"

Instead of the red-haired man's, it was my father's voice that answered, coming from the kitchen doorway behind me.

"I should think it very likely."

Turning, I saw that both my father and Lord Lansdowne had come into the kitchen.

Lord Lansdowne's brows inched up a notch. "Miss James. I see that you have ... met my secretary, Mr. Edward Barton."

"In a manner of speaking." Mr. Barton craned his neck again to look at me. "Do you think you might let go of me now?"

"Of course. I beg your pardon." I stepped back.

"No harm done. I suppose I did look somewhat suspicious." He gave me a good-humored smile.

Lord Lansdowne gave Mr. Barton a quelling look. "Have you determined yet whether the back way is clear, Barton?"

"I beg your pardon, sir. It appears to me that if we leave immediately by the exit here, we should be able to reach Whitehall without unnecessary delay."

"Then let us be gone."

"I will summon the carriage immediately, sir." Before turning to go, Edward Barton faced me again, giving me a bow and another quick smile.

"Miss James, it was a pleasure making your acquaintance."

"Your definition of *pleasure* may be somewhat faulty," I said. "But it was nice to meet you as well. And I apologize again for thinking you a criminal."

"Not at all." Mr. Barton gave me a quick grin, his eyes crinkling at the corners. "I'm rarely threatened with grievous bodily harm in the course of carrying out my secretarial duties. It was quite the most exciting thing to happen to me all week."

"Oh, well." I smiled. "In that case, I'm happy to have been able to oblige."

* * *

"What sort of a person was Royce?" I asked.

Ester, the young maid to whom I was speaking, shrugged. She was a quiet, sallow-skinned girl, with dark hair tucked tightly up under her white cap and dark brown eyes.

"He was all right. Not very friendly. Did his work and kept to himself, mostly."

I suppressed a sigh.

We were speaking in one of the upstairs bedrooms, down the hall from the room where General Pettigrew had died.

The room had been given over to me to speak with the servants, while Inspector Lestrade and my father conducted interviews of the Diogenes Club members downstairs.

Ester was the fifth Diogenes Club maidservant I had interviewed, and every single one of them had given me variations on exactly that same answer.

Royce had been quiet, efficient, had spoken little, and fraternized with his fellow servants not at all.

If his goal had been to ensure that no one at the Diogenes knew the slightest bit of useful information about him, he had succeeded beyond his wildest hopes.

"I understand he had only worked here a short while," I said.

"That's right, miss," Ester said. "About a fortnight."

"Have you any idea where he worked before coming here?"

"No, miss. He never said."

"And when was the last time you saw Royce today, can you remember?"

Ester screwed up her face. "Ten o'clock, maybe? I think he was in the kitchen when I came in to fetch scones and a pot of tea for one of the gentlemen in the dining room."

"Do you remember him fetching General Pettigrew a cup of coffee?"

"Is that what killed him, miss? The coffee?"

"We're not sure yet. Did you see him pouring it for the general?"

Ester looked frightened, but shook her head. "No, miss. I didn't notice particularly what he was doing."

"Did you ever see him interact with General Pettigrew?" I asked. "Did Royce ever seem to have a grudge against the general? Or had the general ever lodged any complaints against him?"

Ester shook her head. "No, miss. Not that I know of. I mean, *none* of us liked—" She broke off, clamping her mouth shut.

"None of you actually liked General Pettigrew? Is that what you were going to say?"

"Well, not to speak ill of the dead, but that's about the way of it, miss. A nasty old curmudgeon, he was. But I never saw him have it out for Royce in particular." She stopped, glancing nervously over her shoulder. "Beg pardon, miss, but is it true that the general's ghost was seen up here?"

"Something was seen." I doubted that Ester was involved in the apparition that Holmes and I had glimpsed. But I still watched her carefully as I added, "Whether or not it was General Pettigrew's spirit is in doubt."

"I wouldn't be too sure of that, miss." For the first time, Ester's face brightened to something like animation. "My aunt goes to séances regular-like and gets messages from the spirit world."

Ester seemed like a nice girl, so I stopped myself from rolling my eyes.

The Fox sisters, who had begun the spiritualist craze with their story of communicating with the ghost of a murdered man, had actually lived not too far from the boarding school I had attended in America.

The fad for séances and mediums and communicating with the spirits of the dead had been spreading like wildfire ever since—never mind that the Fox sisters had eventually admitted the entire thing to be a hoax.

Ester leaned forward, lowering her voice. "My aunt's medium, Madam Giselle, was able to put her in touch with her dead husband *and* her dead sister."

"Remarkable."

It wasn't that I doubted the existence of the soul or of life after death. What I doubted was that the dead had nothing better to do than rap once for yes and twice for no in answer to questions put by women named Madame Giselle.

If that *were* the case, I was going to find heaven unbelievably boring.

"Thank you for your help," I told Ester.

As Ester rose and turned to go, I glanced out the window. The room we were in overlooked the front entrance of the Diogenes Club and Pall Mall outside.

Edward Barton had been entirely right; the street down below was crowded with police and newspaper reporters. The members of the Diogenes were going to loathe everything about the memory of today.

As I watched, a Brougham carriage, drawn by a team of four perfectly matched gray horses, drew up as close as could be managed to the club.

A page boy wearing a royal blue livery uniform hopped down, but before he could open the door, a young woman emerged and climbed down from the carriage herself.

She wore a burgundy colored hat and matching cloak, both trimmed with so much white ermine fur that the woman inside was almost lost to view.

But as she hurried forward towards the club entrance, a man came out meet her.

I recognized Mr. Teale.

This, presumably, must be his wife, whom the dead man had insulted and whom Neville Teale had asked permission to telephone. Suzette, he had called her.

They embraced, and as she tilted her head back to look up at her husband, I caught a better look at her face: round and pretty in a slightly doll-like way, with blue eyes and curls of blond hair artfully arranged across her forehead.

I went still.

At the same moment, she happened to glance up at the window and caught sight of me too. I saw the same jolt of recognition I felt echoed in her expression. Her mouth dropped open, and she looked at me, agape.

If it hadn't been for that, I might have doubted my own memory. But she recognized me too, which meant that I was right; I *had* met her before. I hadn't been acquainted with her well, but when I knew her, she hadn't been married to Mr. Teale or dressed in expensive furs.

And her name definitely had *not* been Suzette.

CHAPTER 8

"What are Mycroft and Lord Lansdowne meeting about?" I asked Holmes. "I assume that is the source of the unpleasantness at the Diogenes you mentioned the other night?"

Holmes looked up from the array of bubbling tubes and beakers on his work table. "Why should you say that?"

We were back at 221 Baker Street.

Uncle John had undertaken to accompany General Pettigrew's body to the St. James mortuary on Golden Square, where an autopsy would be performed. Holmes, meanwhile, had brought the sample of coffee he had taken back here to be analyzed.

Lestrade had hemmed and made slightly disapproving noises at allowing Holmes to remove evidence from the crime scene, but had relented when Holmes pointed out that he would be more accurate and have results a great deal more quickly than the laboratory at Scotland Yard.

Holmes had—uncharacteristically—refrained from mentioning it, but Inspector Lestrade was hardly in a position to criticize anyone else's investigative methods, given that he had managed to lose one of the chief suspects.

Holmes was now giving Becky a comprehensive course in methods of testing for various poisons; she stood beside him, watching with wide, fascinated eyes as he heated various tubes over a gas burner or added a sprinkling of mysterious powders to his beakers.

I was sitting on the couch, out of the way of the chemical proceedings.

"It can't have been the quarrel between General Pettigrew and Mr. Teale," I answered Holmes. "Mycroft wouldn't have bothered to call you in over one man's having insulted another man's wife."

"True." Holmes used a tiny metal scoop to measure out a few grains of another powder onto a tissue-thin sheet of paper, then set the paper on a small set of brass scales. He turned to Becky. "You may add that to the test tube there." He gestured. "Carefully, mind."

"Yes, Mr. Holmes."

Careful wasn't usually a favorite word in Becky's vocabulary, but awe of my father—and the thrill of being allowed to help with gathering evidence—was so far winning out.

At the moment, I could see her trying so hard to stay quiet and calm that she was practically vibrating in place.

She picked up the paper Holmes had used to hold the powder and bit her lip, her eyes crossing slightly as she focused on folding it and tapping the contents, bit by bit, into the tiny mouth of the test tube.

"There has been some trouble with the shipments of arms to the Sudan," Holmes went on. "Lord Lansdowne is looking into the matter."

His voice was guarded, which led me to believe there was more to the story than he was telling me. Though whether that was because it was a state secret or just because my father habitually horded information like a dragon hordes gold I wasn't sure.

"The Sudan." I was only vaguely familiar with the conflict in that part of Africa from what I had read in the newspapers. I knew that Kitchener was leading a coalition of British, Egyptian, and Sudanese soldiers against the Mahdist forces that had invaded and taken over the region. "So nothing to do with General Pettigrew, then—or is it?"

"Nothing to do with him at all. The general's military service was in India, and his career ended five years ago, since which time he has been a crabbed and cantankerous fixture at the Diogenes."

"Had he any family?"

"I believe there is a nephew, but no other near relations."

Holmes's tone was abstracted, which could have meant he was focusing on the chemical experiments before him. Or it could mean that his thoughts were following another track entirely.

"So we still have no motive for anyone's having wished to kill the general?"

"As yet, no." Holmes eyed the test tube to which Becky had just added the powder. "However, we do know one thing: Whatever manner General Pettigrew met his end, it was not through any injurious additive to his coffee."

I looked up quickly. "You're sure?"

"Miss Kelly and I have just tested for all of the most common forms of quick-acting poisons: cyanide, digitalis, strychnine ..."

Holmes gave Becky an approving look before returning his gaze to the arrangement of tubes and beakers. "The coffee is free from all of them."

A light tap sounded on the sitting room door, and Mrs. Hudson entered, holding an envelope.

"This arrived just a moment ago, Mr. Holmes, by special messenger."

"What is it?" I asked.

"I left word at the club for Mycroft that I would appreciate the address of the missing waiter." Holmes ripped open the envelope and glanced at the single sheet of paper inside before tossing it aside. "This is his reply."

I picked up the fallen sheet of paper. "113 Foley Street," I read. "The police will have already been there."

Holmes made an *of course* gesture with one hand, while continuing to hold the vial of coffee up to the light with the other.

"It goes equally without saying that they will have found nothing. A man adept enough to vanish from the Diogenes from under their noses will not be simply sitting in his own home, waiting for Scotland Yard to come and arrest him."

"But you've just established that the coffee wasn't poisoned," I said. "So then why did Mr. Royce run away?"

"This man Royce would hardly be the first to wish to avoid being the subject of a police investigation, regardless of whether he was guilty of murder or no."

I frowned. "It still doesn't seem likely that he would flee if he wasn't involved."

"On the contrary," Holmes said. "I can think of thirteen separate scenarios in which such a course of action would be likely, and twenty-one in which his flight from the club would be a reasonable possibility."

I raised my eyebrows. "Thirteen?"

"One." Holmes held up an index finger. "This man Royce was pilfering money from the club's petty cash box. Two, he had been guilty of some misdemeanor in his old job and feared that his dubious past would be uncovered. Three—"

I interrupted. "All right, I believe you."

"What about a snake?" Becky stepped very slowly and carefully away from the worktable, let out an audible breath of relief, and then—as though unable to contain herself another second longer—spun in a circle, skipped, and landed beside me on the couch with enough force to send up a small puff of dust from the cushions. "The man who died could have been bitten by a poisonous snake, couldn't he? Like in that story of Dr. Watson's?"

My father smiled, which was more than the mention of Uncle John's stories usually elicited from him. Becky had a softening effect, even on Sherlock Holmes.

"That is possible. Though it does not explain the apparition that Lucy and I saw at the dead man's bedside."

"The ghost!" Becky bounced on the seat of the sofa a little. "Do you think the missing waiter is the one who made it appear?"

Holmes had started to dismantle the chemical apparatus and looked at her over the tops of his test tubes with approval.

"I am delighted to hear, young lady, that you place little credence in the supposed spirit having been a genuine manifestation of the supernatural."

"Super—" Becky's forehead wrinkled.

"You don't think it was a real ghost," I supplied.

"Oh. No." Becky shook her head. "I wish there were real ghosts, I'd love to see one. And it would be nice to talk to … them, sometimes."

A trace of sadness crossed her small face, and I wondered whether she was thinking of her mother, who had died three years ago.

"But Jack says that if the dead really wanted to speak to us, they wouldn't have waited this long to figure out a way. I mean, people a hundred years ago didn't have Ouija boards and things like that."

"Your brother makes an excellent point," Holmes said.

He said something more, something about the history of the occult, but I was only half paying attention.

Becky's words—and recalling my conversation with the housemaid Ester—had made me think of something.

I crossed to the cabinet where Holmes kept his files: the one area of 221B Baker Street where organization and neatness reigned.

I ran my gaze over the various ledgers and leather-bound files, trying to remember the name I had heard. *Minton … Marsdon …*

"Maskelyne." Holmes's voice interrupted me. I looked up with a jolt.

"You will find him listed under *p* for paranormal and cross-referenced under *o* for occult and also *l*."

Of course Holmes had had the same thought occur to him—and probably some time before me too. I shouldn't even have been surprised by now.

"L?"

"Levitation," Holmes said. "He is commonly held to be the inventor of that particular illusion."

I quickly flipped through, found the correct file, and carried it with me back to the couch.

"Who is that?" Becky craned her head to peer down at the photograph attached to the file of a mustached man in a smoking jacket and bow tie. "John Neville—"

"Maskelyne," I finished.

Holmes was looking at the clock over the mantel. "I believe if you were to leave directly, there would be just time enough for you to reach the Egyptian Hall for the start of the afternoon show."

"Egyptian Hall?" Becky repeated. Her eyes were wide.

"That's right." I stood up. "Becky, how would you like to come with me to a magic show?"

CHAPTER 9

"And now"—the man in the top hat stepped towards the edge of the stage and lowered his voice impressively—"as my grand finale, I shall make this magnificent animal vanish into thin air."

He waved at the elephant that occupied the stage with him.

The elephant looked fairly unimpressed by the whole proceedings. Though the same couldn't be said for the audience. There were gasps and murmurs all around. Becky, sitting beside me, was on the very edge of her chair.

Two costumed assistants led the elephant into a caged enclosure constructed of bamboo rods. The gate was closed, though everyone could still see the huge animal through the bars.

The magician snapped his fingers, and a black silk cloth descended from the ceiling, covering the entire cage, elephant and all.

He waved his wand, a puff of smoke erupted, and then he whipped the silk covering off the cage.

The elephant was gone.

The room erupted into applause, the magician took a bow to thunderous cheers, and then the stage curtains came down. The lights in the theater came back on.

"Did you like it?" I asked Becky.

Becky's eyes were still saucer-wide. "That was ... *amazing.*"

The rest of the audience was standing up, starting to filter out.

A young theater usher in a brass-buttoned coat appeared beside our aisle.

"Miss James?" he asked. "Mr. Maskelyne will see you now, if you'll just follow me backstage."

* * *

The Egyptian Hall in Piccadilly had been built earlier in the century as a museum and then soon after was converted to an exhibition hall. According to a plaque on one of the walls, the emperor Napoleon's carriage in which he had ridden to Waterloo had once been on display here.

The whole interior was decorated to look like an ancient Egyptian tomb or temple, with columns painted in bright turquoise and gold and stone statues of the Egyptian goddesses and gods lining the walls.

Becky and I followed the usher through a doorway marked *private*, along a hall, and down a flight of stairs. The usher knocked on another door, and a man's voice called out, "Come in."

The room inside was a riot of paraphernalia from the stage: racks of costumes, chairs and tables, and furniture of every description. An entire bookshelf was filled with various decks of cards, and in one corner was a cage with a pair of white rabbits, calmly nibbling on lettuce.

In the midst of the chaos, the magician from the stage performance sat at a dressing table, taking the stage makeup off his face with a cloth and a jar of cream.

"Mr. Maskelyne?" I asked.

He was older than in the photograph from Holmes's files; somewhere in his late fifties, with a few more lines around the corners of his eyes, and more gray in his hair.

"I am indeed." He spoke with something of a showman's flourish, probably the result of having just been on stage.

I knew myself from performing nightly that it was sometimes hard to shift back into normal speaking mode and *stop* performing after the curtain was rung down.

Mr. Maskelyne rose from his chair and smiled with genuine warmth at the sight of Becky, who—in an unusual attack of shyness—was clinging to my hand. He stepped forward, reached out, and pulled a shilling coin from her hair.

"Dear me, how did that get in there?" He shook his head. "And here's *another* one."

He handed the coins to Becky, who narrowed her eyes at him in intense concentration, her shyness forgotten. "Do that again, please."

Mr. Maskelyne obeyed, handing over a third coin, and Becky let out a triumphant shout, turning to me.

"Lucy, I know how he's doing it! He's holding the coins in his palm, see? Then he just pretends to find them. Did you?" she asked Mr. Maskelyne.

"Ah, I can see I must be careful." He winked at her. "A magician never gives away his trade secrets."

If I knew Becky, she would rise to that challenge by making it her personal mission to work out the illusion behind every magic trick in his act. Though at the moment, she was more interested in the rabbits' cage.

"May I pet them?"

"Go right ahead." Mr. Maskelyne made a sweeping gesture. "Just do not allow them to tell you that they are the real stars of the act. Terrible *prima-donnas*, all of them."

Becky laughed and went to peer into the cage.

"Thank you for seeing us," I said.

"It's a pleasure, Miss James. The note you brought with you bore a signature I have not seen in quite some time."

Holmes had sent a note of introduction with me, which I had handed to a theater employee to deliver before the show.

The magician watched me closely. "Am I to understand, then, that the Reichenbach Falls was not the end that Doctor Watson's account would have us believe? An astonishing feat of escape that must have been."

I smiled. "As you yourself said, a good magician never reveals his secrets. But Mr. Holmes sends his regards. He spoke most highly of you."

"He would have made a fine stage magician himself, had he ever decided to make a career of the art of illusion." Mr. Maskelyne smiled. "He possessed the requisite view that people are infinitely easy to confound."

"That certainly sounds like Sherlock Holmes."

"His note mentioned an apparition witnessed by the two of you?"

"Yes, that's right. We were hoping you might be able to tell us how the trick was done."

That was where I had originally heard John Maskelyne's name and where—according to Holmes's files—he had originally gotten his start in the stage business: by debunking the tricks employed by false mediums and phony masters of the occult.

"Well." Mr. Maskelyne rubbed his hands together. "Of course, without seeing it for myself, it's difficult to tell you anything for certain. But I shall do my best. Can you describe to me what you saw?"

"A face—a man's face—glowing faintly and hanging in midair in a darkened room."

"Hmmm." Mr. Maskelyne frowned. "As for the glow, that's easily accounted for." He snapped his fingers dismissively. "Phosphorescent paint may be bought in at least a dozen shops in London alone. A quick coat, and—*presto*—a ghostly glimmer of otherworldly light. As for the hovering, there are wires, of course, or hooks and fishing line. Some of the mediums out there simply use wooden poles painted black—invisible in a dark room, but make it look as though a tambourine or some other apparatus is floating in midair."

"There were no hooks. We were able to examine the room immediately afterwards. There were not ropes or wires—and no one at all to maneuver a painted wooden pole. The room was entirely empty, save for a dead man."

"A dead man." Mr. Maskelyne looked momentarily startled, then frowned. "I see. In that case, I shall have to consider. There are of course various options, such as Pepper's ghost—though that involves mirrors and significant modification of the room in which the illusion appears. Perhaps you might allow me to consider the matter and then contact you when I have come up with a few solutions which we might match to what you saw?"

"Of course." It would have been convenient if Mr. Maskelyne could have pointed me to the exact method our culprit had used, but I had already learned that steps in an investigation were seldom so straightforward. "Thank you for your time."

Mr. Maskelyne waved my thanks aside. "I'm intrigued. I have seen many wonders in my investigations into fraudulent mediums, Miss James. I have seen the ghostly imprints that spirit hands left in a supposedly sealed-off tablet of wax. I have seen tables rock and levitate, mediums apparently float in midair, and the ectoplasm left behind by an otherworldly apparition. What I have *never* seen, however, is a genuine ghost. I look forward to disproving whatever new trickery lies behind this one."

CHAPTER 10

"I think I know how the trick where he sawed the lady in half was done," Becky said. "It has to be two ladies, really—the head of one, and the feet of the other. But I still don't know how he made the elephant disappear. *That* was a good trick."

We were in a cab riding back home to Baker Street from Piccadilly. Becky was silent a moment, her face clouding. "I wish Jack could have seen it. Do you think he's all right?"

"I'm sure he is." Actually, my initial annoyance had faded to an odd, nameless worry that sat in my stomach like a lump of ice. But I was hardly going to tell Becky that. "When we get back to Baker Street, I'll help you write Jack a letter, and we can post it to him in Bath, all right?"

"All right." Becky sounded happier.

I glanced out the carriage window and saw that we were just passing New Cavendish Street. If we turned to the right up ahead, we wouldn't have to go far out of our way to be on Foley Street.

"At the moment, though, would you be willing to help me with something for the investigation?"

Becky beamed—possibly even wider than she had during the magic act—and bounced in her seat. "Of course! What are we doing? Are we going to spy on anyone? Or drag a murderer off to jail? Or sneak into a den of thieves?"

"Nothing *quite* that dramatic, I'm afraid. We are going to make a search of a suspect's lodgings, though."

Becky considered. "I suppose that's still exciting. Where does he live?"

It was nearly five o'clock as our cab rolled up in front of number 113, and the chill dark of an autumn evening had fallen over the city. Gas lamps were lighted at intervals along the side of the road. Pedestrians hurried past, eager to get home to their own firesides and an evening meal.

I turned, handing payment over to the cab driver. I debated asking him to wait, but I wasn't sure how long we would be.

Besides, I didn't want to attract undue attention. I could already see the solid, blue-uniformed officer stationed outside of the address Mycroft had given us. Obviously Lestrade had both been here and thought it worthwhile to leave a constable on guard.

On the positive side, if a police constable was guarding the place, it meant that Royce couldn't be inside. I'd already assumed as much, but the police presence made any possible danger in bringing Becky here practically nonexistent.

It did, though, make our getting inside more complicated.

"How are we going to get in?" Becky asked.

"I'm not sure."

Number 113 was a narrow brick building, new, plain, and box-like in design, with an air of unimaginative respectability.

Like my own old flat in Exeter Street, there seemed to be one main entrance for all the flats in the building. The lock on the door was highly polished, but childishly simple to pick—if we could distract the police constable long enough to let me try it.

"How do you think we should get in?" I asked Becky.

"Lie, probably." Becky spoke calmly. "I'm not supposed to tell lies, usually—and I don't. But this is for a good cause."

"All right. We're visiting our aunt, who lives on"—I scanned the block of flats—"on the third floor. How does that sound?"

Becky nodded approval, following my gaze. "You picked the third floor because there are lace curtains in the window and potted geraniums on the sill."

"Thus making it more likely that there's a woman living there," I agreed. "Not that a bachelor isn't allowed to keep geraniums, but I haven't met very many who do. Now, do you recognize the police constable? Is he anyone Jack knows? Anyone who would recognize you?"

It wasn't very likely. Jack worked out of the Commercial Street police station, and this man was probably from Scotland Yard.

Becky studied him, then shook her head. "I don't know him."

"Perfect. Can you make sure he doesn't look at what I'm doing at the door for ... say, twenty seconds?"

Becky skipped over to the uniformed police officer, who was looking distinctly bored. He'd probably been stationed here all afternoon.

"Hello!" She gave him a brilliant smile. "I'm going to visit my Aunt Alice."

There were advantages to being nine years old. If I'd gone over and started talking to a policeman out of a clear blue sky,

I would have been met with at the very least suspicion. Becky got a nod and an indulgent smile.

The constable was a big, solidly built man who looked as though he might have children of his own at home.

I stepped past them, half listening as Becky told him all about the magic show we had just seen.

The lock was as simple as I had thought. A few quick moments with the set of lock picks I always carried and it snapped obligingly open.

I gave Becky a nod, and she said goodbye to the constable, coming over to join me.

"Did Mr. Holmes teach you how to do that?" she asked once we were inside the building's front foyer.

I shook my head, dropping the lock picks back into my bag. "No, I taught myself long before I met Mr. Holmes. When I was at boarding school, our bedroom wing was kept locked, and I wanted to be able to sneak out at night. Of course, back then, I had to make do with hairpins."

I opened a door and we stepped into a narrow, unlighted stairwell.

The building had only three flats, with the address Royce had given on the second floor. Motioning Becky to keep silent, I stood for a moment outside of the ground floor apartment, listening. But there were no sounds of life from inside, and I'd seen no lights in the windows when we were outside on the street.

"All right, let's keep going," I murmured.

Becky and I climbed up to the second-floor landing, and a door painted in dull gray paint that was labeled 113B.

I took out my lock picks again, crouched down to study the lock—and a sudden crawling sense of uneasiness prickled across my skin.

Holmes would discount the power of intuition out of hand. But I wasn't quite willing to do the same, especially not where Becky's safety was concerned.

In the same way most people could step into a house and know, just by feel, that it was empty, I had the unshakeable feeling that the apartment in front of us was *not* empty now.

I bent down, speaking in a near-inaudible murmur. "You know what would actually be far more helpful? If you go downstairs and wait just inside the front door. That way you can keep watch and let me know if the constable out there decides to come in—or if anyone else does. The signal can be two short whistles if anyone is about to climb up the stairs."

More importantly, if there happened to be trouble, Becky would be practically within arm's reach of police assistance.

Becky nodded, solemn with the importance of her mission, and slipped silent as a ghost back down the stairs. I breathed out slowly, then inserted the first of my picks into the lock, pressed, fumbled a moment, then inserted a second and third. I felt the tumblers slide over with a faint click, straightened, and opened the door to our missing waiter's rooms.

For a moment after stepping into the front vestibule, I thought my sense of not being alone had been misplaced. The curtains were open, letting in the ambient glow of the street lamps outside, and at first glance, the flat appeared entirely deserted.

I was in a sitting room, furnished with a couch and two armchairs, all upholstered in dreary, faded chintz. As though to make up for the furniture, the walls were papered with an almost violently cheerful pattern of flowers in all colors.

The signs of a police search were visible in the cushions that had been pulled askew and the tracks left here and there in the dust on the floor.

There was also a rectangular-shaped mark in the dust by the front door, blurred at the edges—as though someone had slid an envelope under the door and it had lain collecting dust for some days.

But if Lestrade and his men had found anything to point them in the direction of where Royce was now, they had taken it with them.

Save for a painting of a sad-eyed spaniel dog on the wall, there were no pictures, no photographs, no papers or letters on the mantel—nothing of a personal nature of any kind. The shelves of the single bookcase in the corner were entirely empty of books, and the door of the coat closet to my right was partially ajar, showing shelves and a clothes bar that were equally bare.

I stayed very still, listening and letting my gaze travel again around the room. There was a doorway in the wall to my left, likewise partially cracked open. I held my breath and heard it: a faint creak from the room beyond, as though someone had shifted their weight while standing on a loose floorboard.

Maybe the police had left another man on guard inside the flat?

I considered then instantly discarded that possibility. An on-duty police constable would have come out here to arrest me for breaking and entering, not remained hiding in the bedroom.

In addition to a lack of personal items, there wasn't much in the flat that could qualify as a weapon. No helpful iron pokers in a rack by the fireplace. I crept forward, reached the second door, and gave it a swift, violent shove inwards, sending it crashing against the wall and shattering the silence. At least I could be sure that no one was hiding behind it.

The room inside was darker, without any uncurtained windows to let in light. But nothing moved amidst the vague shadows of a bed and other furniture whose shapes I could make out inside.

I inched forward, step by cautious step.

Strong arms—seemingly coming out of nowhere—seized me from behind.

Reflexively, I kicked out, at the same time snapping my head back in a way that should have smashed my attacker's nose. He somehow anticipated the move a fraction of a second ahead of time, clamping my arms to my sides and spinning me around to face him.

Whoever he was, he was incredibly strong. Strong and with good reflexes too.

Not a good combination in an opponent.

I still struggled to wrench myself away. But as I moved, a shaft of the street lights outside happened to slant across us, letting me catch sight of his face.

All the air went out of my lungs, and I froze.

Jack.

If one of the pieces of bedroom furniture suddenly came to life and punched me in the stomach, I would have been less surprised.

He was wearing dark clothes that would blend in with the shadows outside. My one slight consolation was that he looked as shocked to see me as I was to see him.

He opened his mouth.

Becky's voice, small and frightened-sounding, came from outside in the stairwell. "Lucy? Lucy, is everything all right?"

Jack froze for a split second, but then reacted almost instantly, letting go of me and moving to the window in the closest bedroom wall, which I could now see was open. That must be how he had got in.

His leg was hurting him; I could see it in the stiffness of his movements and the compressed line of his jaw. Even still, he ducked under the sash and climbed out before I could manage to make my voice work.

"Lucy?" Becky called out again.

I half expected to hear a crash announcing that Jack had plummeted to his death by falling—or at the least succeeded in breaking *both* his legs.

But a glance out the window showed him climbing down the drain pipe that ran down the side of the house, moving hand-over-hand with a controlled, almost casual grace.

I opened my mouth. But if I called after him, Becky would hear. She would know that he wasn't safe in Bath after all. Instead, he'd been breaking into the home of a possible murderer.

Jack might possibly deserve to be found out for lying, but Becky didn't deserve to have to worry about him.

I turned, crossing back to the outer room. "In here, Becky! Everything is fine."

CHAPTER 11

I swept open the door to the upstairs Baker Street sitting room. It would have been far more satisfying to bang it hard enough to rattle the windows, but I was mindful of Becky, asleep downstairs in 221A.

It was late. After returning from Foley Street, I'd had just enough time to settle Becky in and then leave for the evening performance at the Savoy.

I'd expected to have a hard time giving my full attention to the performance of *The Yeomen of the Guard*. But actually, it had been a welcome change, pretending to be someone else for a few hours.

Now I was back at Baker Street, and I had already heard the murmur of my father and Uncle John's voices from the sitting room, telling me that they were still awake.

Not that I particularly cared; I'd been quite prepared to haul my father out of bed for this conversation if necessary.

Holmes and Watson were seated on opposite sides of the fire. Both gave me startled glances as I swept into the room. Well, Uncle John looked startled. Holmes's eyebrows climbed fractionally towards his hairline, which was as startled as he ever appeared.

"How *could* you?" I demanded. "I know you can be cold—callous at times—but this is *thoroughly* contemptible."

Holmes's brows rose another quarter inch. "You appear to be angry."

"How unbelievably observant!" I curled my fingertips, resisting the urge to sweep everything off the mantel in one giant smash. "You must be some sort of detective."

"However"—Holmes went on as though I hadn't spoken—"in this instance, I believe the conversation would proceed in a more productive fashion if I had the remotest idea what you were angry about."

I faced him. "I *knew* it! I knew you wouldn't actually have sent Jack off to some sort of private clinic for treatment. Jack saved your *life*." My voice wavered briefly. "And he might be permanently crippled as a result. Isn't that enough for you, without roping him into another investigation and sending him off on some sort of secret, dangerous assignment? As if he's in any kind of shape to take that sort of work on!"

"I wholeheartedly agree," Holmes said.

"I—what?" I stared at him, feeling as though I'd just had the ground abruptly drop out from under me.

"That is why I sent Detective Constable Kelly to Bath, in hopes that he might recover, both physically and mentally, from his ordeal." Holmes's voice was calm, but there was an underlying note of grimness. "Am I to understand that he is *not* at Dr. Mortimer's clinic?"

Uncle John had been looking from me to Holmes, rather in the manner of someone watching a tennis match. But now he broke in, his brow creased in an anxious frown. "Lucy, my dear, I don't entirely understand what this is about. But I assure you that Charles Mortimer's clinic is entirely legitimate and aboveboard—an excellent facility. I myself spoke to Charles earlier this week, discussing Constable Kelly's case and inviting his opinion on whether his particular brand of therapy might be helpful."

"But—" I sat down on the sofa, feeling as though my legs had abruptly collapsed under me. I was still staring at Holmes. "Are you saying that when you made your offer to Jack, you were being completely straightforward? *You?*"

"Yes, well." Holmes mouth twitched briefly, though the concern was still in his gaze. "I do occasionally act without ulterior motives or pretense. I admit to thinking that being involved in an investigation again might aid in the young man's recovery. That is my own sovereign remedy for malady. But only *after* he has recovered physically."

"But—" My anger had gone out like a quenched flame, to be replaced by a cold feeling that wrapped all around my spine. "In that case, what was Jack doing at Royce's flat this afternoon?"

Holmes's gaze sharpened, his features becoming even more hawk-like. "He was at our missing waiter's residence?"

"He had broken in through a window."

"Hmmm." Holmes brought his hands together, resting his index fingers against his upper lip. There were disconcerting moments when my father actually looked exactly like one of the illustrations from Dr. Watson's stories, and this was one of them. "That is quite a—"

I took a breath. "I apologize for believing that this was your fault. But if the words *pretty little problem* come out of your mouth next, I may not be responsible for my actions."

Holmes gave me a mildly reproachful look. "I was about to say *conundrum*. And I am not, after all, sure that you are wrong to assign blame to me."

I thought back, trying to remember everything about Holmes's visit to Jack and Becky's lodgings. He had come in, wet because of the rain, and set the leather attaché case down—

"The papers!" I said. "The ones from Mycroft."

Holmes was—unsurprisingly—already in motion, rising and clearing a mountain of papers off the coffee table with a single sweep of his arm. When that failed to reveal anything but the bare surface of the tabletop, he gave an impatient hiss of breath and shoveled another heap of newspapers and other assorted correspondence off the couch.

Mrs. Hudson was going to have her work cut out for her in the morning.

"Aha. Here it is." Holmes held up the leather case, extracting a sheaf of official-looking documents.

"Did Jack see these?" I asked.

Holmes was already frowning over the first of the papers. "He did. They had become wet, and given their importance, I spread them in front of the fire to dry while Constable Kelly and I spoke."

It was a mark of how much Holmes trusted Jack that he would have done that.

I frowned at the papers in Holmes's hands. There were the blueprint documents I had remembered, as well as a few sheets that looked at a glance like police reports.

"I wouldn't have thought these would mean anything in particular to Jack," I said.

"Indeed. However, they must have done. In which case, we had best determine what caught his eye."

With another sweep of his arm, Holmes cleared the table on which he and Uncle John usually took their meals; I barely rescued a teacup and saucer in time.

"You didn't notice Jack looking at any of the papers in particular?"

Holmes looked at me, and I caught myself. "Of course you didn't, or you would already have said."

I bent, peering at the papers as Holmes laid them on the table one by one.

Uncle John got up from his chair and came to stand next to me.

He let out an exclamation of surprise. "These are plans for a machine gun, Holmes!"

"Maxims, to be precise," Holmes said. "There are also plans here for breech-loading rifles." He stopped, looking from me to Uncle John. "It goes without saying that what I am about to tell you is confidential in the highest degree."

"Of course," Uncle John said.

I nodded, as well.

"A shipment of armaments has gone missing."

"Missing?" I repeated.

"Stolen. The weapons were to be shipped out to the Sudan later this month and were being stored in a warehouse here in

London. Six days ago, there was a break-in at the warehouse, and nine crates containing weapons such as these"—he indicated the diagrams on the table—"were stolen."

I stared down at the array of documents spread out in front of us, tension twisting the muscles of my neck.

Three months ago, we had tangled with a group determined to arm themselves by any means possible and kill anyone who stood in their path.

"I didn't tell you what I found in Royce's flat," I said.

Uncle John's forehead creased. "Holmes, weren't you just telling me that Inspector Lestrade told you they'd found nothing?"

"I'm not surprised." I looked at Holmes. "There was nothing there to find. Literally so. No personal items of any kind, no clothes in the closet, no books or food on the shelves."

Holmes regarded the fire in the grate from under half-closed eyes. "Royce was not in fact living there."

"So it would appear. It looks as though the flat was just a sham, a false address in a respectable neighborhood that he could use on his application for work at the Diogenes." I stopped. "You realize what this means, don't you."

It wasn't a question; it was a simple statement of fact. If I had already come to the most obvious logical conclusion, it went without saying that Holmes's mind had leapt there as well.

Uncle John cleared his throat. "I realize I'm the odd man out here, but I personally haven't the faintest idea what any of this means."

I turned to him quickly. "I'm sorry Uncle John. That's because you weren't at the Diogenes today to speak with Lord Lansdowne and everyone else who witnessed General Pettigrew's death. Jack can't have known about the general's death. How could he? It would maybe have been mentioned in the evening edition of the papers, but at that point, Jack was *already* at Royce's flat. Which means that these papers and the whole business of the stolen weapons are somehow connected to Royce, the missing waiter."

Holmes was looking at me across the table, his gray eyes clear and steady. He gave me an almost imperceptible nod of confirmation.

"What Holmes and I are wondering," I went on, "is whether General Pettigrew wasn't actually the intended victim today after all. Lord Lansdowne was."

CHAPTER 12

Holmes spoke into the silence that followed my words. "It will be easier to determine whether our hypothesis is correct once we have ascertained the manner of the general's death." He glanced at me. "Before you, ahem, joined us, Watson was just beginning to relay to me the results of General Pettigrew's autopsy. Watson, perhaps you might give us both the full report now?"

"Certainly. In addition to the hypostasis visible in the general's skin—due to excess oxyhemoglobin—there was a distinct smell of almonds about the body."

I rubbed my eyes. After our trip to Austria, I had asked Uncle John to loan me one of his medical textbooks so that I would understand what he was talking about when he used terminology like *hypostasis* and *oxyhemoglobin*.

From what I remembered, I was fairly certain the first term meant that the general's skin had appeared to be reddened; the second, that his body had been unable to use oxygen. The smell of almonds, though, was the most conclusive.

"So it *was* cyanide poisoning after all."

Uncle John held up a hand. "However, the lungs showed a higher hydrocyanic acid content than the stomach contents."

"The lungs." Holmes expression was hard, focused. "Not potassium cyanide, then, but hydrogen cyanide. Cyanide gas."

"*Gas*?" I looked from my father to Uncle John. "But that makes no sense whatsoever. How on earth did anyone manage to dose General Pettigrew with poisoned gas inside the Diogenes? Wouldn't everyone in the club have died if that were the case?"

Holmes shook his head, but it was Uncle John who answered. "The gas diffuses in a large area. What would be a fatal dose in a contained space would cause no more than a headache or temporary illness when introduced into a larger room."

"Quite so," Holmes said. "If memory serves, there have been instances of a medical examiner becoming ill while performing the autopsy on a victim of cyanide poisoning, the potassium cyanide having been turned to hydrogen cyanide by the acid in the stomach. However, none, to my knowledge have died."

"I suppose that explains why Lord Lansdowne is still alive, even though he was in the same room with General Pettigrew. But it still doesn't answer how the gas got into the general's lungs. Lord Lansdowne didn't mention anything about Royce going over to General Pettigrew's desk and releasing a gas canister."

"Indeed. And such an action is hardly the sort of gambit that can be carried out without anyone—including the victim himself—noticing."

"It's also not easy to imagine how you could gas the wrong man by mistake. If there'd been a mix-up and General Pettigrew had taken Lord Lansdowne's seat, then maybe it would be different. But they were each in their accustomed chairs. And we didn't find any mechanism for delivering a fatal dose of cyanide gas."

"Very true." Holmes's gaze was fixed on the middle distance, his expression making me think more than ever of a bird of prey, poised to take flight. "We must assume that once we establish the method by which the poison was delivered, we will also be more certain of the motive and of the identity of the intended victim."

I studied him. "You still think the intended victim was Lord Lansdowne, don't you."

Holmes was silent a beat; as Watson had often observed, he never relished sharing his own suspicions before a case was solved. But at last he said, "For all the reasons we have outlined already, I think it likely enough that I have already communicated with Mycroft, asking him to put Lord Lansdowne on his guard."

"Then *I* need to find out how Jack is involved."

I turned back to the papers spread out on the table, though they were as frustratingly uncommunicative as before. Machine gun blueprints, reports on safety regulations and testing that at first glance looked like an impenetrable wall of technical jargon. A police report on the warehouse break-in—

"Hello, what's this?" Uncle John said.

I stopped short, looking over his shoulder at the paper he was holding.

It was the second page of the police report on the break-in at the warehouse and showed what looked to be a sketch of a man's face, drawn in pencil.

"What is that?" I asked.

Uncle John read quickly through the notes that accompanied the drawing. "A police artist's sketch of the suspect, as described by the night watchman who reported the theft. Apparently he was making his rounds and came upon this man"—he tapped the pencil drawing—"breaking in through a window. He shouted, and the miscreant attacked him, coming after him with a knife. The night watchman might have been killed, but that he blew on his whistle, summoning reinforcements, and the burglar ran off. However, when they investigated, they found the crates of weapons already gone, thus making it clear that the suspect had accomplices."

"And the location of the warehouse was—" Actually, I knew that; I'd just read it on the first page of the report. With a sick, leaden feeling, I found the address again. Cannon Street, Cheapside.

"Is something wrong, Lucy?"

Uncle John's kindly, concerned voice seemed to come from a long distance off.

"You've gone quite pale."

For the second time, Holmes's gaze met mine from across the table. He hadn't looked at the papers in Uncle John's hands, but I doubted that he would need to. He probably had the entire substance of the report memorized.

"I'm fine, Uncle John." I forced a smile. "Really. I'm just tired. It's very late."

I doubted that Uncle John believed me. He might not have an intellect equal to Sherlock Holmes's, but he was by no means stupid. Still, he patted my hand.

"I shall bid you goodnight, then. Sleep well, Lucy, my dear."

Holmes didn't speak, not until we had heard Watson's footsteps mount to the bedroom upstairs.

"Cheapside would be the turf of the criminal gang with which Constable Kelly was associated before joining the police force?"

"You already know that it is, don't you? You must have made inquiries."

Holmes looked mildly affronted. "In fact, I have not. I may have *theorized* his former membership in a Cheapside gang—the Sloggers, for choice. But he has no criminal record of arrest on file, and I refrained from inquiring of any of my usual sources. I was endeavoring to behave more in the fashion of ordinary fathers, who—or so I am informed—do *not* institute full-scale criminal inquiries amongst the London underworld into the young men of their daughters' choosing."

Despite myself, I laughed, though it came out a little unsteady. "What can ordinary fathers be thinking?"

Holmes cleared his throat. "I firmly believe in the right of any man to rise above the mistakes of his past. Moreover, I trust your judgment—both in regards to Constable Kelly's character and in other matters."

"Thank you."

"In my estimation, however, Constable Kelly is not a young man who shares his burdens easily, and he is very proud."

"Which is another way of saying that he didn't trust me enough to tell me about whatever he's doing now," I said.

Holmes opened his mouth and then closed it again, seeming to change his mind about whatever he had been going to say. "All other questions aside, he may be in a considerable degree of danger. It might be in his best interests to give him a warning—if, that is, you know where to find him?"

I drew in a breath, looking down at the paper that Uncle John had left on the table.

The man in the drawing looked to be somewhere in his middle-thirties, though it was difficult to tell for sure from a pencil drawing. Beneath dark, untidy hair, his features were broad and harsh, like a wood carving formed by rough blades of an axe. A low, heavy brow, deep-set eyes, and a wide jaw.

A pitiless, brutal face, without a hint of softness in its lines. The face of a man who acted without remorse, and expected to be obeyed.

"Not exactly," I said in answer to Holmes. "But at least I have a place to start."

CHAPTER 13

"Now watch closely," Becky said. She glanced up at me. "Actually, don't watch *too* closely. I'm not sure that I've quite worked out how to do this trick properly."

"I will be a very forgiving audience," I promised.

We were in the Baker Street sitting room, with the late morning sun streaming in through the windows.

Holmes's warning from last night sat like a cold block of ice in my chest. But as much I would have liked to go straight out and begin searching for Jack, there was no chance I could start this morning.

For obvious reasons, I couldn't bring Becky with me, and she would see through any excuse I made as to why I had to leave her and then know that something was wrong.

I had an afternoon rehearsal at the Savoy today, which I'd promised that Becky could come along to watch, and then a performance tonight. The task of tracking down Jack would have to wait until afterwards, when Becky would be asleep in bed.

"Good," Becky said. "Now, then." She held up a length of cord and spoke dramatically. "I shall now magically make a knot appear in this string. *Abracadabra!*" She shook her hands, then opened them to reveal the knot in one end of the cord.

I applauded. "Very good."

Mrs. Hudson tapped at the door before coming in. "Morning post for you, Miss Lucy." She handed me a stack of letters. "And there's a gentleman here. He says his name is Mr. Barton and that he's secretary to Lord Lansdowne. He was hoping to see your father, but Mr. Holmes isn't here."

"That's right." Holmes had gone back to the Diogenes Club to examine the scene of the general's death for possible means of introducing cyanide gas.

"Do you want me to show him in here instead?" Mrs. Hudson asked.

"Yes, I'll see him." I ought to be able to speak to Lord Lansdowne's *secretary* without breaking out in a cold sweat. "Thank you, Mrs. Hudson, you can bring him in."

* * *

"Miss James." Edward Barton stretched out a hand to me as he came into the sitting room. He wore a dark gray suit and carried his hat in one hand. His dark red hair was combed neatly back from his face. "Seeing you again is an unexpected pleasure."

I stood up to greet him. "I'm still not sure the word *pleasure* means what you think it does. But please, come in."

Mr. Barton grinned. "And if you knew the life of a private secretary, you would understand that I wasn't exaggerating when I said our first encounter was the most exciting thing to happen to me in quite some time."

"You're lucky Lucy didn't hit you and knock you unconscious." Becky spoke up from her place on the hearthrug. "She's very good at that."

Mr. Barton looked mildly startled, but then bowed. "Then I shall indeed count myself lucky. I don't believe I've had the pleasure of making your acquaintance, miss …"

"Kelly," Becky supplied. "Becky Kelly. I'm staying with Lucy for a while."

Mr. Barton gravely took her hand. "A pleasure to meet you as well, Miss Becky Kelly."

"Do you want to see a magic trick?" Becky asked.

"I should be delighted."

"All right, watch this." Becky held up a shilling coin— probably one of the ones she'd gotten from Mr. Maskelyne yesterday—and skipped over to the breakfast table. "I'm going to make this coin disappear into the table."

She put the coin on the table, balanced on its edge, then covered it with her hand, pushing down.

The coin skidded, bounced, and shot off the table to land with a *ting* in the coal scuttle. Prince, who had been dozing by the fire, sat up with a startled snort.

"Drat," Becky said. "I haven't quite got the hang of that one."

Mr. Barton's mouth twitched, but he bent and gravely handed the coin back to Becky. "Practice makes perfect. I shall stand ready to be astonished at our next meeting, Miss Kelly."

"Would you mind if I asked you a few questions about yesterday?" I asked.

"Not at all." Mr. Barton glanced at Becky.

She had gone back to practicing with the coin, trying to palm it and then let it drop into her sleeve, but she looked up. "It's all right. I know all about that man being poisoned."

"A budding illusionist *and* a detective in training." Mr. Barton smiled. "Very well, then, Miss James, I am at your disposal."

"Were you working with Lord Lansdowne in the writing room yesterday morning?" I asked.

"For a time. His Lordship had some important letters to write. He would write one, then pass it off to me, and I would copy it in triplicate for the War Office files."

"In *triplicate*?" My eyebrows went up.

"I told you, a secretary's work is often dull in the extreme."

"And yet you stay in his Lordship's employ."

"As a boy, I had my heart set on running away to become a sailor, but my father was determined that I should go into politics and found me the post with Lord Lansdowne. The two of them were boys at school together." He shrugged. "There are compensations. At least as his Lordship's secretary I have never had to subsist on hard tack crackers. And I have yet to be marooned on a desert island."

"Or drowned by a huge white whale?"

Mr. Barton laughed. "Now you're just mocking me. I wanted to be Billy Bones of *Treasure Island* fame, not Captain Ahab."

"Did you see the waiter, Royce, while you were working yesterday?"

"I did. At least, I didn't know his name at the time. But I'm told that he was the man who has now gone missing. Let me think." Mr. Barton frowned. "He came in once to ask whether we wished for tea or coffee. His Lordship asked for a cup of tea."

"Tea? You're certain?"

Holmes had determined that the coffee in General Pettigrew's cup was harmless, but it still seemed worth finding out whether there could have been any sort of a mix-up with his and Lord Lansdowne's drinks.

"Quite certain. His Lordship always drinks tea in the mornings. Milk, no sugar. This man Royce delivered the tea, and then"—Edward Barton frowned again—"yes, that's right, then Lord Lansdowne asked for a fresh stick of sealing wax to be brought in so that he might seal up his letters to be posted. And after that, I went out at his Lordship's request to see that the letters were safely delivered into the club mailbag, to be handed in for the collection of the afternoon post."

"So you weren't in the room when General Pettigrew took ill?"

"No." For the first time, Mr. Barton's good-humored face took on a graver cast. "I heard the commotion and came rushing back, but I was too late to be of any use. Has Mr. Holmes any idea how he died?"

"I believe not. Though it is sometimes difficult to be certain what ideas Sherlock Holmes has."

"I imagine it must be." Mr. Barton took a small envelope from his pocket. "I actually came this morning to deliver a message from Lord Lansdowne to you and your father. Well, less a message than an invitation. On this coming Friday night, we are to host a gala evening at Lansdowne House—a charity ball, given for the benefit of the Army and Navy Pensioners' Aide Society. Lord Lansdowne is hoping to raise funds to endow a pensioners' home here in London, where homeless veterans of our army and naval forces may live and receive training in a trade, so that they may become self-supporting."

"That sounds a very worthy cause."

It also sounded like an excellent opportunity for anyone hoping to murder Lord Lansdowne to make another attempt on his life. I said nothing, though.

I hadn't any reason in particular not to trust Mr. Barton. But after the past several months, I didn't trust *anyone* on first or second meeting. I sometimes felt as though I could scarcely manage to trust anyone, ever, anymore.

Mr. Barton's face brightened. "I hope that means that you'll come, Miss James?"

I hadn't been back to Lansdowne House since last May. I would be walking onto the grounds of the place where Mycroft, Becky, Holmes, and I could have died.

I took a breath.

I might not be able to keep from having nightmares, but I could at least refuse to let fear rule my life during my waking hours.

"I can't speak for Mr. Holmes," I said. "But yes, I'll be delighted to come."

* * *

"He seems nice," Becky said when Mr. Barton had gone.

"He does." Always assuming that he didn't prove to be a murderer or a traitor.

"Who is this letter from?" Becky was looking through the stack of mail that Mrs. Hudson had brought in and held up a pink, gilt-edged envelope. Then she dropped it again. "Oh. I'm sorry. My mother told me it wasn't polite to read other people's mail."

"That's all right, I haven't any horrible secrets that I'm aware of."

Becky giggled, but then sighed. "I was just hoping there would be a letter from Jack."

After seeing Jack at Royce's apartment yesterday, I had forgotten my promise to help Becky with a letter. But she had written herself, gotten the address for the clinic from Uncle John, and borrowed a stamp from him, all before I'd woken up this morning.

I hadn't specifically asked that Uncle John keep my meeting with Jack secret from Becky, but then, I hadn't had to. I had known he wouldn't tell her. Though I was sorry now for putting him in the position of having to lie.

Becky wrinkled her nose. "So who *is* this letter from?" She held up the gilt-edged envelope again. "It smells like perfume."

"Let me see?"

I took the envelope from Becky. She was right, it was heavily scented with lavender. I slit it open, automatically noting that the address was written in a round, slightly childish feminine hand. There was only a single sheet of paper inside.

Please—

After the first word, there was a blot of ink, as though the sender had started to write *Lucy* and then scratched it out.

Please, Miss James, will you come and see me tomorrow afternoon at three o'clock?

An address followed, on St. James Square in the West End, and then a signature. *Mrs. Suzette Teale.*

"Teale?" Becky was reading over my shoulder. "Isn't that the name of the man who quarreled with General Pettigrew?"

"That's right." I spoke absently, my eyes still on the note. I hadn't told anyone—not Becky, not even Holmes—about recognizing Mr. Teale's wife, chiefly because I wasn't sure that it was any of my affair.

Mr. Teale was unlikely even to have murdered General Pettigrew, and if we were right that the intended victim was Lord Lansdowne, then Neville Teale dropped, if not quite to the bottom of our list of suspects, then very close to it.

"Suzette is his wife," I said.

Becky's brow furrowed. "Why would she want to see you?"

"I'm not sure. I suppose we'll find out tomorrow afternoon."

Becky looked down at the table, her expression unusually subdued. "Do you think Jack's gotten my letter by now?"

"You only mailed it this morning," I said gently.

"I know." Becky sighed.

Privately, I was thinking that if Jack broke his little sister's heart by getting himself arrested or hurt, the danger of whatever he was mixed up in was going to be the least of his worries, because I would murder him myself.

"I'm sure he misses you too," I told her. "But for now"— I squeezed Becky's hand—"we'd better get ready. I'm due at the Savoy Theater for rehearsal in an hour, and I'm depending on you to help me put my stage makeup on and practice my songs."

CHAPTER 14

"Anyone in here?" Mrs. Budge, the Savoy Theater's costume mistress poked her head around the corner of the dressing room, then drew in a sharp breath at the sight of me. "Why, Miss James, are you still here? I would have thought you'd have left by now."

"I'm sorry to have startled you, Mrs. Budge." I was sitting at one of the big, mirrored dressing tables, ostensibly taking off my makeup, though in reality, I had scrubbed my face clean a while ago. "I thought I'd stay a bit later tonight. I wanted the chance to practice the steps to the dance routine from the second act, and there isn't room in my flat."

Mrs. Budge was a buxom, matronly woman with a Roman nose and gray hair piled into a towering mass atop her head, like a seventeenth-century duchess's wig. Once upon a time, she had an actress herself, though as she told it, rheumatism in her hips had forced her to retire.

She shook her head at me. "You've practically been here all day. Anyone would think you'd be anxious to get home. But just as you like, dear. Just put out the lights when you leave?"

"Of course, Mrs. Budge."

I held my breath as she departed, her arms filled with costumes in need of repair.

I felt slightly guilty for the lie. Although, really, every time I had set foot inside the Savoy for the past three months, I had felt as though I were lying, regardless of whether or not I actually told any untruths.

Maybe that was why I hadn't even managed to make myself audition for a lead part in *The Yeomen of the Guard* and had told Mr. Harris, our stage manager, that I was happy to be in the chorus for this production.

It wasn't that I loved singing on stage any less. But my career at the theater seemed every day to feel a little less real, a little more distant from the life I led out in the non-theatrical world.

I stood up, though not to practice dance steps. What I actually required from the Savoy tonight was a place to change my clothes and depart for Cheapside—someplace away from Baker Street.

In between rehearsal this afternoon and tonight's performance, I had brought Becky home to 221A, where—with any luck—she was now asleep under Mrs. Hudson's watchful care. Holmes and Uncle John ought to be there, as well.

Holmes had as good as told me to find Jack if I could, and he had also said that he trusted my judgment. But I wouldn't at all put it past him to follow me in some bizarre disguise or other, just in case.

I trusted Holmes too—and a part of me would have liked the comfort of knowing that he was watching over me tonight. But I didn't want to put my father in danger, and I wasn't sure exactly how far I might be forced to bend the law while discovering exactly what Jack was involved in.

Holmes had occasionally in the past shown himself willing to uphold the spirit of the law rather than the exact letter. But I didn't want him forced into that position on my account.

I pulled out the satchel of clothes I had brought with me. *Not* the same ones I wore while visiting St. Giles. Male garb would probably be safer in the neighborhoods I was intending to be in tonight, but my intended purpose would require me to talk and come close enough to people to allow my face to be seen—both of which eliminated my chances of passing for a convincing boy.

Instead, I tugged on a gown of cheap green silk, with black lace ruffles around the hem and the three-quarter sleeves. I rouged my lips and cheeks and draped an equally cheap-looking satin evening cloak around my shoulders.

Then I laced on the sturdy boots I wore when passing for a teenaged boy. The trailing hem of the dress all but hid my feet, especially in the dark, and I wanted to be prepared in case I had to run. Or, for that matter, kick anyone.

I tucked a knife into the top of my boot, and my second weapon of choice for the evening—a small but heavy brass paperweight—into a pink satin handbag. Then I stood back from the mirror to survey the effect.

My face was too clean; I would have to smudge myself with a few streaks of grime when I got outside. But overall, I looked the part of a young and inexperienced lady of the evening, hoping to find a protector for the night.

Which was funny, in a way. That was exactly what Jack had mistaken me for the first time we met.

* * *

Before tonight, I had heard the expression *hot as Hades* and thought it an exaggerated figure of speech. At the moment, however, it felt like a literal truth. The gin palace I had shoved and elbowed my way into some twenty minutes ago felt several degrees hotter than the fieriest caverns of the underworld. My skin was itchy under the satin gown.

"What's that you say, dearie?" The barmaid, a stout, middle-aged woman with an improbably golden shade of hair leaned across the bar towards me.

The room was crowded with people packed elbow to elbow like sardines in a can. I had to practically shout to be heard over the noise of the mingle of voices and laughter and snatches of drunken song from those patrons grouped around a piano in the back.

"I said, I'm looking for a man."

The barmaid tipped back her head and gave a gusty laugh. "Aren't we all, dearie, aren't we all."

I drew in a breath. This was the third establishment I'd visited tonight, and so far I had accomplished nothing except to give myself the beginnings of a headache from the smoke, heat, and noise.

"I'm looking for *this* man." I held up the drawing I had made before coming out tonight, carefully traced from the police sketch in Holmes's files.

I'd used a black grease pencil and a sheet of butcher's paper, since a girl of my supposed class wouldn't have proper drawing supplies. My tracing had come out cruder than the original drawing too. But that was all to the good; a young prostitute wouldn't have polished artistic skills. And the distinctive lines of the man's face had still come through.

The barmaid peered shortsightedly at the drawing and looked surprised. "Did you do this yourself?"

"Yeah." I covered my mouth to hide a cough from the smoke in the room. "I've always had the knack." In addition to the dress and makeup, I'd also given myself an East London accent for the night. "Could've made a living at it too, if only I'd gotten a proper chance."

"Well." The barmaid peered at the paper more closely. Something seemed to shift in her gaze, turning her expression suddenly wary. Then she shook her head. "Sorry I can't help you, dearie. Never seen him before."

"Please." I put out my hand, catching hold of her arm before she could turn away.

This was also the third time I had gotten the same reaction to showing the drawing. At the first two public houses I'd visited, the waitresses I'd questioned had taken one look at the drawing and then suddenly remembered urgent business elsewhere.

"Please," I said again. I put appealing quaver into my voice. "Please, I've *got* to find him."

The barmaid looked at me, pressing her lips tight shut. "Look, if you'll take my advice, you'll walk straight out of here and forget all about this. Take it from me, this lot"—she flicked a finger at the drawing—"isn't anyone you want to find if you can help it."

She started to turn, moving towards the next customer at the bar.

"He's my brother!" I said quickly.

The woman stopped, looking at me in open shock. "Your *brother*, is it?"

I sniffed, wiping my eyes with the back of my hand. "I think he is."

Lies were usually best kept simple and as close to the truth as possible if they were to be convincing. But in this case, there was no version of the truth I could share, so a dramatically elaborate falsehood it was.

I let a tear trickle down my cheek. "We were split up when we were just kids, sent to the workhouse after our parents died. I don't even know what name he's calling himself now. That's why I made the drawing. But I saw someone in the street around here the other day—just from a distance, like—and I thought, 'That's the spitting image of my brother Tom.' But he was gone before I could get to him. Must have gone into a shop or up a side street or something. I've been searching for him since." I looked at the woman appealingly. "No matter what he's done or what he's turned into, he's my brother, my own flesh and blood. Please, won't you help me find him?"

The barmaid frowned, her eyes darting back and forth, and I could see nervousness warring with the urge to help. Finally she said, "All right, dearie. You didn't hear it from me, but go up and turn right onto Milk Street, then left onto Clement Court. Look for number fifteen."

* * *

Clement Court proved to be a narrow, crowded lane, with buildings that leaned into one another like a row of drunkards propping each other up. A butcher shop on the corner made me cover my mouth against the reek of blood, and two doors in, a pawn shop appeared to be doing a brisk trade in what were probably stolen watches and handkerchiefs.

An itinerant street vendor had set up camp on the sidewalk. He seemed to be selling pet songbirds, all trapped in small wooden cages that he carried on a pole.

"Buy a bird, miss?" The vendor wore a scruffy-looking gentleman's top hat and a heavy woolen muffler wrapped around his throat. "Beautiful singers, they are." He looked me up and down. "Or I can see you might want something special. This 'ere is a bird of paradise, straight from the jungles of darkest Peru. I'll let you 'ave it for just a shilling."

He whipped the cover off of another cage.

I peered more closely. "That looks like a chicken."

An extremely irritated-looking chicken, whose feathers had been dyed into a rainbow of colors with what appeared to be cheap oil paints. The colors had run in places, blending into a muddy greenish-brown.

The bird let out an annoyed squawk, trying to peck through the bars of the cage, and the vendor gave me a dirty look.

I kept walking.

Number fifteen was at least easy to find, in that it proved to be a coffee house—the sort of establishment where coffee was served for a penny a cup or three half-pence for a pint. The entire house, from the ground floor all the way up to the attic, was brightly lighted and appeared as crowded—and a great deal louder—than the gin palace I'd just been in.

As I stood on the pavement studying the place, the swinging double doors covering the front entrance suddenly burst open, spilling out a pair of men who appeared to be trying to kill each other. One had the other's neck in a choke hold, and they went down to the ground practically at my feet, rolling and grunting and punching each other.

Getting involved wouldn't at all fit with my current persona. Not to mention, I had no idea whose side I ought to be on.

I stepped around them and pushed open the coffee house doors.

* * *

"Haven't seen you in here before."

I turned and found myself staring at the expanse of a man's beefy chest, covered in a none-too-clean blue and white striped shirt and a waistcoat that was strained to the limits of its seams. Adjusting my gaze upwards, I discovered that the waistcoat's owner was a big, red-faced man with hair that seemed to have all fled from the top of his bald head and collected instead into a bushy dark beard. Between the beard and the collar of his shirt, I could see a tattoo of a green snake crawling up the side of his neck.

I took a sip from my coffee, which tasted strong enough that I imagined it slowly eating its way through the cup.

Since I didn't actually want to attract the attention of the man in the police sketch, I hadn't shown my drawing here. But I hadn't seen any sign of him. Neither I had I seen Jack, and I had been here for what had to be close to an hour.

I summoned a smile for the bearded man. "I'm looking for someone."

The one thing I was sure about, after an hour of watching the comings and goings inside the coffee house, was that it was not *just* a place selling coffee and cheap food.

Certain patrons approached the counter, but then stepped around it and vanished through a doorway at the back of the main room. I had been keeping count, and so far eight people—seven men and one woman—had gone inside. None of them had come out again.

The bearded man leaned towards me, baring stained teeth in an answering smile. "Looking for someone, are you, luv? And who'd that be?"

I debated, then made up my mind. "Jack Kelly."

"Kelly, is it?" The man's eyebrows went up, and he eyed me, a calculation seeming to take place behind his gaze. "All right." He turned, jerking his head in a way that meant I ought to follow. "Come along upstairs."

I eyed his broad back. In my experience, practically nothing good ever started with those words—especially not when they were spoken by strange, tattooed men in establishments that were shady at best.

But I couldn't go back to Baker Street without seeing Jack, and neither could I sit here all night.

The coffee house had been an actual *house* at some time, maybe back in the days when Cheapside was a thriving commercial district, the areas around it filled with respectably affluent tradesmen's homes. The bearded man led the way out of the main room and up a flight of stairs that opened off the small entrance hall.

The second floor of the house wasn't as crowded as the ground level, but it was still filled with patrons. Rooms that must at one time have been bedrooms now contained tables and chairs where customers were drinking, eating, and playing rounds of cards or dice.

The bearded man led the way to a room at the end of the hall and pushed open the heavy paneled door. The back of my neck prickled. None of the other rooms had doors.

The realization struck me just as the man's hand shot out, grabbing hold of my wrist with unnerving force.

This of course was the drawback to dressing as a lady of the evening. It disarmed suspicion and gave me access to places where I wouldn't be allowed in more respectable apparel. But it did have its quotient of risk involved.

I looked down at the beefy fingers wrapped around my arm. "You really don't want to do this."

The big man ignored me, dragging me with him into a dark, narrow room that was empty save for a dingy four-poster bed.

I could have broken his grip, but this would be easier without a potential audience from any of the other rooms.

"Kelly's not going to give you any business." The man's beard scratched against my cheek as he whispered, his breath hot in my ear. "Used to be a copper, now he lives like a bloody monk. But I'll give you a—"

I swung my handbag at him, smashing the heavy brass paperweight inside into his face. He howled, clutching his nose, and I gave him the most savage kick I could manage to the groin.

He sank to his knees, groaning, his nose spurting blood.

I stood looking down at him. "Which part of the sentence, *You don't want to do this* was too difficult for you to understand?"

Now I would have to start all over again with looking downstairs.

I turned to the doorway—and came face to face with Jack.

CHAPTER 15

Jack looked from me to the man on the ground. He was breathing as though he'd just run up the stairs, but his voice was almost calm.

"I see you've met Yates."

I recovered my ability to speak. "His notions of hospitality leave something to be desired, but yes. We've met."

Yates was still moaning, his face smeared with blood from his nose and his eyes tearing. "Get that crazy bint away from me."

Jack hauled Yates roughly to his feet and gave him a shove towards the door.

"Keep talking, and I'll leave the two of you alone so that she can finish what she started."

Yates gave us a look that was half anger, half fear, and staggered out.

Jack and I stood looking at each other. He was wearing dark gray trousers and suspenders over a plain cotton shirt, the sleeves rolled to the elbows. His dark hair was tousled-looking, and his expression was grim.

"How did you know I was here?" I asked.

"I'd just come out of the back room downstairs and saw you going up here with Yates. I was hoping I was going crazy or hallucinating or something harmless like that." Jack looked at me, the line of his jaw tight. "What were you thinking, coming up here with him? That has to be the—"

"If you're going to say *craziest thing I've ever done*, I promise you it's not."

Jack rubbed a hand across his face. "What are you doing here, Lucy?"

"What am *I* doing here? You're the one who's supposed to be at a medical clinic in Bath right now!"

"I—" Jack stopped speaking as the door to the room burst open again.

I stiffened, ready for Yates to have returned with reinforcements. But instead it was a man I hadn't yet seen—younger, scarcely out of his teens, with a thin, sallow face and a mop of curly black hair. He was breathing hard, and he looked at Jack with panicked eyes.

"Leave the twist and Botany! Blue bottles in the field!"

He spun, running back down the hall.

I turned to Jack. Working with Holmes had taught me some of the slang used by East Londoners, but in this case, the only term I'd recognized was *blue bottle*.

"Police?" I asked.

"That's right." Jack was already moving towards the window, drawing the curtains back just a fraction so that he could look out into the street below.

"And if you were found here, that would be ... bad?"

Cheapside wasn't too far from Holburn Police Station, where Jack reported—or used to report—for duty. He probably knew all of the police officers who were currently closing in on this place by name.

"Yeah."

Already I could hear a commotion from downstairs, shouts and the sounds of running feet. My heart accelerated.

"Maybe you should leave."

Jack gave me a look. "Right. Never would have thought of that for myself."

"I *mean*, you should get out of here now, without me. You know this area, and I don't, not really. And two people are more conspicuous than one."

Especially when one of them was dressed as I was.

"You'll stand a better chance of getting away if you're on your—"

Jack cut me off. "You want me to just run away and leave you here?"

"You jumped out the *window* to get away from me yesterday."

"That was different."

"How?"

Jack turned fully away from the window to look at me. "On Foley Street, there weren't a hundred different ways you could get into trouble within the first five minutes."

"I can take care of myself!"

"Not arguing. But I'm still not leaving you. You've just seen what Yates is like when he's just getting to know you. He's going to have a score to settle the next time. Not to mention you could get yourself locked up in a prison cell."

Holmes would undoubtedly come and secure my release, but I had to admit it would still be inconvenient. And I wasn't particularly anxious to see Yates again.

"Fine. How are we getting out of here then?"

"This way."

The hallway outside was a crush of people, all shouting and trying to shove past each other towards what I took to be the back stairs. Jack pushed a way through them, keeping close to the wall, and I followed until we reached the stairway as well.

But instead of joining the crowds going down, Jack started *up* the stairs.

There was no one at all going up. The stairwell was in darkness save for lights down below, and the higher we climbed, the darker it grew. I stumbled once, and Jack put out a hand to steady me.

"What kind of business is it downstairs?" I asked. "Illegal gambling? Drugs? Thieving?"

"Some of all three." I couldn't see well enough to be sure, but I thought from the sound of Jack's voice that he was gritting his teeth, probably against pain. I could hear the sound of his footsteps and knew he was favoring the injured leg.

"And the police are suddenly raiding this place tonight because …"

"That's a good question."

We seemed to have reached the top of the stairwell. Jack pushed open a door, and a rush of frigid outside air struck me. I stepped out after him onto what had to be the coffee house's roof, which was luckily flat, and surrounded by a low parapet.

Above us, tattered shreds of clouds drifted across the night sky, though there was too much light from the surrounding buildings to make out any stars.

"Aren't the police just as likely to search and find us up here as they are if we'd stayed down below?"

"Only if we're still here when they come up." Jack moved to the edge of the roof, looking across the gap to the roof of the neighboring building.

I stepped forward to join him. The distance wasn't great, maybe only four feet or a little less, but the drop down to the ground was considerable. I could see a churning mass of people in the street three stories down below us. A fight seemed to have broken out, and small figures in blue policeman's uniforms were struggling to drag combatants apart.

I eyed the gap between buildings. "You realize that this only counts as an escape if we *don't* wind up smashed to smithereens on the pavement?"

Jack didn't smile. He looked at me, his expression taut, braced somehow. He looked like someone facing a fight against twenty opponents: desperately outnumbered, but grimly determined to keep fighting to the end.

"Maybe you're right. Maybe you should take your chances with the police. At least Yates isn't likely to come up here."

"But you're not going to." I scrutinized his face. "You're willing to risk jumping because ... because something even worse will happen to you if you're caught."

I also had a horrible, hollow feeling that if I let Jack out of my sight now, he would disappear into the vast, sprawling mess of London—the great cesspool, my father would call it—and I would never be able to find him again.

Jack didn't answer. But he also didn't deny it.

"All right, fine," I said. "We'll jump."

"Lucy, you shouldn't—"

I interrupted. "When has telling me I shouldn't do something *ever* gone well for you?"

I climbed up, balancing on the edge of the parapet.

Just don't look down.

"Do you want to go first or should I?"

Jack swung himself up to stand beside me, using the strength of his arms. He was keeping most of his weight off the injured leg.

Fear pinched my insides, squeezing.

Jack was unflinching in the face of danger, but not reckless, and I'd never known him to take pointless risks in all the months I'd known him.

If he was willing to do this, there had to be a compelling reason. But I still found myself bargaining with anything or anyone that might be listening, begging God, fate, and the universe not to let him fall.

I heard him exhale, and then he launched himself forward into the air.

He landed on the neighboring roof, staggered briefly, and then regained his balance and turned back towards me.

I made the mistake of letting my gaze stray down to the street below, squeezed my eyes shut, and then jumped before I could think about it anymore. I seemed to be in the air forever—but then the soles of my boots struck the edge of the neighboring roof with a jarring impact.

I was off balance and almost fell backwards, but Jack caught me with an arm around my waist.

"All right?"

My heart felt as though it had stopped beating for a second or two, but I seemed to be in one piece. "Yes. Now how do we get down from here?"

* * *

The building was a tenement house, with an evil-smelling stairwell that opened from a mounted doorway on the roof. We passed by a tired-looking woman with a baby on her hip, four men arguing about racing, and an old man sitting on the landing of one floor and smoking his pipe. But none of them gave us more than a passing glance. In this sort of place, no one was overly curious about their neighbors.

We reached an entrance leading out onto the street. Jack pushed the door open, then drew back into the shadows of the covered doorway, swearing under his breath.

Peering cautiously out past him, I could see that some twenty feet away to our left, the road was blocked by a police wagon, and constables were herding a disheveled band of people into the back, presumably those arrested in the brawl outside the coffee house.

I looked up at Jack. "Stay here?" I asked in an undertone. "Or go the other way?"

Jack glanced in the other direction, but then shook his head. "Stay here. Too much chance we'll be seen if we go out there."

"All right." I leaned back against the soot-stained brick wall behind me. "What do 'twist' and 'Botany' mean?"

Jack quirked up an eyebrow. "That's what you're worrying about right now?"

Actually I was trying to distract myself from thinking about how close Jack and I were standing. The doorway was narrow, and I was nearly pressed up against the hard wall of his chest. I could feel the warmth of his body seeping through the thin satin of my dress.

I shrugged, folding my hands to stop myself from reaching up and brushing the hair back from his forehead or tracing the hard planes and angles of his cheek and jaw.

"I was curious. The boy in there said, *Leave the twist and Botany.* Which I assume means something along the lines of, *Run for your life.* But I have absolutely no idea why."

"Twist is girl." Jack spoke absently, leaning out of our shelter just enough that he could peer into the street. "Twist and twirl— girl. Botany is Botany Bay. So, run away."

"So you only say the first part of whatever makes the rhyme?" I frowned. "Then why does field mean street? He said *bluebottles in the field.*"

Jack turned back to me, suddenly smiling just faintly. My breath caught. He was looking at me the way he used to, before he was shot in July, the way that made my heart feel tightly twisted and my pulse skip.

"Field of wheat." We were standing close enough that I could see the shadow of what looked almost like longing cross his gaze, his gaze lingering on my mouth as though he were wishing that he could kiss me. But then he smiled again. "Don't they teach you Yanks anything?"

"*Kelly!*" A man's furious shout made me startle and look to see a burly figure striding towards us.

The light of a nearby street lamp fell on his face, and a jolt of shock went through me. It was the dark-haired man from the police sketch, the same man who apparently had tried to murder a night watchman a week ago.

Down the street, the police wagon was just rumbling away.

The dark-haired man stepped forward, confronting Jack, and a wave of unpleasant shock whipped across my skin and down my spine.

The sketch even now folded up inside my evening bag had captured the harsh, brutal lines of his face accurately enough: the low brows, the wide cheekbones, the cruel, arrogant twist to his mouth. What the drawing *hadn't* conveyed was the almost animal threat of violence I could see in his eyes.

He was hungry for a fight, just waiting for a chance to explode into violence—and he would thoroughly enjoy it when that chance came.

His glance flicked briefly from Jack to me, and his brows went up in momentary surprise. "Who's the tart?"

His voice was low, grating.

Jack stepped in front of me, planting himself between me and the other man and shielding me as much as possible from his view. "No one important."

Ordinarily, I might have been angry at being kept back, out of harm's way. But in this case, I stayed in the shadows. For right now, I was perfectly happy not to have this man learn to recognize me.

His gaze lingered on me briefly over Jack's shoulder, squinting as though he were trying to make out my face. But then he seemed to abandon the effort and dismiss me, refocusing on Jack.

"Seems funny timing, doesn't it?" The harshness in his voice was like the scrape of knives across stone. "Police raiding us right after you show up, asking to be let back in."

Jack laughed shortly. I couldn't see his face, but he didn't tense or stiffen in any way. His posture was completely easy, relaxed.

"Yeah, you caught me. I didn't have anything better to do, so I thought, why not get myself shot in the leg and kicked off the police force, all so I could turn copper's nark on you."

The man's gaze narrowed, muscles playing along his clenched jaw. "And why should I believe you weren't the one who called the rozzers on us tonight?"

Jack raised one shoulder. "I don't know. Maybe the fact that I'm still here?"

The burly man looked at him for a long beat. I was usually good at reading facial expressions, but I couldn't at all tell what he was thinking.

He licked his lips. "That, and you know what I'll do if I find out you've been lying to me."

The rasp of menace in the words was unmistakable, his face granite-hard. Something ugly—even uglier than before—flickered at the back of his eyes.

For the first time, I saw a hint of tension creep into the line of Jack's shoulders, but his voice didn't change. "And that."

There was another interminable silence, long enough for me to count three, then four beats of my own heart. Then the dark-haired man spun on his heel and walked away without a word.

CHAPTER 16

I watched as the burly man stamped away, heading not for the coffee house next door, but away, vanishing into the darkness across the street.

"How did he manage to escape getting caught up in the raid?"

The chaos next door had died down almost as quickly as it had begun. The house still blazed with light, but its rooms were empty, the patrons—any who hadn't just been arrested—vanished with lightning speed.

A pair of heavily muscled, tough-looking men had appeared seemingly out of nowhere and come to stand in front of the doors, presumably just in case anyone in the neighborhood took the end of the police raid as an opportunity to try their hand at looting.

Unless I was mistaken, the dark-haired man was the owner of the coffee house—and more than that, besides.

"Because he's like an eel." Jack sounded slightly tired. "One hint of the police and he wriggles out of reach under a rock somewhere."

I stepped out of the doorway to join him. "I think I may have just sullied your reputation. He thinks you've been consorting with ladies of uncertain virtue."

Jack glanced at me. "Yeah. Well. If that's the worst thing that happens to me tonight, I'll count myself lucky."

"What's going to happen now that the place has been raided?" I looked at the coffee shop. "Will it be shut down?"

"I doubt it. At most the people they rounded up will spend a night or two in prison for illegal gambling or drunkenness. But there's no way to prove Flint was actually running the gambling ring in there—and that's if they catch him, which they won't. He has lookouts all up and down the street who would have warned him to get things like stolen goods and smuggled liquor off the premises before the police even got inside the door. So they don't have enough motivation to look for him all that hard."

He'd obviously seen this all play out before.

"I—" I started to answer, then cut off speaking as a figure moved into view, coming slowly towards us along the street. It was the same bird vendor I'd seen before, pushing his cart filled with wooden cages.

Despite the police raid, the brawl in the street, and all the other excitement, he was still here.

I marched over to him.

"Buy a songbird, miss?" the vendor started. Then he stopped, catching sight of my face. "Oh, bloomin' 'ell. Not *you* again. Look, I got a right ter make a living, don't I?"

"A bird of paradise?" I planted my hands on my hips. "Even for you, that is preposterous. *And* you can drop the ridiculous accent."

The man gave me a wounded look. "There's no call to get nasty now. All right, so maybe she is a chicken. But she's a good laying bird. Whoever buys her will get fresh eggs every morning—"

I reached out and snatched the ragged-looking top hat off his head.

The vendor reared back. "What the—are you out of yer mind?"

I froze.

When the man jerked back, it had dislodged the scarf from the lower half of his face. Without it—and without the brim of the top hat shading his eyes—it was possible to see the bird seller's features more clearly: plump cheeks, blue eyes, and a short, turned-up nose.

Not even my father was capable of changing his appearance that completely.

The man in front of me was definitely, positively, *not* Sherlock Holmes.

* * *

"Don't say it." I pointed a finger at Jack. "Not one single word."

Jack's shoulders were shaking suspiciously, but he held up his hands. "Did I say anything?"

"You have to admit, it was exactly the sort of insane disguise that would appeal to Holmes. You didn't think even for a second that it might be him?"

Jack shook his head. "The third finger on his right hand had been broken and healed a little crooked. That's not something you can fake easily."

"Ugh. How did you notice that so quickly? I spoke with him twice and didn't see it." Granted it was dark, but still.

Jack shrugged. "Just habit. Out on patrol, noticing details is sometimes the difference between staying alive and ending up dead. It's not all bad news, though." His mouth twitched. "Now you're the proud owner of a—what did he say it was? A bird of paradise?"

"After all of that, I felt as though I owed the vendor *something*."

I looked down at the cage in my arms. The chicken appeared no happier to be in my possession instead of the bird seller's. It regarded me balefully through the wooden bars.

"I ought to give it to Holmes as a present," I muttered. Then I glanced up at Jack. "Are you going to tell me what's going on now? And why you're here instead of in Bath?"

Jack looked at me for a long moment, his eyes dark, his face patched with shadows from the street lamps. But at last he said, "You need to know. You and your father." He looked up and down the street. "We can't talk here, though."

"All right." I frowned, trying to call up what I remembered of the surrounding streets and neighborhoods. "Actually, there is a safe place where we can go. It's not very far, though it will probably feel like it, with your leg hurting as much as it must be right now."

"I'm fine."

"Not counting everything you did tonight, you jumped out of a second-story window yesterday! What were you thinking?"

"I didn't jump, I climbed halfway down. And I was thinking that I needed to get in there and have a quiet look around. I never expected you'd be bringing my sister to the home of a suspected killer."

I stopped short, staring at him. *Blood boiling* was another phrase I'd always thought just a figure of speech. But at the moment, I could have sworn I felt small, hot bubbles of anger hissing through my veins.

I leaned forward. "For the sake of the rest of this conversation, I'm going to pretend that you did *not* just criticize my care of Becky, considering that *you're* the one who's abandoned her to go and spy on a man who looks as though he could give Jack the Ripper a run for his money in the category of Most Unpleasant Men in London!"

Jack let out a slow breath, running a hand across his face. "You're right. I'm sorry. Thank you for letting Becky stay with you. There's no one else I'd trust with her more."

"You're welcome."

"How is she?" Jack asked.

I looked up at him. In a way, I wished I could hold onto my anger. But I couldn't. Not when I could see the shadow of the same grimly trapped look at the back of his gaze.

Not when relief at finding him safe and fear of the danger he was in were forming a churning mixture inside me—and awareness of how close I'd already come to losing him was so sharp it was almost physically painful.

"She's developed a new passion for magic tricks. When I left her tonight, she was trying to work out how to arrange all the household mirrors so as to make Prince disappear. You should probably reconcile yourself to being sawed in half the next time you see her. Or at the very least, buying her a white rabbit so that she can pull it out of a top hat."

Jack laughed. "Maybe she can use your new friend there." He nodded at the caged chicken.

"She misses you," I said.

"I know." Jack's voice was quiet. He rubbed his eyes again. "I'm sorry."

I waited, but he didn't say anything more. Finally I straightened. "All right. Let's be on our way. The sooner you tell me what this is all about, the sooner we can end it, and you and Becky will be able to go back home."

CHAPTER 17

Despite the night having started out perfectly clear and dry, a chill, gusting rain had started to fall by the time we made our way to Dorset Street, near Blackfriars Bridge. I shivered. My thin cloak and gown were soaked through and felt like cold, slimy seaweed against my skin.

From inside the cage, the chicken was making irritated clucking sounds that sounded like the avian version of profanity.

I glowered up at the sky, wiping rain from out of my eyes. "How is it that even after two years here, I'm *still* surprised when it suddenly starts raining out of nowhere in London? You don't even have a proper summer."

"Sure we do. That's when the rain's warmer." Jack glanced at me. "Sorry I don't have a coat to give you, though."

"That's all right, we're nearly there. That's the place, right up ahead."

I pointed.

The shop was tiny and narrow, sandwiched between a restaurant selling battered and fried fish on one side and a cobbler's shop on the other. A sign over the doorway proclaimed the place to be *Griggs' Meats*.

Jack looked at the hams and chops, sausages, and cuts of beef on display in the small front window. "A butcher's shop?"

"Yes. Although not entirely."

Most butcher's establishments wouldn't be open at this hour of the night, but in this case I wasn't worried. I pushed open the door, making a bell above our heads jangle.

"Why, Miss James!" A stout, balding man in a white apron came bustling out of the back. "This is a surprise. Always nice to see you, of course."

"Hello, Mr. Griggs." I smiled and accepted the butcher's outstretched hand. "This is"—I glanced at Jack. Mr. Griggs was as far as I knew entirely trustworthy, but it seemed safer that he not hear Jack's name—"a friend of mine. I was wondering if you could let us in to the room upstairs?"

"Certainly, certainly."

Mr. Griggs had left the door to the back area of the shop open, and a smell like old, boiling washing was filtering out.

"I've just been trying my hand at *bouillabaisse*," he said. He looked from me to Jack with a hopeful gleam in his eyes. "Would you care to sample a bowlful?"

Jack looked as though he were trying valiantly not to flinch back at the smell.

I smiled. "Oh no, that's incredibly kind of you, Mr. Griggs. But we just had supper before we came here. We couldn't possibly eat another bite."

"Oh." Mr. Griggs looked slightly crestfallen.

I mentally crossed my fingers behind my back and added, "But if you have any of those delicious scones of yours, would you mind wrapping them up so that I can bring them back to Mr. Holmes and Dr. Watson? They said last time that no one makes scones quite like yours."

That was, in fact, the literal truth. Mr. Griggs' scones accomplished the outstanding feat of being even worse than mine.

He brightened at once. "Of course! I just baked a fresh batch today, in fact. I'll wrap some up directly. And here is the key."

He reached behind the shop counter and drew out a heavy, old-fashioned key on a ring, handing it over to me with a flourish. "Go right up. Oh, and here are a candle and some matches. You'll want those so that you can find your way."

I wrapped my soaked clothes more tightly around myself, trying not to drip all over the floor as we squelched our way up a narrow, creaking flight of stairs at the back of the shop. We reached the second story, where our way was met with a locked door.

"What is this place?" Jack asked.

"One of my father's bolt-holes. The places he keeps around London in case he needs a safe place to elude pursuit or assume a new disguise."

I handed the lighted candle over to Jack so that I could fit the key into the lock.

"Holmes pays Mr. Griggs a monthly fee to let him use the upper floor of the shop whenever he needs it. Mr. Griggs is a nice man—and a very competent butcher, or so Holmes says. You just don't want to make the mistake of eating anything that he actually cooks."

I pushed the door open.

The room inside was small, with a low, slanted ceiling that reflected the pitch of the roof outside. A big wooden wardrobe containing all manner of wigs and changes of clothing took up nearly a quarter of the floor space, but there was also a comfortably upholstered sofa that could serve as a bed if needed and a mirrored dressing table similar to the ones I used at the Savoy.

I deposited the dripping chicken's cage on the floor beside the couch while Jack used the candle flame to light the two twin lamps that stood on the dressing table.

"Wait a moment," I told him. "I want to see whether Holmes has any dry clothes I can borrow."

I opened the wardrobe and quickly rifled through the articles of clothing. A man's tweed suit in a size that would swim on me, a woolen overcoat, a polo uniform …

Did my father actually play polo?

In any case, the white riding breeches and dark purple waistcoat weren't particularly useful to me at the moment.

I rummaged in the back of the wardrobe and finally found a silk dressing gown in a paisley print. Not perfect, but at least it was dry.

There was a dressing screen in one corner of the room. I stepped behind it, undid the hooks and buttons on the soaked green gown, and stripped it off.

"So why were you at the flat on Foley Street?" Jack asked from the other side of the screen.

I bent, unlacing my soggy boots and kicking free of them too. In addition to a lack of clothes in my size, Holmes's wardrobe options didn't run to things like female underthings. I left my shift on, but rolled down my wet stockings and took them off.

"I wanted to see whether Royce might be our ghost."

There was a creak of furniture springs, as though Jack had just dropped down onto the couch. "I know you didn't hit your head when we jumped from the roof. So I'll just go ahead and ask. What ghost?"

"Oh. That's right, I haven't had the chance to tell you. A man died at the Diogenes Club yesterday morning. And the man who had rented the rooms on Foley Street—a waiter, named Royce—fled the scene, as though he'd had something to do with it. Also, Holmes and I—and a charwoman who works at the club—saw a ghost hovering above the dead man's bed."

"Maybe I was wrong about you not hitting your head."

I rolled my eyes. "Not an *actual* ghost. An illusion of one. At least, we're assuming so." I slipped on the dressing gown and belted it around my waist. "That was why I took Becky to the magic show, to consult an expert on how the trick might have been performed."

My hair was wet and coming down already, so I pulled out the pins. It would dry more quickly if I left it loose.

"Your turn, if you want it." I stepped out from behind the screen, still combing my fingers through my loosened hair. "Holmes's clothes would probably fit you better than they do me."

"I'm—" Jack started to say. Then he stopped short as he caught sight of me.

One of the benefits of being Sherlock Holmes's daughter was that I practically never had to worry about things like chaperones and social conventions.

The dressing gown actually covered more of me than many evening dresses I had worn, but even still, something about the way Jack was looking at me reminded me that it was the height of impropriety to be here with him this way.

I sat down beside him on the sofa, and Jack stood up—so quickly that I saw him wince as his weight landed on the injured leg.

"I'm all right. I'll dry out eventually." He crossed to the room's small brick hearth. "Though it'll be faster if we get a fire started."

There was a box of safety matches on the mantel and coals in the scuttle by the grate. Jack measured coal out and struck a match.

I watched him work, wishing that I knew what he was thinking. Wishing that I could ever tell what he was thinking anymore.

I'm afraid was probably my least favorite phrase in the entire English language. But a part of me *was* afraid to hear what Jack's answer would be if I asked him what he felt for me—or if I told him how I felt about him.

"Then you can tell me now what *you* were doing at Royce's flat," I said.

Instead of answering, Jack was silent for a second, his shoulders braced as he looked down at the kindling fire. His back was to me, but I could see his reflection in the mirror above the mantel, frowning.

"Why did you say I was spying on Flint?" he asked.

"Flint? That's the man you spoke to in the street?"

"Yeah. Flint Bayles. He goes by just Flint, though. You said that I'd left Becky to spy on him."

I drew my feet up, hugging my knees. "Well, that's what you're doing, aren't you? You saw the picture of this man Flint in my father's notes on the break-in at the munitions warehouse. And you recognized him. So now you've persuaded Flint that your leg injury has caused you to lose your job with the police and that you've been forced to return to your old life, the one you had before you joined the force. He is a gang leader, isn't he? And you knew him before?"

"He is. And I did," Jack said. He was still frowning. "What I mean is, how did you know that wasn't the actual truth? That I haven't gone back to the Sloggers?"

"Oh." I stopped, looking at him in surprise. "Why would I have thought that?"

"Flint and the others believed it," Jack said. "And they've known me half my life."

I shook my head. I didn't need to consider. "No, you would never do that to Becky, for one thing. Besides, you have to know what I'll do if it turns out that all those reading lessons were wasted and you don't take the sergeant's exam after all. What I did to Yates tonight absolutely pales by comparison."

Jack laughed, though the smile vanished as he finally turned to face me.

"You're right about everything you said. I did recognize Flint's picture from the police report in your father's files."

I looked at him in exasperation. "If only there were some way of conveying that to Holmes or Mycroft." Or me, for that matter. "Something involving—oh, I don't know—*telling* us, instead of going off on your own and risking your life without anyone having the faintest idea what you were doing."

Jack raked a hand through his hair. "I know. I couldn't tell you or anyone else, though. Not until I knew some things for certain. I—it's a lot to explain."

"I'm listening. But sit down before you tell me, you're making me hurt just looking at you."

"It's not that bad."

"I once heard Uncle John tell Holmes that he didn't mind listening to him practice the violin at three o'clock in the morning—and he was more convincing than you right now!"

Jack sighed and came back to the couch, which was probably a mark of how much pain he really was in. He sat down on the opposite end, as far away from me as he could possibly get.

Maybe I really had only imagined the momentary flicker of heat or need in his gaze before.

"When I left Flint's gang, it was for good," Jack said. "No going back. But I also knew I couldn't use what I knew from when I was part of his crew to inform on them. It wouldn't have been honest, when I'd been one of them myself. And the boys who work for Flint ... they're not all like he is."

"I understand," I said. I *did* understand.

Growing up on the streets as Jack had, stealing wasn't so much a moral question as it was a matter of survival. Steal or starve. Those were the choices homeless young men and boys faced. And Jack had been lucky, in that he'd never been arrested. Most boys with his background had criminal charge sheets dating from the time they were barely out of childhood.

Some were sent to Australia, some served prison sentences. But there was almost no way out of the life they'd been trapped in from the time they were born.

"And then I knew what Flint would do, if I ever turned on him and gave the police what I know about him and his operations."

"He would have had you killed." It wasn't a question so much as a statement. From what I had seen of Flint tonight, I didn't doubt that he would deal swiftly and mercilessly with anyone who betrayed him.

But Jack shook his head. "No. He would have gone after Becky."

I caught my breath, staring at him. "That's why you couldn't let yourself be caught by the police and be recognized tonight. Flint might assume that you really *were* the one who'd called in the raid. And then he would have—"

I stopped. I had seen my share of the ugliest parts of life, but I still felt sick at the idea of even saying the words out loud.

Grimness tightened the edges of Jack's mouth. "A few weeks ago, before this all happened, Becky told me she'd seen strange men hanging around in the street outside our lodgings' house once or twice. Like they were watching the place."

"You think Flint sent them?"

Jack turned his head to look at me. "When I got out of Flint's gang, I told him I was leaving. And I said that if anything ever happened to me or to Becky, I'd left a sealed letter with my station house inspector, telling him everything I knew."

"Insurance," I said. "That was a wise move."

Jack raised one shoulder. "It worked. At first, anyway. Flint wasn't happy, but I wasn't worth enough for him to risk his whole line of operations on killing me. But then … the Jubilee happened. It was in the news. Written up in the papers. Some of the other boys in the Sloggers would have seen it. It makes Flint look weak, letting me walk away from the gang without any reprisals."

It made a horrible, chilling kind of sense.

"So you think he'd already started arrangements to keep watch on you and Becky, trying to work out a way around your insurance policy?"

"And then I saw the sketch of him in your father's papers," Jack said. "But I couldn't risk saying anything. Not until I was sure we could get enough evidence against him to bring him down once and for all."

I wanted to scrub away the thought of Becky falling into Flint's hands—of her ever even coming within a hundred yards of him. But it was lodged in my head, immovable.

I took a steadying breath. "All right."

Being terrified wouldn't keep Becky safe. Finding a way to see Flint Bayles locked up behind bars for the rest of his miserable *life* would keep Becky safe.

I drew my feet up, tucking my legs under me on the couch. "Tell me what you've found out, then."

"Not much." I could hear the underlying frustration in Jack's voice. "He doesn't share a lot of details with new arrivals. Which is what he considers me, until I prove to him that I'm back and loyal to him again. The one thing I do know is that the man who rented the place on Foley Street wasn't called Royce. His name's Stephen McHale."

"He's one of Flint's men?"

"He is."

"What does he look like?"

"Tall, medium build, dark hair. Maybe thirty. Can speak like a toff when he wants to."

Toff meant gentleman; I did know that one.

"That fits the description of Royce that Holmes and I were given at the Diogenes." I bit my lip. "Have you seen this man McHale since yesterday? Has he come back to report to Flint?"

"No. As far as I've seen, he hasn't come around."

"So he could be anywhere."

And unless he did come back to Flint and the house on Clement Court—or returned to Foley Street—he would be depressingly hard to find.

"The man who was killed yesterday died of breathing in cyanide gas," I said. "We still don't know how it was administered. But we think that the intended victim was actually Lord Lansdowne. And that this is all tied up with the theft of armaments—rifles and machine guns—intended for the Sudan."

"Stolen weapons." Jack's brows went up.

"And the night watchman at the warehouse identified Flint as having been there the night of the crime. That was the police report you saw." I stopped. "Would Flint want crates of guns?"

Jack gave a short laugh. "Flint would steal his own grandmother's wedding ring if he thought he could sell it again for a decent price. He doesn't usually deal in stolen guns, though. Besides …" His gaze shifted focus, and I could see him thinking. "That doesn't account for tonight's raid on the coffee house."

"Oh." I stopped short. I should have thought of that for myself. "You're right. We both know you didn't summon the police to make the raid. And we can also take it that it wasn't the world's most improbable coincidence."

"No."

"No you don't agree, or no I'm right?"

"No, I'm not buying coincidence either."

"Then someone else ordered the raid. And the question becomes: who?"

"I don't know," Jack said. "But if Flint had made a deal with someone—say, accepted money in exchange for doing this person's dirty work for them—"

"—then whoever he was working for might have decided to tie up loose ends by having Flint and his gang members arrested," I finished for him.

I leaned forward, my pulse quickening as the pieces slid together in my mind. "That would fit in with the rest of what we know too. We're saying that Flint was hired to steal arms and to murder Lord Lansdowne. McHale—Royce, as he called himself—killed someone at the Diogenes by mistake, after being sent there on Flint's orders to carry out the murder."

"And maybe spy on Lord Lansdowne and the other club members," Jack said.

"You're right! The first sighting of the ghost was two weeks ago. It could have been a distraction, set up so that Royce could get a look at Lord Lansdowne's private papers."

"So we're looking for someone else connected to the Diogenes," Jack said. "Someone with the power and influence to get McHale—Royce—hired on."

"Because it couldn't have been Flint who got him the job. A man like Flint's influence doesn't extend to exclusive gentlemen's clubs. Although unfortunately that doesn't narrow down our list of suspects by all that much. The sort of men who frequent clubs like the Diogenes are always trading favors based on who knows who. Not necessarily with each other, they're not supposed to talk to other club members on the premises. But they're still part of … they'd call it an old boy's network in America. I don't know what it's called here. But if Lord Somebody sidled up to Admiral Someone and said over a whiskey and soda that his second cousin's nephew had a friend who needed a job, and could he recommend him for a waiter's post at the Diogenes, you can be almost certain that Admiral Someone would say, *Certainly, old man, only too pleased.*" I let my voice drop into a gruff imitation of a military rumble.

Jack smiled. "That was good. You should be an actress."

"Thank you."

I stopped.

Somehow, without my even being aware of it, Jack and I had both leaned inwards while we were talking. My knees were almost touching his leg, and our faces were close enough that I could see the individual dark points of his lashes, the fine white scar that ran across one of his brows.

Something sharp stabbed me, straight through the heart.

For as long as I could remember, I had been aware that my mind simply didn't work the same way that other people's did. I had learned to keep quiet about things like studying the reports of criminal trials in the newspapers or noticing the pattern of shoe prints or tire treads as a matter of course.

That was part of why I'd loved reading Uncle John's stories, even before I knew that Sherlock Holmes and I were in any way connected: Reading the stories, I had always felt that Holmes would understand the way I thought about the world.

He *did* understand. But I still wasn't Sherlock Holmes and never would be, and speaking with my father, I was constantly aware that his powers of logic and deductive reasoning were exponentially ahead of mine.

With Jack, I never felt that.

He was handsome and brave and honorable and made me laugh, but he could also finish my sentences for me, and talking to him felt almost like an extension of talking to myself, because he always understood what I was thinking and why without my even having to explain.

I sat back before Jack could leap off the sofa to get away from me again.

"I'll have to find out whether Lord Lansdowne was in the club at the time the ghost was first seen. And find out whether the letters he was working on yesterday were properly delivered."

"That's a good idea. I take it your father's already told Lansdowne about the danger?" Jack asked.

"He has."

Jack gave another short laugh. "No wonder McHale hasn't been back to see Flint if he killed the wrong man by mistake. Flint doesn't look too kindly on those who fail him."

"Which makes it likely that McHale will try again?"

"Or whoever hired Flint will."

We looked at each other. "Do you have any idea who could have hired Flint to steal those weapons?"

"No." Jack's expression was set. "But I need to find out. Because anyone who'd hire Flint and his boys is someone we don't want getting their hands on a shipment of machine guns."

CHAPTER 18

Gray dawn was just lightening the sky over Baker Street when Jack and I alighted from our cab. I had told Jack he didn't have to bother with seeing me safely home, but hadn't argued when he insisted.

I wasn't worried about getting myself back home to 221B in one piece, but every minute that Jack spent in my company was a minute I didn't have to imagine something horrible happening to him without my being there.

Now he glanced down at the wooden cage in my arms, a smile tugging at the corners of his mouth.

I grimaced. "I know, I know."

Before leaving the shop, Mr. Griggs had offered to kill and dress the bird for me. *A nice little roasting chicken*, he had proclaimed it.

Now I adjusted my grip, causing a flurry of squawking and outraged flapping from the bird inside.

"The poor thing has already been painted all these ridiculous colors, though. It felt like injury added to insult to make her end up in an oven somewhere."

The rain had stopped, and I had borrowed the overcoat from the bolt-hole wardrobe. But the early morning air was still raw with a damp chill. I tried not to shiver as I looked up at Jack.

"Be careful. If whoever hired Flint is cleaning house by having the Sloggers broken up and arrested, then they're not likely to stop at a single police raid."

Jack would be in constant danger, both from our unknown adversary and from Flint, if Flint ever discovered the truth behind Jack's return to the gang.

"I know."

We started slowly down the street. For safety's sake, I had given the cab driver the address of number 134 instead of the real one.

A milk wagon rumbled by, pulled by a tired-looking team of gray ponies. But otherwise the street was empty of traffic.

"Do you want me to keep from telling Holmes about Flint?" I asked. "I don't think he would move against Flint unless we were sure that Flint was neutralized as a threat to Becky. In fact, if I do tell him, I'll make absolutely *certain* that he doesn't. But she's your sister. I won't say anything at all if you don't want me to."

Jack was silent, looking at the street ahead of us, and I could see the struggle playing out behind his eyes. He was probably thinking of all the same nightmarish possibilities that had already occurred to me.

But finally he shook his head. "No. You should tell him. We have a better chance of putting Flint away if your father's not kept in the dark and is on our side. Just—" his jaw locked.

"I'll do everything I can to keep Becky safe, I *swear*." I held Jack's gaze. "Anyone who tries to hurt her will have to go through me first."

Jack looked away from me. "I'm not sure that makes me feel any better. But thanks."

"What about Becky?" I asked. "At the moment, she has no idea that you're not at a clinic in Bath. But I can't guarantee that she won't begin to suspect something. She's incredibly bright. I could ask Uncle John to take her away somewhere safe, of course, somewhere entirely out of London, even. But we both know—"

"—she'd give him the slip and be right back here within the first half hour," Jack finished for me.

"Exactly."

Jack studied me. "Maybe—"

"Stop." I held up my hand. "I already know what you're going to say. You're going to tell me that this is dangerous and that I should leave you to cope with Flint and whatever underhanded connections he's made on your own."

Jack's brows drew together. "It is dangerous, and you *should*—"

"No. I promised you that I'd keep Becky safe, and I will. But you are *not* going off, getting yourself killed, and leaving me with the task of telling Becky that maybe I could have done something to stop it, but I agreed to stay safely out of the way."

Even as I said it, the nightmare flickered to life at the back of my mind, making my whole body flash cold.

"I'm not living with that on my conscience."

Jack's scowl deepened. "Maybe I don't want to live with knowing that I'd gotten *you* hurt or killed."

"Fine." I glared back at him. "I suppose neither of us had better die, then. *I'm* not planning to, what about you?"

Jack looked down at me, shaking his head in slow disbelief. "I've been a beat constable for two years, and before that, I was with Flint's gang for ten. I've been in bar room fights and street brawls, I've been shot at, I've arrested murderers and thieves—and all of it was less frightening than a single conversation with you!"

"It will be all right." I spoke more quietly. "When have you ever known me to run into danger without thinking or take unnecessary risks?"

Jack opened his mouth and then closed it again without saying anything.

"Exactly." I nodded. "You're trying to find a more tactful way of saying *all of the time*. To which I will say: *Then you ought to be used to it by now*."

Jack let out a smothered sound, half-exhale, half-laugh. "God, Lucy, you make me—"

The door to the house just ahead of us opened, and a woman's figure popped out. I suppressed an inward groan.

Sophia Highbridge, who lived at number 203, was about my age, or possibly a year or two older, with a frizz of pale blond hair around a plump face and slightly prominent blue eyes.

She and her husband were newly married, without any children as yet. Sophia was bored and lonely—and so far as I could tell, had absolutely nothing to do but sit and look out her windows all day, trying to spy on her neighbors.

"Miss James!" Despite the early hour, she was already dressed in a pink ruffled tea-gown, with a lace shawl wrapped around her shoulders. She came down her front steps and marched towards us, her shoulders back, her blond curls almost quivering with indignation. "Miss James, is this man annoying you?" She turned to Jack, waving her hands. "Be off with you! Shoo! This is a respectable neighborhood, and we will not tolerate the likes of you coming here and causing a nuisance. Now take yourself off, or I shall call the police!"

She probably wouldn't believe that Jack *was* the police. With his clothes rumpled and dirty from being caught in last night's rain and a stubble of beard tracing his jaw, he did look somewhat less than respectable.

Although I wondered what Sophia would say if she knew that beneath my borrowed overcoat, I was wearing nothing but a man's silk dressing gown.

Jack had already stepped back into the deeper shadows that lined the edges of the street. But I still didn't want Sophia or anyone else taking a close look at his face.

He had been a visitor at 221B before, and I couldn't take the chance of Sophia recognizing him from one of those visits.

So I allowed her to take my arm and draw me away.

"*Really.*" Sophia clucked her tongue. "The way these tramps think they can go anywhere is simply shameless. Why just the other day …"

I let her words wash past me without registering more than a handful. As we reached the door of number 221, I looked back over my shoulder. Jack was already gone.

CHAPTER 19

"Lucy?" Becky's whisper filtered in through my dream. "Lucy, are you awake?"

I opened one eye and found her perched on the side of my bed. "I am now."

"I'm sorry!"

I sat up. "It's all right."

In fact, I truly didn't mind being woken, even though I'd slept only a handful of hours since climbing into bed at dawn. The nightmare had barely started, the chill of the ice house only just beginning to creep over my skin when Becky's voice had broken the spell.

The relief I was feeling now was akin to being let out of prison after only serving a single day's worth of a five-year sentence.

"It's just there are a lot of important-looking people upstairs meeting with Mr. Holmes," Becky said. "Mr. Holmes's brother and some other men. And then there was that letter, remember? The one from Mrs. Teale? Asking you to come and see her this afternoon at three?"

"Of course."

I was actually lucky that I had Becky to remember for me. I had completely forgotten the letter from Suzette Teale.

I pushed back the blankets and stood up.

"Was it raining when you came home from the theater last night?" Becky asked.

"What? Why?"

"Your overcoat is still wet. You left it hanging by the door." Becky gestured to the sitting room outside. "But it's not the one you usually wear. Did you have to borrow someone else's?"

This was exactly why I flinched at the thought of trying to keep Becky ignorant of Jack's presence in London: She missed absolutely nothing.

And Sophia Highbridge had interrupted Jack and me before Jack could say whether he wanted me to tell Becky the truth.

I picked up the brush from my dressing table and started brushing out my hair, willing myself to sound as-usual.

My mirrored reflection still showed traces of last night's rouge on my cheeks and lips.

"Yes, it started raining quite suddenly, after the performance was over at the Savoy. So I had to borrow an overcoat."

Strictly speaking, I hadn't *lied*, but I still felt slightly sick telling Becky even a half-truth, when I had never tried to conceal anything from her before.

But then she had never been in this type of danger before, either.

Memories flashed before me, like colored projections in a lantern slide show: Becky, following me to Lansdowne House and single-handedly confronting the guard placed at the ice house door. Becky, captured by Griffin—

She hadn't been hurt that night. But she so easily could have been. And if I told her any part of the truth now, I wouldn't put it past her to climb out the window the second my back was turned and go to find her brother.

Becky sat down on the edge of the bed, seeming to lose interest.

I exhaled, slowly and silently, while I continued to watch her in the mirror.

"Becky, about the meeting upstairs ..."

Becky had already anticipated what I was going to say. "I know, I can't come. Those sorts of people always think children should be seen and not heard." She sounded slightly disconsolate, but then smiled. "Tell me all about it afterwards?"

"If I can, I will."

"All right." Becky frowned. "Also, why is there a chicken in the sitting room?"

I closed my eyes briefly. I had almost succeeded in forgetting about the chicken. It had been so late when I'd come home that I had just set the cage down on the sitting room floor and gone to bed. But the hen probably needed water and ... whatever it was that chickens ate by now.

"I rescued it from a bird vendor last night," I told Becky. "Give me a minute to get dressed, and we can go and introduce her to Mrs. Hudson together."

* * *

Mrs. Hudson blinked at my edited account of having adopted a chicken, but then shrugged philosophically.

After twenty years as Sherlock Holmes's housekeeper and landlady, very little could surprise or rattle her.

"Ah, well, I've dealt with stranger things, heaven knows, since Mr. Holmes and Dr. Watson moved in here."

Becky was on her hands and knees on the kitchen floor, studying the bird through the bars of the cage. "Do you think it would be disrespectful if we called it Sherlock?"

I almost choked trying to smother a laugh. Usually I thought of my father's features as hawk-like, but there *was* something about the chicken's close-set, sharp eyes and jutting beak ...

"I'm not sure Mr. Holmes would see the humor of the comparison. Besides, I have it on authority that it's a lady chicken."

Becky tapped her chin. "I'll have to think of another name, then."

Mrs. Hudson hefted the cage into her arms, glancing at Becky. "Why don't you get her some water in a dish, and some of yesterday's bread. I'll put her outside in the yard for now."

I followed Mrs. Hudson out while Becky stayed in the kitchen, assembling the water and food.

There was no garden behind the house, just a small, square paved yard that opened off the kitchen door and was chiefly frequented by tradesmen when they came to make deliveries.

Mrs. Hudson set the bird's cage down in a patch of watery sunshine that was just beginning to break through the morning clouds.

"Later on I can see about getting Fred the carpenter's boy to come and build a coop for her."

"Thank you, Mrs. Hudson." I glanced at the kitchen window, but I could see that Becky was still at the table, tearing up scraps of stale bread. "There was one other thing. Try not to let Becky out of your sight. Definitely don't let her go outside alone. And if anyone comes to the door, make sure that it's someone you know before you let them in."

Mrs. Hudson looked no more shocked than she had at the arrival of the chicken. "Ah. I take it there's some trouble brewing, is there? Well, don't worry about the child. I'll keep her with me every moment you're not here."

"Thank you." I hugged her.

"That's all right, dear." Mrs. Hudson patted my arm, her plump, motherly face hardening with determination. "And if a stranger tries to force himself into my kitchen, he'll soon find himself on the business end of my heaviest frying pan."

* * *

I paused on the stairwell, just outside the door to 221B's sitting room, listening.

I was dressed in the plainest and most conservative skirt and shirtwaist I had in my wardrobe, with my hair neatly smoothed back into a low bun and all traces of last night's rouge scrubbed away.

I didn't doubt that some of the important personages in the room would still regard me as no more fit to take part in the conversation than they would Becky. Although that was their trouble, not mine. What was making me pause was the anticipation of who exactly I would be facing in there.

I could hear the murmur of masculine voices from inside the sitting room: Mycroft's deep baritone rumble, followed by another voice I didn't recognize. I couldn't hear Lord Lansdowne, but it was more than likely that he would be present. He was Secretary of State for War, after all.

Get it over with.

I opened the door and rapidly took stock of the men assembled.

Mycroft and my father. Lord Lansdowne and Edward Barton.

And three gentlemen I didn't recognize, all of whom looked as though they were trying to murder each other by sheer force of will.

The tension in the room was so thick it felt like an almost physical presence weighting the air.

Mycroft and all of the other men immediately got to their feet at sight of me, all of them far too well trained in proper behavior to sit while a lady was standing.

"Ah, Lucy, my dear," Mycroft greeted me. "I am grateful that you could join us. Gentlemen, this is Miss Lucy James, with whom you may speak as freely as you would before my brother and myself."

I had sometimes reflected that dealing with thugs like the man Yates in the coffee house last night was actually easier than dealing with men of the English Establishment. Men like Yates could be impressed—or at least intimidated—by hitting them in the face, as needed.

Gentlemen who had lived their entire lives with the intrinsic, often unconscious belief of being physically, morally, culturally, and intellectually superior to the entire female population were far harder to sway.

The three men I didn't know had stopped glaring at one another, their faces smoothing out into polite, if stiff, expressions. Now they gave Mycroft startled glances, as though checking to be sure that he wasn't playing some elaborate joke.

"Allow me to introduce you," Mycroft went on. "Lord Lansdowne and his secretary Mr. Barton I believe you already know."

Lansdowne and Mr. Barton were positioned at the small breakfast table.

I could feel my father's gray eyes lingering on me as I smiled a greeting in their direction. Holmes had risen with the other men from his customary chair by the fire, and he didn't look worried, precisely. But his expression was certainly watchful.

I concentrated on standing straight and unflinching. I was fine. Just because Lord Lansdowne was here did not mean I had to let myself fall into another waking nightmare. Besides, my own memories scarcely mattered, compared to the danger hanging over Becky and Jack.

"Hello."

Lord Lansdowne gave me a polite nod of greeting, and Mr. Barton flashed a friendly smile.

"And these gentlemen are Sir Andrew Noble and Lord Armstrong, of the Sir W. G. Armstrong and Company armaments firm," Mycroft said.

I turned to the men who had risen from the chairs flanking Holmes.

I might not have met either of them before, but Uncle John had mentioned them to me, in connection with his journey to Newcastle in June. I knew Lord Armstrong to be the founder of the arms' manufacturing firm, while Sir Andrew, his business partner, was responsible for most of the day-to-day running of the company.

Sir Andrew Noble appeared to be somewhere in his sixties, with a bald, domed head, bushy gray mutton-chop whiskers and equally bushy brows. He gave me a keen look and a *pleased to meet you, Miss James* before subsiding into silence.

Beside him, Lord Armstrong looked ancient. His age had to be approaching ninety, and his back was slightly bowed. His skin, mottled and papery-looking, had pulled back, stretching tightly over the bones of his face and his prominent beak of a nose, and his eyes were rheumy.

"It's nice to meet you, gentlemen," I said.

Lord Armstrong also looked unsteady enough on his feet that I was afraid a strong breeze would knock him over. I sat down quickly, taking a place at the breakfast table, so that he would be free to regain his own chair.

He did sit down, though he continued to eye me with interest. "American, are you? Well, I don't hold it against you. During the War Between the States you had over there in the 1860s, the Americans were some of my best customers."

Beside me, Mr. Barton murmured—so quietly I doubted anyone else could hear—"On both the northern and the southern sides of the conflict."

I glanced at him, but his face was bland.

"And this is Mr. Alexander Dimitrios," Mycroft finished. "Of Blackthorn Munitions."

The last man to be introduced was middle aged, with dark hair growing into a pronounced widow's peak on his forehead. His face was broad and craggy, with deeply scored lines around the edges of his mouth. His eyes were dark, and somehow sad, almost haunted-looking, as though life had in the past dealt him a crippling blow from which he had never quite recovered.

He tipped his head in my direction. "I am pleased to make your acquaintance, Miss James."

I had expected a Greek accent, to match the name Dimitrios, but he sounded more Russian.

His profession also probably explained the lethal quality of the glares being exchanged with the two men from the Armstrong armaments company. If the three men were business rivals, they had probably had occasion to meet—and dislike—one another before.

"They were Mr. Dimitrios' weapons that were stolen," Mycroft continued. He settled back onto the sofa, that being the only seat in the room capable of supporting his bulk. "But both firms of weapons manufacturing have experienced, shall we say, unexpected setbacks in their production of late."

"By which you mean sabotage?" I asked.

Mr. Dimitrios sat up, looking past Mycroft to give Sir Andrew a hard stare. "We assumed that the difficulties originated with the same source as they had in the past."

Sir Andrew's jaw locked. If it were literally possible to look daggers at someone, Mr. Dimitrios would currently have a six-inch steel blade sprouting from his chest.

"Were these *difficulties* you speak of at Blackthorn armaments similar to the time we had an important fleet of diplomats from the Spanish government coming to bid against the Japanese on our latest design in breech-loading rifles? And somehow, mysteriously, the car in which the Spaniards were traveling chanced to break down, forcing them to abandon the trip? Or the time that the prototypes for our new design of armored ships' turrets were mysteriously hacked to pieces before they could be brought to testing?"

Mycroft held up his hands in a pacifying gesture. "Gentlemen, please. What is in the past must necessarily remain there, if this meeting is to proceed towards anything resembling a productive outcome."

The two men subsided, though Mr. Dimitrios continued to look surly and white dents appeared at the edges of Sir Andrew's mouth.

Lord Armstrong turned to me. He had been silent during his partner's exchange with Mr. Dimitrios, his face stiff. But there was now a faint gleam in his eyes that made me suspect the elderly man was rather enjoying himself.

"I'm afraid, Miss James, that ours can be a somewhat ruthless profession."

I bit my tongue before I could say *imagine that* or something equally sarcastic.

I couldn't scrape together much surprise that the profession of creating weapons designed for the sole purpose of killing and maiming one's enemies should be a ruthless one.

But then, I wasn't sure whether I was in a position to judge. I had in the past used physical force to defend myself. I had fired weapons—possibly weapons manufactured by the men before me—in self-defense or to defend Holmes.

My father had been leaning back in his chair, his eyes half-closed as though he were scarcely listening to the conversation around him. But now he murmured, "Both Armstrong and Company and Blackthorn Munitions have suffered sabotage of a particularly subtle variety, the sort that only becomes apparent during the final rounds of weapons testing. However, Blackthorn Munitions is the only firm—to our knowledge—to have weapons outright stolen."

I looked at my father closely. "You believe that to be significant? As I understand it, the weapons were all stored in a warehouse owned by the War Office, where they were to be kept before they could be shipped off to the Sudan. You think that someone deliberately targeted the crates of weapons manufactured by Mr. Dimitrios' firm?"

I glanced at Mr. Dimitrios as I said it and saw him heave a sigh.

"My family were Jews. Forced to flee Russia during the *pogroms* after the death of Czar Alexander. Unfortunately, escaping the threat of death does not mean that one will not face other, more subtle ways of persecution."

Sir Andrew sat up straighter, looking as though he were about to burst a blood vessel. But I could see Mr. Dimitrios' point. Even here in London, the Jewish immigrant neighborhoods were often threatened by violence, their houses burned or their businesses defaced.

Holmes only tilted his head slightly in answer to my question, his face inscrutable.

"I will show you the list of the stolen munitions, as well as the reports on the weapons that were sabotaged," Mr. Dimitrios said. "I have them with me here."

He lifted a black leather attaché case up onto his lap, flipped back the clasps to open it—

And then stopped, staring at the three tubes wrapped in brown paper and attached by wires to what looked like a timing mechanism.

Holmes was the first to break the silence. "It would appear that, at some point this morning, you came into possession of a bomb."

CHAPTER 20

Mr. Dimitrios made a quick, convulsive movement, as though to throw the attaché case off his lap and onto the floor, but the motion was checked by Holmes, who had somehow leapt from his chair and manifested at Mr. Dimitrios' side while the rest of the room was still frozen in shock.

"Be still, Mr. Dimitrios, I pray you. Sudden movement may jar the mechanism and precipitate the bomb's detonation."

Mr. Dimitrios sagged back, his face slack with terror and so pale the skin looked almost gray.

I spun to face Edward Barton. "Down in the kitchen you'll find Mrs. Hudson and the little girl you met here the other day. Go down and get them out of the house. *Please.*"

Mr. Barton jumped up, racing out of the room without a word. A second later, I heard his footfalls, clattering at breakneck pace down the stairs.

"You!" Mr. Dimitrios remained rigid, unmoving under the weight of the bomb. But his head swiveled to face Sir Andrew and Lord Armstrong. "It's not enough that you seek to destroy my business, you must also threaten my life!"

Sir Andrew's face turned a shade redder. "Are you daring to suggest—"

"Gentlemen!" When Holmes liked, his voice could crack like the snap of a whip. "Scarcely productive right now."

He was studying the bomb apparatus and spoke without looking up. "In fact, I suggest that you all file, calmly and quietly, out of the room and into the street. Mr. Dimitrios, if you will just remain still a moment more."

Holmes dropped to his knees and placed his long fingers around the edges of the attaché case, easing it slowly, inch by painstaking inch, off the Greek man's lap.

I held my breath, but no explosion came.

Mr. Dimitrios let out a gusty exhale, his face quivering as though he were about to weep with relief. Then he struggled to his feet, almost knocking over Lord Armstrong in his headlong rush from the room.

Lord Armstrong and Sir Andrew followed more slowly, the elderly man hobbling and leaning heavily on a cane.

"Let me help." Lord Lansdowne came to take hold of Lord Armstrong's arm on the other side, helping to support his weight and hurrying them from the room.

I bit my lip, waiting to hear the sound of the front door opening and closing.

"You know," I said in an undertone, "it might not be a terrible plan for us to leave along with them. The bomb can't kill anyone in an empty house."

"You may if you like." Holmes's gaze flicked briefly up from the arrangement of wires and timer to land on me. "I have long since abandoned all attempts to order you towards the safest course. But I encourage you to proceed outside without delay. You also, Mycroft."

Throughout the hurried exit of the other men, Mycroft had sat unmoving on the couch.

"I, however"—Holmes returned his attention to the bomb in his hands—"take exception to someone trying to blow up my place of residence just when I have become accustomed to living here again. Also, I am not entirely sure that I can set the bomb down without jarring the mechanism and inducing an explosion. That spring and wire arrangement there"—he nodded towards a coil of coppery colored metal near the edge of the case's interior—"was, I believe, intended to trigger the detonation the instant the case was opened. It is similar to the trip-hammer mechanism that fires a pistol. Although whether by sheer chance or due to some flaw in the design, this one here appears to have stuck. But I am afraid that any sudden movements will jar it into motion."

My heart lurched into my throat. "So there's a timing mechanism *and* a device to set off the explosion if the case were to be opened before time? Someone wished to make very sure that the bomb went off today."

"Indeed."

Mycroft remained unmoving on the sofa. Apparently he was ignoring Holmes's admonition to leave. "It might be helpful to know how many minutes are left on the timing device, Sherlock."

No one looking at Mycroft and Sherlock Holmes would ever suspect that the two of them were brothers. But inwardly, they were in fact quite alike, both in intellect and in their habit of even in the darkest moments of crisis sounding as though they were doing nothing more exciting than ordering a cup of tea.

I had known them both long enough to find it almost reassuring—when it didn't make me want to strangle them.

I peered down at the timer. "It looks like … five minutes?"

Holmes nodded. "Five minutes and perhaps a second or two more."

Don't think about what happens at the end of those five minutes. "Tell me what to do to stop it from going off."

The two paper wrapped sticks were dynamite; during the Jubilee affair, I had seen enough of it to last a lifetime.

Holmes looked as though he were about to argue. I cut in before he could speak.

"You can't defuse it when you're using both hands to hold it steady. Yes, you might be able to shift the case into one hand, but that's risky, and you'd only have one hand left for trying to disconnect the timer."

Mycroft cleared his throat. "I would offer my assistance, but I am afraid that Lucy's fingers will be far more nimble than mine."

As Mycroft's hands matched the rest of him for sheer bulk of size, that was patently true.

"Very well." Holmes refocused on the bomb. "Since it is clearly a waste of our remaining four minutes and thirty-nine seconds to argue with you, I would ask that you go to my work table and find the pair of wire cutters in the top drawer."

My hands shook slightly as I did as he asked, rummaging quickly through the work table drawer, which was about as neat and orderly as the rest of the flat. Rubber tubing, a packet of some unidentified chemical substance, a newspaper clipping from three years ago, a mousetrap …

There. I picked up the wire cutters. "Why do you even *have* wire cutters here in the flat?"

"They were purchased for use during a case in which I spent several days as a workman, charged with fixing the electric lighting in a large seaside hotel."

I came back to Holmes's side. "Which wire should I cut?"

"I believe the furthest to the left."

I resisted the urge to ask Holmes just how secure he was in that belief.

Holmes eyed me as I angled the blades of the cutters into position, trying not to touch any other component of the bomb. "I need hardly emphasize that delicacy of touch is of the essence here."

My hands were still shaking more than I liked. "Really? How lucky you said that, or I might have decided to just hit the whole contraption with a meat mallet."

I managed to get the blades of the snips around the wire Holmes had indicated. "This one?"

Holmes gave a short nod.

In the room's silence, I could hear the faint *tick tick* of the timer, counting down the seconds. I squeezed, severing the wire and bracing myself.

But there was no explosion.

The ticking had stopped.

* * *

"Can you tell us who might have had access to your attaché case this morning, Mr. Dimitrios?" Holmes asked.

We were seated once again in the Baker Street sitting room: Mycroft, Holmes, myself, and Mr. Dimitrios. The rest of the men had already given us their statements and gone.

The attaché case lay open on the tufted ottoman in front of the sofa, sticks of dynamite still exposed.

Mr. Dimitrios was staring at it as though it were a poisoned viper.

"It must have been one of those *svolotch*—the swine from Armstrong's company." His face reddened. "As I said, they are not content with sabotaging my business, they—"

Holmes broke into the tirade, holding up one hand. He was leaning back in his armchair, the stem of his pipe clamped between his teeth, and seemed to have entirely recovered from the experience of nearly being blown up half an hour earlier.

"Since Lord Armstrong and Sir Andrew would both have perished in the explosion, had you not chanced to open the case when you did, I believe we may reasonably eliminate them as suspects. Unless, of course, we discover the two gentlemen to be possessed of violent and simultaneously suicidal urges."

Mr. Dimitrios looked sullen, but apparently couldn't find any counter-argument.

Directly after the bomb's failure to go off, Mycroft had left the room to use the telephone. He hadn't specified, but I imagined him alerting various higher-ups in the government and setting into motion a plan for keeping Lord Armstrong under constant protection.

Now, though, he sat in his former place by the sofa, his hands resting on his knees and his large, jowly face as unreadable as Holmes's.

"One also doubts whether Lord Armstrong, as a man of nearly ninety, would have the physical stamina to shadow you without being seen, abstract your case, and plant a bomb in it. Which returns us to the question, Mr. Dimitrios, of who might have gained access to your attaché case." Mycroft's eyes narrowed as he studied the other man. "You took the train to London this morning, from the departure point of … Covington?"

"Birmingham, I think," Holmes murmured.

"Birmingham, of course," Mycroft agreed. "You had breakfast at the railway station house restaurant—poached egg on toast, some of which has unfortunately clung to your waistcoat. You then took a cab—"

"A growler," Holmes put in. "The spatter of mud left on the cuffs of his trousers by the wheels is quite distinctive."

"That might reasonably be considered splitting hairs, Sherlock. But yes, a carriage of the standard four-wheeled growler variety here, to Baker Street," Mycroft finished. "Which leads me to believe that the likeliest points at which the bomb might have been introduced would have been either in the restaurant or on the train. Now, did you open the case at any point during your journey?"

Mr. Dimitrios' scowled in concentration, then nodded. "On the train. I opened the case to consult some new business contracts that I had brought along to read."

"And we can take it that all was as normal within the case at that point," Holmes said. "Very good. These were the papers that you wished to consult?"

He lifted the sticks of dynamite and the disconnected timer aside, pulling out a sheaf of documents.

Mr. Dimitrios flinched and swallowed visibly, his eyes on the bomb. "Mr. Holmes, is that wise—"

Holmes gestured dismissively. "It is perfectly harmless. Now, will you kindly cast your eye over these papers and tell us whether anything is missing?"

Mr. Dimitrios leaned forward, grasped the furthest edges of the papers from Holmes's hand, and quickly sat back, pressing himself into the sofa and looking as though he still expected the bomb to explode at any second.

Holmes set the dynamite back down, and Mr. Dimitrios gave an audible sigh of relief, turning his attention to the documents and shuffling quickly through them.

"They are all here. Everything I brought with me from Birmingham. None are missing," he said.

"Thank you." I couldn't tell from Holmes's expression whether it was the answer he had been anticipating or not. "Now, was the case out of your possession at any point in time?"

"No." Mr. Dimitrios' answer was instantaneous, but then he gave an irritable shrug of his shoulders. "At least, not that I noticed. I may have dozed off at some point on the journey, with the case at my feet. But when I awoke, nothing had been disturbed."

I leaned forward, watching him. "You noticed no one following you? No familiar faces, either on the train or in the restaurant?"

"None."

"Did you speak to anyone at all?"

Mr. Dimitrios' brow furrowed. "There was a man. He sat next to me on the train. He kept talking to me of vegetables."

"Vegetables?" For a moment, I thought I must have misheard.

Mr. Dimitrios grimaced. "Apparently he grows—what did he call them?—vegetable marrows as a hobby and wins prizes for the size. He went on and on, speaking of quality of soils and different fertilizers. I assure you, I now have more knowledge of the merits of sheep versus cow manure than I ever cared to possess."

"Did he make any effort to pick up your case or see inside it?"

"No."

"Do you know where he came from? Or his name?" I asked.

Mr. Dimitrios shrugged. "He got on the train with me in Birmingham. I did not ask him his name. I said as little to him as possible so that he would cease talking."

"Can you describe him at all? Was he old? Young?"

"Neither old nor young. I think he had brown hair. Or perhaps blond." Mr. Dimitrios shrugged again. "There was nothing to make me look at him in particular. He was an ordinary Englishman, nothing more."

Holmes sat back in his chair. I saw him exchange a brief glance with Mycroft, and then he said, "Very good, Mr. Dimitrios. Thank you for your assistance. You will be staying in London for the next few days?"

"At the Clarendon, on Bond Street."

"Then we shall know where to find you should any further questions arise," Holmes said. He studied the attaché case again. "I presume you will not mind leaving this in my possession for the time being?"

Mr. Dimitrios followed Holmes's gaze with a barely concealed shudder. "You are welcome to it."

* * *

"Do you think this was another attempt on Lord Lansdowne's life?" I asked, when Mr. Dimitrios had gone. "Whoever wanted to kill him failed in the attempt at the Diogenes. And now they're trying again?"

Mycroft pursed his lips. "If that is the case, we are dealing with an individual possessed of a remarkably high tolerance for collateral damage. If the bomb had gone off, up to seven people besides Lord Lansdowne might have been killed."

Nine, if you counted Becky and Mrs. Hudson downstairs.

Holmes stood up, crossed to his worktable, opened one of the lower drawers, and began flinging objects out one by one. A medical scalpel hit the ground, followed immediately afterwards by a small bronze bust of the composer Brahms.

"The assumption that Lansdowne was the target also presupposes that whoever planted the bomb knew of the meeting here this morning. And not only that, but was able to assemble the bomb, discover Mr. Dimitrios' travel plans, intercept him, and find an opportune moment for introducing the bomb."

"When was the time for this meeting set?" I asked.

"Eight o'clock last night," Holmes said. His head was still half-buried in the drawer. "I would have told you, but you were already at the theater." He tossed out a jeweler's loupe before emerging with a fine horsehair brush and a metal tin.

"Are you going to test Mr. Dimitrios' attaché case for fingerprints?"

Holmes flicked open the tin, revealing the gray powder inside. "It will probably be an exercise in futility, considering that Mr. Dimitrios has been handling the case all morning, thus in all likelihood wiping any other prints away. However, in the spirit of leaving no stone unturned ..." He tipped a fraction of the powder onto one clasp of the attaché case.

"Do you think Mr. Dimitrios' vegetable marrow enthusiast could have been the one to plant the bomb?" I asked. "He might have done it after Mr. Dimitrios fell asleep."

Holmes flicked the tip of the brush lightly across the clasp, smoothing the powder. "It is possible. It is also possible that he was a perfectly ordinary bore, of the sort that seems to invariably sit down next to one when traveling by train. In either case, however, the odds of our finding the gentleman in question are small. We have not even a reasonable physical description to go on. Unless this man hunted down a railway station attendant, lectured him on proper fertilizing techniques, and then was good enough to leave a card bearing his name and address, I fear we must approach the problem from another direction."

I could forgive Holmes the sarcasm; he had a point.

"What about the bomb itself? Could anything about the materials tell you where it was made, or who by?"

Mycroft was already shaking his head. "The Irish nationalist campaigns of the 1880s, along with the rise of readily available scientific journals, have had the unfortunate side effect of making the construction of such devices almost common knowledge. At one point, there was even a so-called dynamite school in the United States—in Brooklyn, I believe. We may perhaps track down suppliers of dynamite, with an eye to determining the origin of these sticks here. But considering that they might have been purchased by order from anywhere in England or even further abroad, it will likely be a tedious line of investigation, unlikely to bear any fruit."

"There is one other possibility," I said. "Mr. Dimitrios could have planted the bomb himself, deliberately jammed the mechanism meant to detonate it when the case was opened, and then made sure to open it before the timer ran out."

Both Mycroft and Holmes looked at me, near-identical frowns furrowing their brows.

"Why would he have done that?" Mycroft asked at last.

"To win our trust, make us believe him an innocent victim in all of this."

"Possible," Mycroft said. "Although considering the risks involved in transporting sticks of dynamite—whether controlled by a timer or not—it seems a long way to go, especially as we were not even seriously considering him as a suspect."

Holmes was still looking at me oddly.

"What is it?" I asked.

"Nothing." Holmes bent to dust fingerprinting powder on the other clasp of the attaché case, used the brush, then made a noise of disgust as he studied the resulting marks. "Smears only, nothing useful."

He put the lid back on the tin of fingerprint powder before looking up at me again.

"I realize I am the last person on earth to chide anyone for possessing an overly suspicious mind. However, you do seem to be taking the exercise of refusing to take anyone at face value to new heights."

When Sherlock Holmes of all people suggested you were too untrusting, it was probably time to admit that there was something wrong.

I opened my mouth, but before I could answer, the sitting room door opened and Uncle John came in.

He must have spent the morning at his surgery; he had his medical bag in one hand. He saw the sticks of dynamite on the ottoman and blinked.

"Has something happened?"

"Ah, Watson." Holmes looked up from his fingerprint dusting. "One of the gentlemen present this morning, a Russian arms dealer named Dimitrios, was either inadvertently or by design in possession of a bomb, which we managed to defuse. We are now attempting to discover whether the individual who planted the bomb left us with any identifying clues."

"I see." Watson sat down on the opposite end of the sofa from Mycroft. "In other words, an average morning, then."

I smiled despite myself. Uncle John could almost always make me feel better.

"I'm glad you're here, Uncle John," I told him. "I need to tell you—all of you—about how I found Jack last night and what he told me."

CHAPTER 21

Holmes leaned back in his chair, his eyes closed, as I gave an account of everything that had happened the night before.

Almost everything. For the sake of my father's nerves, I left out my encounter with Yates.

"So we now have a culprit for our warehouse burglary," Holmes murmured when I had done.

"A culprit, but not an orchestrator," Mycroft said. "As Lucy and Constable Kelly surmised, this man Flint is unlikely to have acted alone."

"But surely you can now go to Lestrade with what you have learned, have him arrest Flint, and—"

"On what grounds?" Holmes interrupted. "Apart from Constable Kelly's word and the description given by the night watchmen, we have not a shadow of hard evidence that Flint Bayles was responsible for the weapons theft. Their two testaments might possibly lead Bayles to be brought to trial, but they are unlikely to elicit a conviction. And a man like this Flint is not of the type to obligingly confess to his crimes under police interrogation. He would be back on the streets in under a month's time, and—"

Holmes stopped speaking. But I could finish the thought for him.

"And rabid to get revenge on Jack for betraying him," I said. My heart squeezed into a cold, painful knot.

"Both Constable Kelly and Miss Kelly would be in a considerable degree of danger," Holmes agreed. "No, I believe we must have more solid proof than is currently in our possession before we can move against Flint Bayles."

At the moment, Becky was downstairs in the kitchen with Mrs. Hudson again. She knew of the dynamite, but I hadn't told her how close it had come to exploding, only that we had sent her and Becky outside as a precaution. Becky had no idea how close we had all come to dying today or that there was a man at large who would hurt her, just to revenge himself on Jack.

I trusted Mrs. Hudson completely, but I still had to fight the urge to run down to the kitchen just to be absolutely certain Becky was there and safe.

"Have you any ideas on how we might go about getting that proof?" I asked Holmes.

He pursed his lips. "We must be careful in how we go about it, lest we alert Flint to our intentions. I am afraid that this may prove to be a slow game, in which patience and prudent consideration are our watchwords."

I took a breath, trying not to grind my teeth together. Neither patience nor prudence were exactly strengths of mine. Though I couldn't argue with anything Holmes had said.

Holmes opened his eyes, glancing at the clock above the mantel. "Mr. Carey, General Pettigrew's nephew, is expected in about ten minutes. Mycroft contacted him and asked him to come here. I believe young Miss Kelly mentioned earlier that you have another appointment this afternoon, but will you stay for the interview?"

"If you wish me to," I said. "But why?"

"The man has lost his only living relative." Holmes reached for his pipe. "And I have been informed in the past that my manner lacks sympathy when dealing with the recently bereaved."

"You don't say."

There might have been a brief flicker of humor about my father's eyes, but he got up, reaching for the Persian slipper where he kept his shag tobacco.

My father's character in a nutshell: He could defuse a bomb without turning a hair, but needed the comfort of nicotine to face an interview with a murder victim's family.

"Of course I can stay," I said.

* * *

Holmes's worries about General Pettigrew's nephew being in any kind of violent paroxysms of grief over his uncle's death proved to be unfounded.

Actually, Reginald Carey hadn't been in the room five minutes before it was clear that he wouldn't recognize a grief-stricken sensibility if it tapped him on the shoulder, introduced itself, and then invited him to waltz.

He was a tall, elegantly slender man of around thirty or thirty-five, with very fair hair plastered down over his skull by brilliantine cream and eyes of such a pale, washed-out blue that they looked almost colorless.

As he came through the door and shook hands, I could almost see both Holmes and Mycroft ticking off the points of his appearance: immaculately cut and tailored suit, probably made by an exclusive haberdasher in Savile Row. Gold pocket watch tucked into the pocket of his waistcoat, with a diamond-encrusted watch fob decorating the chain. Lemon-colored suede gloves and shoes polished to an almost mirror-like shine.

A rich man with expensive tastes, keen to display his wealth for all to see. Fond of taking snuff, as witness the slight scattering of tobacco on his left sleeve—

No, wait a moment. As Reginald shrugged out of his overcoat, I caught sight of a pawn shop ticket protruding from the inner pocket.

Not as wealthy as he would like to appear to be, if he was pawning his belongings for ready cash. Maybe his expensive tastes had caught up with him.

Holmes made the introductions, then offered him a chair. Reginald looked at the seat of the chair a moment, drew out a silk handkerchief and dusted the cushion, then … he didn't so much sit down, as drape himself languidly on top of the chair seat.

"Are you something to do with the lawyers?" he asked Holmes. He had a high voice for a man, with a north-country accent overlaid with Oxford or Cambridge, and he spoke with an affected drawl, as though speaking each word were almost too much trouble. "I didn't quite understand why you wished to see me. Is there some question over my uncle's estate?"

"We are investigating the circumstances surrounding your uncle's death," Holmes said.

Reginald blinked, then waved an airy hand. "I cannot concern myself with such trivialities. Surely that is a matter for the police."

"It does not concern you that your uncle was murdered?" Mycroft asked.

Reginald yawned. "My uncle has shuttled off this mortal coil. *How* he died is of little importance to me."

"Shuffled," I said.

Reginald blinked again, turning as though noticing me for the first time. "I beg your pardon?"

"The quotation is *shuffled off this mortal coil*. Shakespeare. Hamlet."

"Oh." Reginald gave me a slightly bored look. "Jolly good. As I say, I really cannot be bothered to worry over the manner of my uncle's death."

Uncle John was looking as though he were suppressing the urge to haul Reginald up by the collar and kick him down the stairs.

"You don't feel a duty to see your uncle's killer brought to justice?" he asked.

"Oh, justice, duty." Reginald covered his mouth to hide another yawn. "How terribly boring. Almost as boring as my uncle. He was forever going on about his service in India and his heroic deeds in some petty little uprising or other in Manipur. I suppose if I knew who had done the deed, I might be inclined to send him some flowers, but I assure you, that is all."

My father might be able to do better, but for myself, nothing about Reginald's appearance, per se, would lead me to deduce his family background. At the moment, though, I was penciling him in as an only child, born late in life to parents who had given up all hopes of having a son. Neither could I prove his father had died when he was a young child, but I would still be willing to bet money on it.

I could picture Reginald as a child of ten or eleven: odiously spoiled and indulged by his doting, widowed mother, saying rude or shocking things just because he knew he wouldn't be punished for them.

If he was hoping to shock us now, he was disappointed. My father gave him a calm look. "We are to take it that your uncle's estate comes to you?"

"Yes, thank God. It was all entailed so that it descends through the male line, and since he had no heir of his own, it all comes to me. The only good the old buzzard ever did me in his life. I'm amazed he allowed himself to be poisoned, I had expected him to live to be a hundred just to spite me." Reginald crossed one leg over the other and studied the glossy toe of his shoe. "He was forever preaching at me about squandering the family fortunes at the gambling tables. But I ask you, what is a family fortune *for*, if not to be squandered?"

"Had your uncle any quarrels of late that you know of? Anyone who might wish him ill?" Holmes asked.

"Quarrels?" Reginald tipped back his head and laughed. "My dear man, my uncle had a quarrel with the entire human race. Quarrelsomeness was his *modus operandi*."

"Did he ever mention missing self-powered machine guns?" Holmes asked.

"Maxims?" Reginald looked momentarily startled out of his bored, languid pose. But then he waved a hand. "I really couldn't say. I couldn't be bothered to listen to more than one word in ten my uncle spoke. Besides, I hadn't seen him in some months. I didn't make a habit of spending time with him if I could otherwise help it."

I saw Holmes and Mycroft exchange a brief look, and then Holmes said, "I believe that will be all, Mr. Carey. Thank you for your time."

Reginald unpeeled himself from the chair and stood up. "Is that all? There's no trouble about my inheritance, then?"

Holmes rose, as well. "Provided you did not murder your uncle, Mr. Carey, I see no trouble whatsoever."

"Me?" Reginald looked momentarily taken aback, but then recovered, giving us a supercilious look. "I won't pretend I felt any affection for the old boy or that my favorite thing he ever did in his life wasn't to pop off and leave me his money, but I didn't kill him. I wouldn't lower myself so much as to commit a murder."

I personally suspected the number of crimes that Reginald Carey wouldn't lower himself into committing was in fact quite short. But Holmes merely asked for an address at which Mr. Carey could be reached and allowed him to slouch his way languidly out of the room.

I waited until I heard the downstairs front door close behind him. "Charming."

"Indeed." Holmes's gaze was fixed on the door through which Mr. Carey had gone. "As a doting nephew, young Reginald leaves a great deal to be desired. A thoroughly venial character." He glanced at Mycroft. "You observed, of course, that he addicted to laudanum?"

"And that he spent last night in a gambling den, losing a considerable sum at the card tables," Mycroft agreed. "He is not, however, as vapid and unintelligent as he would have us believe."

"Maxims," I said. "He guessed right away that the machine guns you mentioned were Maxims. That shows at the very least a passing knowledge of military armaments."

"It does."

Uncle John was frowning. "He as good as shouted aloud the fact that he had a motive for wishing his uncle dead. Surely he wouldn't have done that if he were involved in the general's death?"

"On the contrary." Holmes pursed his lips. "We were bound to discover Mr. Carey's financial incentive to hurry his uncle's demise. By fairly rubbing our faces in his callous disregard for his uncle's life, he created what at first glance one might believe to be a more honest impression than if he had made a pretense of grief and shed crocodile tears. It is a peculiar quirk of human nature that we tend to believe a rude man is more honest than one who observes the social niceties."

"We thought at first that General Pettigrew's death had nothing to do with the stolen weapons," I said. "Have you reason to think he was somehow involved after all?"

Holmes made an airy gesture that was almost the equal of Reginald's. "Merely covering all the possibilities. And now I believe Mycroft and I have interviews to conduct in Whitehall, and you have an appointment to be kept."

He was right. If I was to reach St. James Square by three o'clock, I needed to leave. Still, there was an abstracted quality to Holmes's voice that made me give him a searching glance.

"What are you thinking?"

"I?" Holmes rose, putting his pipe back into its holder on the mantel. "I was merely reflecting on the question of whether Mr. Reginald Carey prefers to squander his money at dice or cards."

CHAPTER 22

"How is Constable Kelly?" Watson asked in an undertone.

We were on Marylebone Road, walking in the direction of Regent's Park. Becky was skipping along a few feet ahead of us, holding tightly to Prince's leash.

Uncle John planned to take both Becky and Prince to the park while I met with Suzette Teale. I was trying to ignore the cold thread of fear that tightened inside me at having Becky out here, on a public street this way.

But I couldn't let Becky feel as though she were a prisoner or she would start trying to break free. Besides, I had been watching very, very carefully for any sign that we were being followed, and I had seen no one—no sign of anything suspicious at all.

If we were right in our suppositions, Flint Bayles had more urgent business to attend to just now than thinking about Becky or Jack.

"He's worried about Becky, of course." I spoke quietly so she wouldn't hear. "And I don't think he's doing his injuries any good, with all the physical stress he's putting on them."

"Hardly surprising in either case." Uncle John was watching Becky's blond braids thumping against her shoulders as she skipped and hopped over puddles in the street. "But not what I meant." He rubbed his grizzled mustache, then glanced at me. "I don't believe I've often spoken to you of my time here in London before I met Holmes."

"No. But I have read what you wrote about how you and my father met. You needed to find cheaper lodgings and a flat mate to share them with."

"Yes, quite. But the reason I needed to economize in my mode of living—" Uncle John stopped, looking at the street ahead of us as though he were staring back across the years. "It has been years since I wrote those first stories about my association with Holmes. But as far as I can remember, I glossed over my initial few months here in London in a few brief generalities about my comfortless, meaningless existence and the habit I had fallen into of spending what little money I had more freely than I ought."

A big, four-wheeler carriage rumbled past us in the street.

I frowned. I had read those words of Watson's, but strangely it only now occurred to me that I had never really stopped to visualize what they *meant*.

"I hadn't descended to the levels of our visitor Mr. Carey. But I was gambling." Uncle John's voice was blunt. "Drinking more than I ought, as well. Not because I particularly enjoyed it. I didn't. It was more because ..." He stopped, as though searching for words. "Because I felt an urge to punish myself in some way."

"*Punish* yourself? But why?"

I couldn't help but stare at him. Up until this minute, I would have said that Dr. John Watson was sober, careful, steady, and above all *dependable* to his core. What he had just told me was like a stray puzzle piece that refuses to fit in anywhere with the picture you happen to be working on.

Uncle John rolled his shoulders almost as though trying to settle a physical weight. "I was wounded in Afghanistan, as you may know. Wounded, and then I contracted a fever and nearly died. You might think that an experience like that would leave me grateful to be alive, determined to make my existence in this often cold world of ours *matter*." He glanced at me, a brief, dry twist of a smile touching his mouth. "I suppose that eventually I did manage to struggle through to something approaching those feelings. But only by way of a lengthy sojourn with anger—at the world, at life. But chiefly at myself."

"But it wasn't your fault—getting shot, catching a fever. You weren't to blame for any of that."

Up ahead, Becky had paused at the corner to wait for us, with Prince sitting down beside her. Even sitting, the top of the big dog's head came up past Becky's shoulder. He was panting, his mouth lolling open to reveal teeth nearly the size of my little fingers. Most of the other pedestrians on the road took one look and then gave them a wide berth.

Uncle John stopped walking, turning to me. "If only human emotion were as subject to logic and reason as Holmes's mind. I *felt* as though I must have done something to deserve my misfortunes. I cannot count the number of nights I lay awake, replaying the Battle of Maiwand in which I was wounded, asking myself whether I could not have avoided injury if I had been faster, or …" He trailed off and was silent a moment. "There was a cannon ball," he said at last.

Uncle John's voice lost color, as though he were holding emotion tightly in check. Listening, I didn't have a doubt that he had relived the scene he was speaking of countless times.

"The cannon ball struck one of the infantrymen to my right. Stevens. I knew him slightly. It took his leg entirely off. He was dead—or as good as. I knew it; no man survives a field injury like that one. But I still went to him, fighting my way across the field of battle to his side. That is when I was struck."

He touched his leg as though remembering the jezail bullet that had shattered the bone and nearly cost him his life.

I squeezed Uncle John's arm. "You were very brave."

Watson smiled at me again, an easier smile this time. "Brave and stupid, I'm afraid, and with an unshakeable belief in my own heroism. An extremely dangerous combination."

Becky was hopping from one foot to another, impatient for us to catch up to her. Another moment or two and she would probably come running back to demand that we hurry.

"You're saying that Jack may feel as though it was his fault he was shot during the Jubilee?"

"I wouldn't go that far." Uncle John's smile was brief and rueful. "Just because *I* behaved like an idiot does not mean that Constable Kelly will."

I thought of Jack dropping from the second-story window and then jumping from the roof last night.

"*Idiot* might possibly cover it. Although to be fair, I'm not sure Jack has a choice. He has to protect Becky."

Uncle John's kindly face took on a determined cast. "We all must do our utmost to ensure the child's safety. In that task, at least, Constable Kelly will not be alone."

We started down the street again.

"Uncle John?" I asked.

"Yes, my dear?"

"What helped you to recover? Was it meeting my father?"

"In part. My association with Holmes certainly gave me a new interest in life and a sense of purpose. But if you ask how I finally regained some measure of inner peace, for that I would have to credit Mary."

"Oh." He meant Mary Marston, his wife. I had never met her, but I had heard both Holmes and Watson speak of her.

Uncle John had loved her so much, and they'd had so little time together. Just a few short years of marriage before she died. "I'm so sorry, Uncle John."

"Don't be." There was grief in Uncle John's face, but it was a grief plainly worn smooth by years. His eyes were steady, calm. "I count myself fortunate to have what time with her I did. Do not mistake me. I would have given anything for more time—a year, even a single day—with her by my side. But the days of our marriage were still a gift." Watson turned to me, his gaze steady. "Love is always a gift, Lucy. One that should never be wasted."

* * *

I raised my hand and tapped at the door of 33 Saint James Square.

Like most of the other houses on the square, number 33 was a tall Georgian building, with a handsome brick facade and a columned door. Behind me, in the garden at the center of the square, loomed a statue of William III astride a horse.

The door was opened by a stately gray-haired butler. I gave my name, and he stepped back, allowing me to enter. "Certainly, Miss James. Mrs. Teale is expecting you in the drawing room."

I followed the butler up a white marble staircase to the drawing room, then stopped, trying not to stare, open-mouthed, as he opened the door and announced, "Miss James to see you, madam."

The room inside was long and rectangular, with clean Georgian lines like the exterior of the house and a classical plaster frieze running along the top of the walls near the ceiling.

And every inch of the floor space was crammed with furniture: upholstered chairs, shield-back wooden chairs, sewing tables, coffee tables, velvet-covered sofas, curio cabinets … the effect was like being inside the crowded showroom of a curiosity or antique shop.

But what was actually making me stare were the figurines that in turn covered every square inch of surface on every available table, cabinet, and shelf.

Dogs. Dog figurines of every breed, from collies to bulldogs and from setters to spaniels and terriers. Glass dogs, china dogs, bronze dogs, and dogs enameled in the Chinese style.

It took me a moment of standing in the doorway and blinking to even manage to pick out the room's human occupants from amongst the jumble.

But there were two women, sitting side by side on the sofa in front of the fireplace. The first was Suzette Teale: blond and pretty, dressed in a pale lavender-colored gown with so many layers of lace and ruffles that she looked somewhat like a wedding cake.

The second woman was older, with snowy white hair piled high on her head and a sweet, pink-cheeked face. She wore a high-necked dress of black satin, edged with black crape, and no jewelry—plainly mourning clothes.

It was the older woman who stood up and came to greet me, beaming. "Miss James, I am so very pleased that you could come to see us today. I am Mrs. Josiah Teale, Suzette's mother-in-law. Neville is my son. But of course, you may know all that already, since you are acquainted with Suzette."

I looked over Mrs. Teale's shoulder at Suzette, hoping for some direction, but she only gave me a look of helpless appeal.

"It's nice to meet you, Mrs. Teale," I said.

Mrs. Teale drew me over to the sofa, still talking. She seemed scarcely even to draw breath between sentences, though she had a pleasant voice and was obviously anxious to be kind.

"Suzette told me all about how you met at Lady Selfridge's bridge party last month. It's so good for Suzette to have a friend come to call. Most of the time she's cooped up in here with only me for company, and I'm afraid I'm *very* dull."

Suzette straightened at that, speaking for the first time. "You are not at all dull, Mother Teale. I always enjoy your company very much."

She spoke in a low-pitched voice, heavily tinged with a French accent.

Mrs. Teale smiled. "That is kind of you, my dear. Now." She looked anxious. "Have you had enough to eat? I could ring for another plate of toast or some fresh tea? And are you sure you're not too cold? I thought I felt a draft in this room earlier."

Suzette smiled. She looked slightly pale, with shadows beneath her eyes and a flicker of a troubled look at the back of her gaze. But there was genuine affection in her expression as she turned to her mother-in-law.

"I could not eat another thing, truly. And I am not at all cold. In fact, I thought perhaps Lucy and I might take a turn around the square outside. We can walk once around the garden."

Mrs. Teale's look of alarm deepened. "Oh my dear, are you sure that's wise, in your condition?"

Suzette stood. All the ruffles and lace on her dress had hidden it while she was seated, but now I realized that she was clearly expecting a baby soon.

"I feel quite well."

Mrs. Teale looked as though she might protest again, but then caught herself. "Oh dear, I'm fussing again. I'm sorry. Of course you should go out if you wish to. The fresh air will no doubt do you good." She leaned towards me, speaking confidingly. "I don't mean to be such a worry-monger, but it really just seems like such a miracle. For so many years, I believed my son lost to me forever, but now to have him back home again—and with a wife and child …"

She glanced up at the mantel, where I now saw hung a portrait of a young man in army uniform.

"Is that—" I began.

The young man's face in the portrait was clearly Neville Teale's, though somewhere about ten years younger than he was now. In the painting, he looked barely out of his teens, and though I was certain the portrait had been designed to flatter, the artist hadn't entirely been able to erase the slightly nervous, uncomfortable look in his eyes.

"Yes, that is Neville." Mrs. Teale's smile was tinged with sadness. "The only time his father was ever really happy with him, poor man. Though for myself, I was never so relieved in my life as I was when Neville got his discharge papers. But still,

I used to look up at that portrait and think that I might have escaped losing my son to some nasty, foreign war. But that he *was* lost to me, all the same—"

Her voice caught and she dabbed at her eyes with a handkerchief, then gave Suzette a determined smile. "I'm sorry. Do please go out and enjoy your visit with your friend."

* * *

Suzette relaxed visibly, breathing a sigh of relief as we stepped out onto the street.

"Mrs. Teale is very sweet," she said, eyeing the house behind us. "It is just that every time I open my mouth lately, she tries to cram a teacake or a sandwich—"

She was trying to hold onto the French accent, but it slipped on the last word, making her break off.

"Blast it." She slipped back into the voice I remembered, English, with a slight country burr. As far as I could remember, she came from a family of dairy farmers in Devon. "I never was any good at accents."

"You want to soften your *g*'s more. And make your *th*'s sound a little bit more like a *d* instead of a *z*."

I didn't ask why she was masquerading as a native French speaker; presumably, I was here so that she could tell me.

"Thank you." She looked at me as we started across the street towards the square garden and the William III statue. "You recognized me at the Diogenes Club the other morning. I wasn't sure whether you would remember me."

"Of course I do. It hasn't been that long."

Suzette—or rather, Susan Watkins, as she was called back then—had been a member of the D'Oyly Carte opera company up until about six months ago. Like me, she sang soprano, and we had performed in last year's production of *The Gondoliers* together. We had been friendly enough acquaintances, if never growing close enough to really be friends. Susan had dropped out of the company soon after, and I had never found out where she had gone.

"But if you're worried about me telling anyone—" I began.

Susan shook her head. "It's not that." She nodded to a bench a short distance away. "Do you mind if we sit down?" She put her hand on her rounded middle. "I actually can't walk very far these days. Not without feeling like a waddling duck, at any rate."

"When is the baby due?" I asked.

"November. Another month, about." She dropped heavily down onto the bench, then looked up at me, her expression almost helpless. "I'm not sure where to start."

I wasn't sure, either. I hardly qualified as an expert, but if she had only another month before the baby came, that meant that six months ago when she was singing in *The Gondoliers*, she had already been expecting a child. And she had never mentioned a husband to me back then.

Besides, men like Neville Teale—men with stately family homes in St. James Square and membership to an exclusive club like the Diogenes—didn't marry country farm girls from Devon; that was simply not how London high society worked.

"Why don't you tell me how you met your husband?" I asked.

"I met him at a party someone from the theater was having. Last April."

I didn't say anything, but Susan glanced quickly up at me all the same. "So no, the baby isn't his. Are you horrified?"

"My own father and mother were never married, so I hardly think I have the right," I told her.

Susan looked down, plucking at one of the frills of lace on her dress. "Mrs. Teale bought this for me. She picked out all my clothes and gave them to me as a present after Neville and I came to live with her. I feel like a walking millinery advertisement." She made a slight face, but then sighed. "She's really very nice, though. And she's not nearly as eccentric as you'd think, from all those dog figurines of hers. It was just she got bored and lonely, too, when she and Neville were estranged."

"Mr. Teale and his mother were estranged?"

"Yes. Well, no. The estrangement was really between Neville and his father. Neville's father insisted on Neville joining the army—you saw the portrait—and being shipped off to war. But Neville hated everything about the army. He never wanted to fight or be a soldier. And then there was some trouble. I don't know the details, exactly. Some quarrel with his commanding officer. He's never said, but I think Neville may have gotten into trouble on purpose, just so that he would be able to leave. At any rate, he was discharged, and his father disowned him—turned him out of the house and cut off Neville's allowance too. Neville hasn't a penny of his own, it was all his father's. And even after his father died, it was all tied up in trust until Neville's thirtieth birthday or until his marriage, whichever came first."

"When did the elder Mr. Teale die?"

"Five months ago."

"Ah." I was beginning to understand the direction in which this story might be heading.

Susan's cheeks flushed. "I know this next part is going to sound bad ... *greedy*. But it wasn't like that, it really wasn't.

Neville had heard his father was ill—dying. He didn't want his father to disinherit him. The house here has always been Neville's home, and Neville didn't want to lose it. Anyway, why should Mr. Teale have the right to deny Neville the family house and fortune? Just because Neville didn't want to live the life his father had picked out for him?"

She drew a breath, not waiting for me to answer. "It wasn't just the money, though, Neville wanted to come home and make things up with his mother too. Mrs. Teale couldn't stand up to a goose, much less her old tartar of a husband, and Mr. Teale had forbidden her to see Neville. But she had been sending money to him sometimes, in secret, whenever she could."

"And Neville thought that if he arrived home with a wife who was expecting a child, he would stand a better chance of reconciling with his parents?"

Susan bit her lip, nodding. "That's about the way of it. I needed a husband, and he needed a way back into his father's good graces. We told his parents that I was Suzette DuPris, great-granddaughter of a French marquis who lost his head during the reign of terror. Neville told them that we'd met and been married in Paris over the winter."

"And they believed that?"

Susan's shoulders twitched. "Mr. Teale was getting very vague and wandery in his mind towards the end. He could hardly remember his own name. But he liked the idea of his son having married a descendent of royalty. He was a terrible old snob. And Neville's mother was just happy to have her son back again."

I thought of the tears that had come into Mrs. Teale's eyes when she spoke of her son's return. I could easily believe that was true.

Susan cheeks flushed. "You're thinking it's a mean trick to play on an old, lonely woman." She looked at me, appeal in her gaze. "But wouldn't it have been crueler if she'd been left alone after her husband died, without anyone to keep her company? If Neville's father had disinherited him, the estate would have gone to a cousin in Australia. He might have sold the house, and Mrs. Teale would have been turned out of her own home! This way, everyone is happy. Neville gets his inheritance and can live here with his mother. And Mrs. Teale has a family again—and a grandchild." Susan's hand rested fleetingly on the curve of her stomach. "She's so happy about the baby. She spent weeks picking out furniture and linens for the nursery."

I nodded slowly. "She certainly does seem happy to have you here."

"I love *being* here!"

"You don't find it ... strange? Everything about the way the Teales live must be so different from what you're used to."

Susan frowned, opening her mouth, but I held up a hand.

"I'm not suggesting that you're somehow not good enough for them, just because you didn't grow up in a place like St. James Square. I just wondered whether you can really be happy. You don't go out very much, do you?"

Susan's eyes widened. "How do you know that?"

"Your shoes." I gestured to Susan's fine white kid walking boots, the leather embroidered with blue and red satin roses. "They're last summer's fashion, but you've scarcely worn them outside at all. The soles are hardly even scuffed."

"I *don't* go out very much. It isn't considered proper, with the baby so close, and besides—"

Susan broke off, biting down on her lower lip.

"Someone might recognize you?" I guessed.

"Yes. There's not so very much chance of it. It's not as though I was in any way well known for being on the stage, we're just being careful. But Mrs. Teale has people—her lady friends—come to the house, and they're all very nice to me."

"They don't make you feel as though you don't belong?"

"Well, but everyone—Mrs. Teale and everyone she knows—think that I *do* belong here," Susan said.

"Yes, I suppose that would make a difference."

Susan gave me a confused look. "But why do you want to know all of this?"

"No reason. Never mind."

I'd actually been thinking of Jack—thinking that it was all very well for me to say that the difference in our backgrounds shouldn't matter. I wasn't the one who would be looked down on by London society.

But probably I should stop letting Jack intrude on my thoughts every five minutes.

Susan went on. "I never really knew my own mother. She died when I was just a baby. Mrs. Teale has been like a mother to me these past few months. I'm not just trying to sponge on her for the sake of the money. I love her."

There was a note of something almost like pleading in Susan's voice.

"Yes, I can see that you do."

I didn't doubt the affection that Susan felt for her mother-in-law.

I might privately doubt that you could build a happy life on a foundation of lies. But I hadn't come here so that I could judge Susan's choices.

"If you're worried that I'll tell Mrs. Neville the truth, I promise you, I won't. I haven't breathed a single word to anyone about seeing you at the Diogenes."

"Thank you." Susan let out a breath, but then shook her head. "That's not why I asked you to come, though." She leaned back against the wooden bench, shutting her eyes briefly and then opening them again. "I'm being blackmailed."

CHAPTER 23

Susan's eyes had flooded with tears. "I'm sorry." She fumbled in her reticule. "I cry about absolutely everything lately. *And* I don't have a handkerchief."

The last word broke on a choked-off sob.

"It's all right. Here, take mine." I handed my handkerchief to her and waited while she mopped her eyes and blew her nose. Then I asked, "Who is trying to blackmail you?"

"I don't know." Susan drew a shuddering breath, balling the handkerchief up in her hands. "That's just it, I—" She stopped. "Before I tell you any more, I need to ask you something. I should have asked it right away, but apparently I can't *think* anymore, either." She rubbed her forehead, then looked at me. "Are you somehow connected to the police? After I saw you at the Diogenes, I asked Neville who you were, and he said that you'd been with the police, asking questions."

A breeze rustled through the bare branches of the trees over our heads, making the boughs creak and clatter, swaying.

I felt the ever-present knot in my chest tighten.

Susan had far more to risk by being honest in this conversation than I did. I hadn't any reason to mistrust her or to think that it would do any harm to tell her of my connection to Holmes. It was something of a secret, but not a very closely guarded one. With every case I worked on with Holmes, the circle of people who knew of our association grew.

I still had to clamp down on a wave of uneasiness at the thought of sharing that part of my life with Susan. The last two women I'd been honest with hadn't exactly come to good ends. And Susan's story of being blackmailed *could* be a ploy—

Somewhere in the back of my head, my father's sardonic voice repeated his earlier comment about my taking suspiciousness to new heights.

"I sometimes assist the police in their inquiries," I told Susan. "But I'm not officially associated with them in any way."

I braced myself for more questions, but Susan only nodded, apparently satisfied.

"I don't know who it is that's behind this," she went on. "Whoever it is has only ever communicated by letters."

"How long has it been going on?" I asked.

"The first letter came three months ago." Susan spoke in a flat voice, her shoulders sagging as though she were suddenly exhausted. "It demanded that I leave fifty pounds behind Queen Anne's alcove in Kensington Gardens. Otherwise, it said, the writer would tell Mrs. Teale exactly who I really was and how Neville and I met."

"Do you still have the letter?"

Susan shook her head. "I threw it in the fire. I hoped it was just a nasty joke. I thought that maybe if I ignored it—" She stopped, swallowing. "But a few days later, there was a letter for

Mrs. Teale. She was ill with a cold that day and just by chance stayed in bed instead of coming down to breakfast. So *I* was the one to see the letter first, instead of her, and I knew what it was."

"How could you tell?"

"It looked just like the other one. The writing had all been made from newspaper letters, cut up and pasted on one by one."

"Crude, but an effective way of keeping one's handwriting from being recognized," I murmured. "What did the letter say?"

"It told Mrs. Teale *everything*." Susan scrubbed at her eyes again. "All about my being on the stage and not really a member of the French royalty and ... everything else."

"What did you do?"

"I burned the letter before Mrs. Teale could see it, and then I went straight out and left the money behind the Queen Anne alcove, just as the first note said. I thought everything would be all right. I *hoped* everything would be all right. But then, about a month later, I got another letter, just like the first one, demanding that I leave another fifty pounds behind the bust of John Milton in the poet's corner of Westminster Abbey."

Susan's blackmailer was beginning to sound slightly like a Baedeker's guidebook to London's most famous sights.

"What did you do?"

"I paid. I didn't know what else to do. Then three weeks later, another letter came. For a hundred pounds, that time. That one said that if I didn't pay, the blackmailer would send proof of who I really am to all the gossip columns in all the London society papers." Susan took a shuddery breath. "So I paid that too."

"Have you had any more letters since then?"

"No. But I'm afraid it's only a matter of time—"

Susan didn't really need to say it. The blackmailer was unlikely to leave her alone now that he or she had discovered such a rich source of easy income.

"No, obviously you haven't heard the last from whoever it is," I agreed.

Susan looked at me with red-rimmed eyes. "I thought perhaps you might know—" She stopped speaking, her attention caught by something behind me. "Oh, Neville. I'm glad you've come home. I was just telling Lucy everything."

I turned to find Neville Teale standing beside our bench. He was dressed in a gray suit and a black bowler hat that made his fair hair look fairer still.

"Of course." He nodded to me. "Thank you for coming, Miss James."

I couldn't help looking at him in quick surprise. Susan hadn't said as much, but I had somehow unconsciously assumed that she'd kept the matter of the blackmail from her husband. Apparently I'd been wrong.

"We'd be grateful for anything you can suggest, Miss James. Any help you can give in dealing with this bounder." He came to stand behind Susan, resting a protective hand on her shoulder. "If it were only the two of us, I would say publish and be damned. But there's my mother to think of."

"You could tell her the truth," I said.

"I could," Neville agreed. "She would probably forgive us both too. My mother is not a vengeful woman. But if the truth were to be spread about town, my mother's reputation would be tarnished by the scandal. Many of her friends would cease to receive her in their homes. She would be cut and scorned wherever she went."

That was unfortunately true. It was another of those basic truths of the way London high society functioned.

Neville started to push his hair back—evidently forgetting that he was wearing a hat because he knocked the bowler onto the ground, swore, and then bent to pick it up before it could roll away.

"I've already brought my mother grief enough, Miss James." His eyes were earnest. "I cannot be the cause of inflicting on her any more pain."

"I understand." I looked from Neville to Susan. "I'm afraid that until you hear from the blackmailer again, there's very little that I can do. But I can make a few inquiries for now. And once you do have another letter, let me know at once."

"Thank you." Neville shook my hand. "I suppose I should be getting back to the house."

"Susan, would you mind staying out here with me just a few moments more?" I asked. "There were just one or two more questions I had."

Susan looked at me, a flicker of something like nervousness in her gaze, but then nodded. "Of course. You go ahead, Neville, I'll join you shortly."

I waited until I had seen Neville Teale cross the street and ascend the front steps of number 33. Then I turned back to Susan.

"Do you know who it is that's behind the blackmail?"

"What?" Susan's hand flew to her throat, shocked. "No, no, of course not."

"You do suspect, though."

Susan didn't say anything, so I went on, speaking as gently as I could. "Whoever sent these letters is someone who cares more about hurting you than they do about the money. At least, they did at first."

Susan's eyes went wide. "How can you tell that?"

"After you ignored the first letter that came, the blackmailer wrote to Mrs. Teale straight away. He didn't make any more threats, he didn't try to bargain, he just straight away revealed your secret. It was just sheer chance that Mrs. Teale never saw the letter. The blackmailer couldn't possibly have known that she would be ill in bed with a cold that day. And he hadn't yet threatened to go to the papers. If he'd told Mrs. Teale the truth, you would have had no motivation to ever pay him. Which means that he wanted to hurt you, expose your secret, more than he wanted the fifty pounds. Although once you did pay, he must have decided that he was onto a good thing, and that he might as well keep on with it." I looked at Susan, still speaking as gently as I could. "So who do you suspect would want to hurt you that much? Is it your baby's father?"

"I don't know." Susan's face seemed to crumple again, her voice wobbling. "Honestly, I don't know. But it could be. He was ... angry when I broke things off with him."

"Why did you break things off?"

"Because I found out he was stealing." Susan searched fruitlessly for a dry patch on the handkerchief, then gave up and wiped her eyes with the back of her hand. "He had a job as a theater usher. Not at the Savoy, he was at the Lyceum. But I found out he was just using the job to get close to the rich people who came to the shows and pick their pockets while he showed them to their seats. So I stopped seeing him." Susan's face hardened with determination. "I wasn't going to have my baby grow up with a criminal for a father."

The story was close to what I had already suspected, but a prickle of unease ran through me all the same. "Could he be dangerous? If he is the one blackmailing you, he's shown that he wants revenge. Do you think he would hurt you physically?"

"Not him." Susan's face was contemptuous. "He's too much of a coward for that. Sneaking around sending anonymous letters is just his style, though."

"Will you tell me his name—and his address too, if you know where to find him?" I asked.

Susan looked worried. "What are you going to do?"

"At the least, have a look around and see if he seems likely to be your blackmailer. If I discover that he is, we can take steps to see he gives up on the whole enterprise."

"Do you really think you can do that?" Susan's voice trembled, her eyes filling with tears all over again.

"I can't make any promises. But I will try."

"Thank you." Susan squeezed my hand. "Oh, thank you, Lucy. I can't tell you what a relief it is to have told you."

"You're very welcome. Can I ask you one last question?"

"Of course."

"Did Neville ever mention a General Pettigrew to you? From the Diogenes Club?"

"Pettigrew?" Susan repeated, slowly shaking her head. "No, I don't recognize the name. I don't think Neville has ever spoken of him. Neville doesn't go to the Diogenes often, even though it's just down the road from here. His father was a member. It was *exactly* the sort of place to suit an old toad like Mr. Teale. Then when he died, the members offered his place to Neville."

"I see."

Susan's brow furrowed. "Why do you ask?"

"No reason." If General Pettigrew had quarreled with Neville Teale over the subject of Susan, it seemed likely it was because the general had recognized her from the stage. But there was no need to worry Susan with that, especially not with General Pettigrew dead.

"Just give me the name and address of the man you suspect of being your blackmailer, and I'll get back in touch with you the moment I have any news."

CHAPTER 24

I knocked at the door of Jack and Becky's lodgings, then held my breath. *Please be here.*

After parting from Susan, I had made sure that Becky and Uncle John returned safely to Baker Street.

Now it was nearly dusk. I had to be at the Savoy in just under two hours, but there ought to be time enough for me to call at the address that Susan had given me.

I had also spent nearly the whole of my journey here convincing myself that this wasn't just an excuse for trying to find Jack again. But if I was wrong and he wasn't here after all—

The door swung open, and I worked at not exhaling a long breath of relief.

Jack went motionless at the sight of me. He looked as though he was either just getting up or just going to bed, his shirt collar partly unbuttoned, and his dark hair still damp from the washbasin.

"Is Becky—" he began.

"She's fine," I interrupted quickly. "I'm sorry, I didn't mean to worry you, coming here like this. Becky is back in Baker

Street with Holmes and Uncle John, quite safe. I think Holmes was going to spend the evening teaching her to use a chemical re-agent to test for hemoglobin."

Jack stepped back, letting me come in.

"Is this place still being watched?" I asked.

I had waited a solid quarter of an hour on the street outside before I approached Jack's door, watching for any signs that Flint was keeping him under observation.

I hadn't seen anyone, but the streets in St. Giles were always a jumble of foot and street traffic, horse carts and pickpockets and dockyard workers on their way to or from work. It was impossible for me to be absolutely certain that there were no men here on Flint's orders.

"Not that I've seen. Doesn't hurt to be careful, though."

Jack closed the door behind us, shutting out the noise of a spirited fight that two of the neighbors were having over who had spilled ashes over whose clean washing.

"All right, I give up. How did you know I'd be here?" he asked.

Everything about the Kellys' small home was substantially the way it had been the last time I had visited here: everything orderly and neat, if threadbare. But somehow, without Becky's liveliness and warmth, the rooms had a grim, empty feel that made me wince to think of Jack staying here alone.

At least he was still alive.

"The spots of candle wax on your shirt last night. You had a few specks on your sleeve, just there"—I gestured to the cuff of the clean shirt Jack was now wearing—"as though the candle had spattered when you blew it out. The wax was green. Like the candles on your mantel." I pointed to the rough wooden shelf over the fireplace. "I was with Becky when she bought them three weeks ago. I was the one to take her marketing that week, remember, while you were on duty? She picked the green bayberry ones because she thought they were pretty."

"Candle wax." Jack shook his head.

"Well, I owed you for being the one to notice the bird vendor's crooked finger last night and realize he wasn't Holmes."

"Has something happened?"

"No, nothing. But I wanted to visit the home of a possible blackmailer this evening, and I thought it would be more sensible if I didn't go alone. It's nothing to do with the Diogenes case," I added. "Just something I'm looking into for a friend."

Jack looked at me strangely. "Since when do you ever worry about doing the sensible thing?"

"I can be *eminently* sensible when I wish to be!"

Jack didn't say anything.

I blew out an exasperated breath. "Don't you have something better to do than stand there looking skeptical?"

Jack grinned. "Sure. Apparently I need to come along and visit a possible blackmailer."

* * *

"I think that must be the place there." I pointed to a narrow building between a store advertising meat for cats and dogs and a pawn shop. "Susan said that he had rooms over a tavern called the White Hart."

The address Susan had given me was on Maiden Lane, just to the south of Covent Garden and not far from the Lyceum Theater.

This wasn't the most dangerous neighborhood in London, but someone hoping to find a brothel could throw a stone in any direction and be reasonably sure of hitting one. And a pickpocket would be right at home.

Jack eyed the tavern, which looked decidedly down-at-heel, with paint peeling from the sign over the door and windows sagging in their frames.

"Who exactly are we looking for?"

"His name is Fred Miller. I don't know too much more about him, except that he works as a theater usher, with a bit of petty larceny on the side."

"Do we know what he looks like?"

I had gotten a description of him from Susan. "About five foot five inches tall, slim build, brown hair, and hazel eyes."

Jack tilted his head to look up at the windows over the White Hart. "Looks like there should be an entrance around back. Do you want to go knock on his door and see whether he's at home?"

Jack was wearing his blue police uniform since I'd thought a conversation with Fred Miller might carry more weight if I was accompanied by an officer of the law. As we made our way down the narrow alley that bordered the tavern, several of the men loitering in doorways looked at him and then abruptly decided that they had urgent business somewhere else.

"Have you seen Royce at all since last night?" I asked.

"No, but then Flint's orders have been for everyone to lay low since the police raid. Why?"

"Someone planted a bomb in the luggage of a Greek armaments dealer. It was on him when he came to meet with Holmes this morning. I was just wondering whether it could have been Royce."

Jack stopped walking. "That's your definition of nothing happening?"

"Well, the bomb didn't go off." If I ignored the sick feeling in the pit of my stomach at the memory, I could almost pretend that the *nothing* part of my answer was true. "I know Holmes is still worried about another attack happening tomorrow night, though. Lord Lansdowne is hosting a gala ball for charity at Lansdowne House. You haven't heard Flint mention anything about it, have you?"

"No." Jack and I had started down the alley again, but he glanced at me. "What's wrong with Lansdowne House?"

"What?" I startled. "Why should there be something wrong?"

"I don't know, your voice just sounded strange when you said it."

Saying *it did not!* would only make me sound as though I were younger than Becky. I took a slow breath instead, then went motionless. We had reached the end of the alley and the back entrance to the tavern.

Glancing up and to my right, I could see a set of external stairs running up the back of the building to what had to be the door to Fred Miller's rooms. And standing at the top of the stairs was a man in tattered clothes trying to pry open the door with a crowbar.

The man caught sight of us at the same moment, gasped audibly, dropped the crowbar, and launched himself headlong down the stairs, trying to run away.

There was a stack of empty wooden packing crates leaning against the side of the tavern. I gave them a quick shove, and the whole pile toppled over, landing at the foot of the stairs just as the would-be burglar's feet hit the ground.

He tripped, crashed, and landed in a tangled pile of splintered wooden boards.

Jack hauled him up by the back of his collar, studying him. "Doesn't look like he's our man."

"No," I agreed.

By Susan's description, Miller was dark and slim. This man was fair-haired, with a scruffy, unkempt beard and watery blue eyes.

"I wasn't doing nothing!" The man's voice was high, frightened-sounding, and he dangled in Jack's grasp, not even trying to free himself. "The place belongs to a friend of mine. He said I could bunk there for the night."

"Using a crowbar as a back door key?" Jack didn't relax his hold. "Try again."

"Fine, fine!" The man's voice slid into a despairing whine. "I was breaking in, but I wasn't going to steal or nothing! I just wanted a warm place to sleep, and I knew it would be empty."

Jack glanced at me, and I stepped forward. "How did you know that?"

The man blinked, his watery gaze flicking in my direction. "I've been keeping an eye on the place, off and on. I haven't seen any lights inside or anyone come near it in the last week, night or day."

Now that I was closer, I caught a breath of a sickly sweet, smoky odor that seemed to roll off his clothes.

"Do you know the man who usually lives there?" Jack asked.

The man shook his head. "No. I just noticed the place was empty, like I said. Someone must have paid the rent on it, but then left."

Jack gave me another questioning look.

I didn't doubt that the man would have stolen whatever was of value inside the upstairs rooms, but he didn't seem to be in any fit state to lie about knowing Fred Miller.

In the ambient light coming from the downstairs floor of the tavern, I could see that his skin had a yellowish cast to it. His facial muscles were twitching oddly, and his hands shook.

"I swear I didn't mean any harm!" He gave me a look of miserable appeal.

I studied him, then gave Jack a slight nod.

Jack released his hold on the man's collar. "You've probably never heard this from the police before, but I'm going to take your word for it. Now move along."

The blond-haired man looked momentarily dazed, as though he couldn't quite process that he was being set free. Then he ran off, loping down the alley with a clumsy, shambling gate.

"Opium," Jack said, watching him go. "He was probably hoping to steal enough to cover the cost of his next pipe." He glanced at me. "So what now? Do you want to wait and see if Fred Miller comes back? Or go in ourselves and have a look around?"

I considered, but then shook my head. "No, it's not worth the trouble. If Fred Miller hasn't been home in the last week, either something has happened to him or else he's used the money he made from his blackmailing enterprise and moved on."

Either way, it wasn't worth our waiting here. If I was going to help Susan, I would have to find some other way of tracking

Fred Miller down. But that would take more time than I had this evening.

"Besides, I have to be at the Savoy soon."

"I'll walk you," Jack said.

I stopped myself from asking whether he was sure he felt up to walking. The Savoy was only a bare few minutes from Maiden Lane in any case.

"May I ask you something?" I said instead.

"Will it make any difference if I say no?"

"Well, it might make me abandon all efforts at being polite and bring out the thumbscrews ..." I shook my head. "No, you don't actually have to answer if you don't want to. I just wondered ... you've hardly ever spoken of the time you spent as part of Flint's gang."

Jack's gaze was on the street ahead of us, ticking off shadowed doorways and entrances to darkened alleys, watching for any hint of disturbance or danger. I knew it was automatic habit with him by now, picked up from all the nights he'd spent patrolling a constable's beat.

But at that he glanced at me. "I suppose I was hoping to convince you I'm a decent person. Telling you about all the times I've broken the law didn't exactly seem like my best bet."

We had turned from Maiden Lane onto Lumley Court. About a block up ahead, a pair of supremely intoxicated men were staggering along towards us, walking arm-in-arm, their voices clashing in drunken song.

Jack watched them for a moment, then said, "Mostly while I was with the Sloggers I worked in Flint's gambling operations. Breaking up any fights that started. Making sure no one tried to leave without paying their depts. Guarding the door. Or if a rival gang was cutting in on Flint's territory, sometimes a group of us would get sent out to make them stick to their own neighborhoods."

"That doesn't—" I caught myself.

"Sound so bad?" Jack finished. There was a faint bitterness in his voice, but then he shrugged. "It wasn't. A lot of the time."

We were passing under the glow of a street lamp. The light reflected in his dark eyes. "I'd be lying if I said I'd never done anything I wish I could wipe out now, though."

I took a breath and said, quietly, "You're not the only one who's ever done things they hated, because there was no choice or because all the other choices were worse still."

Even now, I could feel the memories—memories of Harriet, of Mary, of Adrian Arkwright—like hungry ghosts, trying to crowd their way back into my mind.

Without thinking about it—without even consciously realizing it—I had taken Jack's hand. Now I looked up at him. "I think that sometimes we don't have a choice about what we have to do. We only get a choice about who we are."

Jack looked down at our joined fingers and was silent a long moment.

"So what's bothering you about Lansdowne House?" he asked.

"That was the most glaringly obvious change of subject in the history of conversation. But fine."

I had never told Jack about being held captive in the Lansdowne estate's ice house or about my nightmares.

But Jack had been honest with me. Maybe I owed it to him to give him honesty in return.

My heart sped up. "I—"

Just ahead of us, two shadowed figures stepped out of a side street, blocking our path. Beside me, Jack went perfectly still.

A carriage rumbled by without stopping, but the two figures didn't move. They were dressed in dark breeches and coats, with cloth caps pulled down low over their eyes. Both of them carried knives, the blades glittering in the overhead gas lamps.

Shock and fear coursed through me like fire, though I forced both down. I still had the knife in the top of my boot, and Jack was armed with his heavy police truncheon. That ought to give us at least even odds—

Two more men stepped out of the shadows, one likewise armed with a knife, the other carrying a double-bladed axe.

My heart jolted.

I recognized the man closest to us. It was Yates from the coffee house. His nose was still crooked, bruised, and swollen, and both his eyes had turned black.

He should have looked ridiculous, but anything comic was canceled out by the ugly look in his eyes.

The street was nearly empty, save for the two drunken men I'd seen before, both of them still too far off and too inebriated to even realize that anything was wrong, much less offer help.

Snatches of slurred song punctuated by bursts of hilarity drifted to us through the cold night air.

> In Dublin's fair city
> where the girls are so pretty
> I once met a girl named sweet Molly Malone.

My pulse skittered, hard and fast. The world felt as though it had narrowed, shrinking down to just the scant few feet of space between us and the four men. Other sights and sounds all faded away.

The man with the axe—big and heavy-set—shifted the weapon in his hands and flicked a look from me to Jack and then growled, "We can either do this the easy way, or we can get unpleasant about it. Either way, you come with us."

I held still, my mind racing as I tried to run through our possible courses of action. I knew that beside me, Jack was doing the same.

The trouble was, I couldn't think of any alternatives that would allow Jack and I to fight our way out of this and still walk away alive.

Even as I thought it, Yates lunged—not for me, but for Jack—the blade of the flick-knife he held slashing towards Jack's face.

My breath caught, but somehow Jack anticipated the attack. He leaned out of the way of the knife, spun, and swung with his truncheon, shockingly fast. The blow caught Yates on the arm, making him let out a yell of pain. The knife clattered to the pavement.

But Jack was still fighting with the weakness of his injured leg, and the maneuver had left him off balance. I saw him catch himself against the wall of the building next to us.

Another of the men made a grab for me. I kicked his kneecap, making his leg collapse under him. But there were still two more men behind him …

As I fell back a step, trying to take rapid stock of our position, I realized that the two drunkards had crossed over to our side of the street and come up behind the attackers.

Now, the pair of men abruptly ceased their intoxicated stumbling, stopped leaning on each other, straightened … and resolved themselves into Holmes and Uncle John, both pointing revolvers at Flint's men.

CHAPTER 25

"Stop." Holmes's voice cracked like the flick of a whip.

Yates was on the ground, cradling his injured arm against his chest. The man I'd kicked was on hands and knees, struggling to rise.

The other two men spun to face Holmes, and I saw the big man with the axe eye my father speculatively.

"Don't try it." Uncle John's voice was as clipped and harsh as Holmes's. "I assure you, I've shot far better men than you. Drop your weapons."

The men must have believed him; knives and the axe fell with a clank to the ground.

I finally managed to decide that I was awake and not hallucinating, though I was still having difficulty in forming words.

"How—"

"Later." Holmes was eyeing our four attackers with distaste. The steadiness of his hand as he trained the revolver on them never wavered. "Our present circumstances are somewhat melodramatic. Besides which, I believe further conversation will be more productively carried out in private. Watson and perhaps

Constable Kelly, if you would be so good as to remove these specimens from our presence?"

Uncle John produced pairs of handcuffs from an inner pocket of his brown ulster overcoat.

Jack appeared to be recovering from the shock much better than I was. He moved to take two of the pairs of manacles, snapping them first onto the man at my feet, then onto Yates.

A plain black carriage rumbled down the street and drew to a halt beside us. The driver was so muffled in overcoats and scarves that I couldn't see his face, but he gave Holmes a respectful wave and a tip of his hat.

Uncle John and Jack hauled the four handcuffed men up and loaded them into the body of the carriage, while Holmes kept the revolver trained in case any tried to get away.

My voice finally worked. "You almost never carry a firearm."

Holmes shot a sidelong look at me. "I am also not in the habit of rescuing my daughter from marauding street gang members. But unfortunately, this appears to be a case of there being a first occurrence for everything."

Uncle John slammed the door to the carriage closed, the driver picked up the reins, and the carriage rumbled away up the street.

"Where are they being taken?" I asked.

"To a secure location, where some men in my employ will keep a close watch on them until we can decide what is best to be done with them."

"Isn't that otherwise known as kidnapping?"

"I find it unlikely in the extreme that any of them will press charges, considering where they themselves stand in relation to the law. However, Lestrade is aware of our operations tonight. I requested his cooperation in ignoring justifiable means to an end."

"Requested?"

Uncle John had come back to us. "Say *demanded* and you would have a more accurate description."

"In any case, thank you. Both of you," I told them.

Jack turned and came back to face Holmes, his posture braced. "This is my fault, sir. I didn't think we were followed tonight, but I must have been wrong. Those were Flint's men. And he'll only send more of them."

His voice was even, but I could almost feel the anger rolling off him in waves. He didn't look at me.

"It's me he's after. If I go to him now, without a fight, he'll leave Lucy alone."

An invisible hand wrapped around my chest and squeezed.

Jack would do it. I could see it in his expression. He would walk straight back to Cheapside and Flint—and possibly not survive whatever happened next.

"You don't know that!" I said. "And I'm the one who came to St. Giles tonight. Even though I was watching for any signs that I was followed, I could have missed it. I could have led them straight to your door."

I'd also dragged Jack out—and wearing his police uniform too, something that would make it infinitely harder to persuade Flint of his loyalty. Sickness lurched through me.

Holmes held up a hand. "While a willingness to admit fallibility is usually an admirable quality, in this case, you are wrong. I believe it unlikely that either of you were followed."

Jack frowned. "What do you mean?"

A pair of theater-goers—a man and woman—hurried past us, no doubt on their way to an evening performance. Holmes waited for them to pass before saying, "You have not yet asked how Watson and I came to be here tonight. We are here because I have had Flynn and some of the other Irregulars watching the Savoy Theater for any signs of trouble. Tonight I received an urgent message, saying that groups of tough-looking men were positioning themselves at various points on the streets surrounding the theater. Covering all possible routes by which you might approach."

I went cold. "They were waiting for me."

Holmes tipped his head in acknowledgement. "In our guise of inebriated revelers, Watson and I made a complete circuit of the Strand. We identified no fewer than six groups of men such as the ones who accosted you here."

"But why? What could Flint possibly want with me? He shouldn't even know that I exist, except—" I broke off, pieces slotting together in my mind like the parts of a puzzle. "He must have been acting on orders. Orders from the same person who hired him to steal the weapons, the same person who tried to have Lord Lansdowne killed at the Diogenes and who planted the bomb on Mr. Dimitrios this morning. Flint's headquarters were raided by the police, but Flint himself escaped. He must have gone to the person who hired him and bargained—negotiated—for the police attention to be withdrawn."

Jack was listening, a grim set to his mouth. "Whoever it was must have given Flint one more chance to show he could be useful."

"By kidnapping me," I finished for him. "But why? For leverage? Or information?"

"Either of those, I should imagine," Holmes said. "You were present this morning during our meeting with Lansdowne and the armaments dealers. Your name was given. Anyone wishing to pressure Mycroft and myself to leave off the investigation of the stolen weapons—or to learn how far our investigations had progressed—might reasonably move to kidnapping you as a solution."

Holmes spoke calmly, but I could hear the undercurrent of anger in his voice as well.

This was exactly what he had feared, from the moment I had joined him in our first criminal investigation.

"So you think that one of those men—" I mentally ran through them. Lord Lansdowne. Edward Barton. Sir Andrew and Lord Armstrong. Mr. Dimitrios.

"Not necessarily. Our association has become known to a widening circle of people. And you were also at the Diogenes Club."

I scarcely heard him. Fingers of ice were compressing my lungs, stealing my breath. "This *is* all my fault." I turned to Jack. "Flint's men have just seen you with me. That puts you in danger. And Becky—" My breath caught and I spun back to Holmes. "Where is she? If she's back in Baker Street, she could still be—"

Holmes interrupted me. "Miss Kelly is as safe as the four police constables stationed by Lestrade at the front and back of the house can make her. And the men who saw you and Constable Kelly together tonight have not—and will not—have the opportunity to make their report to Flint."

"We can't hold on to them indefinitely, though."

"We will not need to. A short delay will be all that is required, one in which we change our approach to Flint and his gang from a defensive stance to an offensive one."

Jack studied my father's face. "You have a plan, sir?"

"I believe so."

Uncle John was watching me with a worried expression. "Lucy, my dear, perhaps you ought not to perform at the Savoy tonight. I could go there now and make your excuses, say that you were unavoidably detained—"

The Savoy and tonight's performance of *The Yeomen of the Guard*.

I couldn't imagine the two separate parts of my life—acting and detection—ever feeling more completely divorced from one another as they did right now. But I shook my head.

"No, I'm all right, I can go on." I glanced at my father. "As long as it's safe for us to wait until after the performance is over to move against Flint?"

"Indeed, if you could smuggle us all into the theater after the rest of the company has departed, it might be to our advantage. Our other alternative involves a return to Baker Street for theatrical supplies, which with the police guarding the door would involve a good deal of tedious explanation as to the nature of our activities tonight."

Holmes still spoke with his usual equanimity. But something in his voice sent a chill dancing across my skin all the same.

"How much am I going to hate this plan?" I asked.

My father's lips bent at the edges in a very faint, wry smile. "I assure you, not nearly so much as I will."

CHAPTER 26

The dressing room door was slightly ajar, spilling a chink of yellow light into the darkened corridor and letting Holmes's and Jack's voices filter out to me. Jack was speaking, though I caught only the end part of what he said.

"—we're sure this is going to work?"

I paused with my hand on the door handle. All around me, the Savoy was quiet, deserted save for ourselves and Mr. Evans, our night watchman, who was comfortably snoring at his post by the front door. The smells of the theater—grease paint and the varnish used on wooden pieces of scenery, powder for wigs, and old fabric—hung in the air.

I heard a creak, as though Holmes had shifted position in his chair, and then he said, "Among the colorful American expressions I have heard my daughter employ is one that describes a person of considerable mettle as *tough as nails*. Lucy is more than capable of dealing with a man like Flint Bayles. I would not have suggested this scheme if I thought otherwise."

A shiver went through me: one part warmth at my father's high opinion, two parts fear that I wouldn't live up to it.

The last time I had walked, eyes open, into a plan like this one, I had wound up chained up at the hands of a deranged, sadistic killer. Of course, that plan had been entirely of my own devising. This time, I was trusting in Holmes's ability to construct a more foolproof trap than mine.

Holmes cleared his throat. "It would perhaps be as well if you were to make yourself scarce immediately once your part of the scheme has been carried out. Lestrade may be willing to turn a blind eye to some of tonight's proceedings, but not all of Scotland Yard will be as understanding. If you are found on the Clement Court premises, the consequences to your career may be severe."

"I'm not so sure I care about that right now, sir."

"*I* care." I pushed the dressing room door open and went in. "I don't want you risking your job over this."

Jack was already risking far too much as it was.

"Ah, you're ready." Holmes gave me a critical scrutiny. "Excellent."

"Thank you."

I was wearing a high-necked gown and a cloak from last winter's production of *His Majesty*. Both garments were of plain, unrelieved black satin that almost seemed to swallow the light. With the hood of the cloak drawn up to shadow my face, I would look like an incarnation of death itself.

Holmes rose. He was in his ordinary clothes and, barring the addition of a pair of gray, mutton-chop side-whiskers, had done very little to alter his appearance.

"I shall go and see whether Watson is ready."

I waited until the door had closed behind him before turning to Jack.

"Don't bother," Jack said. He had changed from his police uniform into trousers and shirt, borrowed from one of the costume racks in the men's dressing room, and was sitting on a spare wooden chair.

I hadn't even opened my mouth yet. "How do you know what I was going to say?"

"Because we've done this before, remember? You're going to say that this is too dangerous, and I shouldn't risk it."

"Yes. But usually you're the one warning me about the danger."

"True enough." Jack stood up, crossing to stand looking down at me with a crooked half-smile. "I remember once I was in prison, framed for a murder I hadn't done, and this stubborn American girl marched in and told me she was going to get me out again, no matter the danger. Besides." Jack's expression changed. "If this gets Flint locked up, it's worth it. Just be careful."

"I will be."

I looked up at him, at the lean, dark lines of his face, his dark lashes and eyes.

What would he do if I put my arms around him or kissed him goodbye?

Instead I said, "What you said before. You *are* a decent person. Better than decent." I reached to touch his cheek. "You are *good*."

I heard Jack's breath hitch momentarily at the touch, and he shut his eyes. "Lucy—"

The dressing room door opened behind me as Holmes and Uncle John stepped into the room.

"If we are all of us ready," Holmes said, "I believe we should move without delay. We have a full night's work to carry out."

"Don't worry," Uncle John murmured in an undertone. "Holmes knows what he is doing. He always does."

"I know."

We were huddled in a doorway across from Flint's coffee house on Clement Court—not at the front of the business, but around the back, where the rear entrance to the shop opened onto a cold and dingy side street.

True to Jack's prediction, the coffee house seemed to be doing as lively a business as ever tonight, the brightly lit windows revealing rooms crowded with customers.

Here outside, the street was nearly deserted, thanks to both the lateness of the hour and the chill, sullen drizzle of rain that had begun to fall.

Though at least tonight the weather was more or less a match for my mood. My heart had squeezed into a cold, painful lump of anxiety that Uncle John's words of reassurance did nothing to dispel.

"It's basic human nature," Uncle John went on.

His voice, steady and reassuring as ever, formed an almost ludicrous contrast with his appearance.

Holmes, aided by the greasepaint and theatrical paraphernalia of the theater, had used the full powers of his skill in the art of disguise on Uncle John. Now one of Watson's eyelids drooped, marred by a thick, ropy scar that ran from his brow to his chin. His upper lip was twisted into a permanent leer, and his head was covered by a gray wig that looked as though it ought to contain an entire colony of lice and other wildlife.

He patted my arm. "When trapped in a burning building, we instinctively race to save whatever is most precious to us."

I stopped myself from pointing out that the last time Holmes had relied on that same principle of human behavior was during the Irene Adler case, and the episode hadn't exactly turned out in Holmes's favor.

Instead, I focused on the back door to the coffee house, where somewhere inside, Jack was at this moment setting Flint's house—in a metaphoric if not a literal sense—on fire.

"What if Flint has already sold the weapons?" I hadn't meant to speak, but the anxiety inside me seemed to crank tighter with every passing moment, the words coming out on their own. "Or what if he's handed them over to his buyer and doesn't know where they're being stored now?"

"Then Holmes will come up with an alternative plan." Watson's answer was unhesitating. "He always has one of those too."

"I'm sorry." I forced my clenched fingers to relax. "I hate having to sit and wait."

"Do you really?" Uncle John's voice was mild. "I would never have guessed."

The back door to the coffee house opened, and both of us stopped speaking, drawing instantly back into the shadowed cover of our doorway.

Footsteps echoed on the cobbles, moving down the street away from us. I waited a count of ten before risking a quick look out.

Flint. His head was slightly turned, and I could see his profile in the glow of light from the coffee house.

Holmes's plan was designed to drive as much of a wedge between Flint and the rest of the Sloggers as could be managed, but all the same, Uncle John and I had been prepared for him to bring a bodyguard or two.

Perhaps the fates had decided that we were finally due a stroke of luck tonight, though, or maybe I should simply get used to Holmes always being right.

Flint was alone, dressed in a navy cloth coat with the collar turned up and a cap pulled down over his brow.

I watched, waiting as he strode towards the end of the street. Then I moved silently out of the doorway and followed, keeping to the deepest part of the shadows that lined the edges of the road.

Behind me, I knew that Uncle John was skulking along at a safe distance, since two followers together were more likely to attract Flint's notice than one at a time. And somewhere close by, though I didn't know where, Holmes was likely watching, as well.

Flint turned twice, heading at a rapid pace towards the river. We walked past beer halls and penny theaters, tenement houses and matchstick factories. At first it was easy to blend in with the other people on the road. Though as we drew closer to the Thames, the traffic thinned to only the occasional pedestrian, head ducked, shoulders hunched against the damp chill.

After twenty minutes of walking, my cloak and gown were growing damp with the rain, and I was halfway tempted to simply catch up with Flint, knock him down, and demand that he get on with leading us to where we were going.

Finally, though, we reached the warehouse district that bordered the docks. Flint turned left and then left again before finally fetching up at the door of a narrow building sandwiched between two larger warehouses.

He never looked back.

The sound of the rain did at least cover any noise from my or Uncle John's footsteps. And, true to what Holmes had predicted when he had outlined this scheme, Flint was too enraged to worry about whether he was followed.

I stopped, drawing into the shadows of the nearest warehouse, and watched Flint reach into his coat pocket. He drew out a ring of keys, selected one, then bent his head, fitting the key into a padlocked chain on the door.

I held my breath, my pulse beating as fast as the rain pelting the pavement all around.

Back at the coffee house, Jack had gone to Flint and reported rumors of weapons being sold illegally on the London streets— weapons exactly matching the description of the guns stolen from Blackthorn Munitions.

According to Holmes, if Flint were guilty of the theft, he would hear those rumors and wonder whether one of his subordinates had betrayed him and taken the weapons to sell for his own profit. In any case, Flint would wish to check whether the weapons he had stolen were still where he had left him.

That—I devoutly hoped—was what he was doing now.

I inched forward, peering through the mist and darkness.

Flint opened the lock, the chain rattled as it was dragged aside, and then he flung the door open. A lantern hung on a nail just inside the door. Flint lighted it and held it up, taking a few steps inside.

The room inside was small—a little bigger than a stable stall— and stacked, from floor to ceiling, with wooden crates. The glow of lantern light showed me the words stamped on the sides of the crates: *Property of Blackthorn Munitions*.

Relief swept through me, along with hot, angry satisfaction. *Got you.*

Turning, I lifted up one hand in signal.

Immediately, Uncle John strode out of the shadows behind me to the storage room door, raised a small wooden club, and struck Flint a mighty blow on the back of the head.

CHAPTER 27

I struck a match and touched the glowing flame to the tips of the two candles on the table in front of me. Then I changed my mind and blew out the first candle. I wanted the room to be dim, almost dark.

"Lucy, I believe that he is coming around," Watson said behind me. "Another few minutes and he should be reasonably coherent."

I turned. Uncle John was bending over Flint, who was slumped in a hard wooden chair, with only the ropes that bound his wrists, ankles, and chest keeping him upright. His head was flopped onto his shoulder, but I could see that Uncle John was right; his eyelids were beginning to flutter.

The curtain was just about to rise on our performance.

"You should get into position, Uncle John," I said.

Uncle John moved to stand beside the plain wooden door.

We were about a mile from the warehouse where we had followed Flint, inside another of Holmes's bolt-holes, though this one, unlike Mr. Griggs' upstairs room, had no caretaker or landlord. The place was part of a candle-making factory that had gone bankrupt and been abandoned some years ago.

The room we were in had once been the factory foreman's office, and the remnants of the business's furnishings still remained: an old roll-top desk covered with a thick layer of dust and a set of shelves that were empty save for thick wisps of cobwebs.

The air of must and decay hung thick in the air, and something—rats or mice—scurried and squeaked in the shadows outside our small circle of candle light.

I drew the black hood of my cloak over my head, partially shading my face, then checked to be sure that the rest of what served as the stage for our performance was effectively set.

The single lighted candle. A row of knives and other surgical implements laid out on a small table, their blades the only bright, polished surface in the room. Three small glass bottles with stoppered lids and dark, murky contents. And of course, Uncle John looming by the doorway, his countenance still stretched by Holmes's makeup into a scarred, horrible leer.

I drew a breath to steady myself, then reached out and slapped Flint across the face, hard.

I didn't usually hurt people. I didn't *like* hurting anyone, not even Flint. But at the moment, what I did and didn't like made no difference. This man would have hurt Becky and could easily kill Jack if I didn't succeed tonight.

I locked away the part of me that hated what I might have to do and struck him again.

"Wake up, Mr. Flint." I made my voice eerie, whispery-soft. "It's time that you and I had a talk."

Flint blinked and groaned, trying to raise his head, his arms and legs beginning to stir. I saw the precise moment he realized that he was bound: his muscles all tensed, instinctively lashing out against the ropes, his breath went out with a hiss, and his head snapped up.

He blinked again, his bleary gaze struggling to focus on me. "What the—"

I interrupted him, speaking in the same ominously hushed tone. "You will not speak until I tell you that you may."

Flint shook his head as though trying to clear away the lingering haze of unconsciousness. I could see him assessing me, registering me as young and obviously female, even with the folds of the cloak shading my face.

His upper lip drew back into a contemptuous snarl. "Are you trying to make me laugh?"

"I assure you, your amusement is of no interest to me whatsoever."

I straightened, the black cloak and the black skirts of my gown swirling around me, and crossed to the table where the array of knives was laid out.

Flint's gaze, cold and reptilian as a snake's, followed me. Although as I reached to select a sharp surgical scalpel, borrowed for the purpose from Uncle John, I saw a brief shadow of uncertainty cross the back of his gaze.

But then he growled and struggled again, twisting, trying to rock the chair he was bound to.

"I wouldn't bother," I said. I tested the point of the scalpel with the tip of my finger. "The ropes are quite tightly tied, I made sure of it. And the chair is bolted to the floor. I made sure of that as well."

Flint's expression darkened, muscles standing out along his jaw. "What do you want?"

I turned back to him, the scalpel in my hand, letting a smile curve the edges of my mouth.

"We are going to play a game, you and I. It's called *guess what I do to lying, thieving criminals who send men to abduct me*."

As I spoke, I brought the scalpel slowly up, nearer and nearer to Flint's face, until the blade was barely an inch from his right eye.

Instinctively, he flinched back.

"Who the hell are you?"

"You know exactly who I am. You sent your men after me earlier tonight. However, that is not the issue we are here to discuss."

Holmes's voice echoed at the back of my mind.

A man like Flint is well-versed in intimidation.

That was what my father had said back at the Savoy, when we were discussing my part of this scheme.

Flint views other men as a threat to his authority. He expects it, and he expects to win. What we must aim for is to throw him off balance by giving him something he does not *expect. A* woman *who can make him uneasy and afraid.*

I needed Flint off balance, helpless, and unsure.

I twitched the scalpel back and forth, like the arm of a metronome. Flint swallowed, his eyes reflexively following the motion, but then he bared his teeth, a red flush of anger sweeping up his throat.

He didn't actually believe that I would hurt him. I could see it in his face.

"When I get out of here, I'll tear you to pieces, and—"

I brought the scalpel down and stabbed him, fast and hard, in the back of the hand. Flint gasped, jerking back, hitting his head against the back of the chair.

Blood oozed from the stab wound and clung to the scalpel when I pulled it out, but I forced all trace of sickness down.

I kept my voice steady, my expression cold.

"Please do not bother with threats. I find them tedious. What I require from you, Mr.—do you prefer Mr. Flint or Mr. Bayles? In either case, you are here because I want some information."

"I'm not telling you anything," Flint ground out.

I smiled coldly once again. "You know what is really quite funny? The fact that you seem to think you have any choice about the matter."

I paused, looking down at him. The knuckles of his hands were crisscrossed with a network of fine white scars, and his ears were slightly thickened by repeated blows. Obviously he had spent his fair share of time fighting for his position in the London underworld with his fists.

He also tilted his head in a way that made me think he might carry some slight residual hearing loss from repeated blows to the head.

I lowered my voice, so that he would have to strain to make out my words. Forcing him to be aware of his own weakness would serve to push him further off balance and drive home his current helpless position.

"I have poisons here." I picked up one of the small, dark vials from the table. "Extremely deadly ones."

Flint bared his teeth. "You want to poison me? Go ahead. I've looked death in the face before. Come to that, you'd *better* kill me, because otherwise I'll track you to the ends of the earth and—"

I brought the scalpel up, this time just touching the point to the skin of his throat.

I had been where Flint was now, almost exactly: a prisoner, shackled and helpless. I wasn't letting those memories surface now. But I also knew from experience how it felt and what would make the horror greater still.

"Threats, Mr. Flint," I snapped. "Tedious. I am not proposing to kill you with these poisons. One or two drops in each of your eyes and you will be blinded. Permanently. I'm sure a man in your position has enemies. How long do you think you will last out there on the London streets if I turn you out of here, blind and helpless, unable to see an opponent coming?"

Flint swallowed again and, for the first time, I saw genuine fear flicker at the back of his gaze. A man like Flint feared humiliation and weakness far more than he did death or physical pain. The scenario I had just outlined was probably close to his worst nightmare. Which of course was exactly why I'd chosen it.

"Now." I held up the small vial between my thumb and forefinger. "I wish to know the name of the person who hired you to steal crates of weapons from the Cannon Street warehouse."

My heart quickened as I spoke the words.

This was the reason that we hadn't just handed Flint over to Inspector Lestrade and allowed him to carry out the interrogation.

Even as I stood here, fighting to break Flint's will, Holmes was engaged in transferring the crates of weapons from Flint's hidden storage location to the basement of the coffee house, where they would be found a few hours from now, after the police received an anonymous tip that they should search the place.

As Holmes had pointed out, Flint might not own the warehouse building where the weapons had been stored. He might have gotten one of his subordinates to rent or buy the place for him, or he might have bullied or bribed someone into letting him use the place for storage purposes.

We needed the case against him to be iron clad, without any hope that he would wriggle out for lack of evidence.

But we also needed the name of the person behind all of this.

That was why I was here.

Flint does not fear the police, Holmes had said. *Neither does he fear imprisonment or even the hangman's noose, which are the worst our system of justice can offer.*

Lestrade will never be able to force answers out of him. That is our job.

Now Flint's eyes were focused on the vial in my hand. Sweat beaded his upper lip and brow, but his jaw remained clamped shut.

I sighed. "Very well." I turned to where Uncle John stood by the door. "Hold his head for me, please."

Flint jolted in place, his head swiveling to Uncle John. He clearly hadn't noticed him before.

Without a word, Watson strode forward and took up a position behind Flint's chair, locking one arm around Flint's head and dragging his chin up, holding him in place.

"Now, Mr. Flint, do you wish to begin with the right eye or the left?" I used my thumb to nudge the cork out of the bottle's mouth. "I am perfectly willing to be flexible if you have a preference."

"I don't know!" The words burst out of Flint in a ragged shout.

I raised my eyebrows. "You don't know?"

"I never got a name." Flint dragged in air, his chest heaving like a bellows. "Men like him—they don't exactly hand you a calling card with their name and address."

"That's not particularly helpful, Mr. Flint. How did he initially get into contact with you?"

"I never spoke to him in person. One of my men, Ewan Granger, came to me with a message. A job offer: lift some crates from the Cannon Street warehouse and get paid for it."

"And you accepted?"

Flint's upper lip drew back again. "I said no thanks. Me and my boys aren't anyone's lackeys for hire. The next day, I got a package in the mail. Know what was inside it? Granger's hands and feet."

"His—" I had to work not to let myself jerk back in shock or let the sickness that roiled through the pit of my stomach show.

Muscle played along Flint's jaw. "Envelope that came with it had a hundred Bank of England notes and a message saying I'd be paid double that again if I pulled off the job and got the crates of weapons. Or I could refuse, and it would be my hands and feet that got hacked off next time."

"So you agreed."

Flint jerked his head impatiently. "There was money to be made. I like money."

That might be so, and it was undoubtedly what Flint had tried to tell himself. But the methods used by his mysterious employer had also shaken him. Shaken *and* angered him.

Flint wanted to get back at the man who had murdered one of his men and threatened him. I could see it in every harsh, furious line of his expression, the tension that corded his muscles.

If the man who had hired him to steal weapons had been standing in the room with us now, Flint would have struck him dead.

Good for us, bad for our nameless adversary.

Flint evidently had a similar thought. His eyes narrowed, a look of calculation cross his face.

"Look, you want the man who hired me. I want him too. We've a score to settle, him and me. Maybe we can work out a way we both get what we want."

I stood motionless, regarding him steadily for a long moment, then nodded at Uncle John. Uncle John released his grip on Flint and stepped back.

"I'm listening," I said.

"I don't know his name, but he arranged for McHale to get a job at a men's club in Pall Mall."

"The Diogenes. And I knew that already." I leaned forward, still holding the small glass vial between my fingers. "You aren't exactly bargaining from a position of strength at the moment, Mr. Flint. You'll need to give me something more helpful than that if I'm to even consider letting you out of here. If all you have to offer is the fact that your employer has ties to the Diogenes or to someone at the Diogenes I had already surmised as much for myself."

Flint held himself stiff and straight, as though he were fighting the urge to flinch back again. "That's not everything. McHale was ordered to … take care of some business at the Diogenes."

"By which you mean murder."

Flint jerked his shoulder in as much of a shrug as he could manage with his hands bound. "That's not the point. The order came to him—to McHale—direct, in care of the club."

I raised my eyebrows. "And?"

"And I saw the instructions. McHale showed them to me. The message was addressed and stamped, like it'd been delivered by post. But it hadn't." Flint leaned forward slightly. "The stamp hadn't been canceled, like it would have been if the letter'd really been through the post."

I regarded Flint in silence. Brutal and dishonest he might be, but he certainly wasn't stupid.

"The message was delivered by someone with daily access to the club."

A club member, most likely. Someone who was actually there on the premises in the days leading up to General Pettigrew's death.

"That's it." Flint jerked his head in agreement.

"Where is your man McHale now?"

Flint's gaze shifted. "I don't know."

I leaned forward. "Did you know that most people look to the left when they're about to tell a lie? Precisely the way yours did, just now. The truth, Mr. Flint."

"I don't know!" A red flush of anger darkened Flint's cheeks.

"Really, Mr. Flint? We need to go through *again* who is in charge of this conversation? This grows even more wearisome than your threats, but very well." I held up the vial, at the same time nodding to Uncle John, who took a step forward.

"Stop!" Flint breathed heavily in and out. "I don't know where McHale is now. But I was given an address to use, to report back on when I'd finished the job of robbing the warehouse."

"The flat on Foley Street." I thought of the marks where letters had landed through the letter slot, just inside the door.

Flint jerked his head in acknowledgement. "After the raid on my place the other night, I sent another message saying that was it. Another trick like that, and I'd torch the whole lot of crates and then throw what was left into the Thames."

"Go on."

"This afternoon I got a message back, saying—"

I interrupted. "How did the message arrive?"

"I own properties all up and down Cheapside. I was making the rounds to inspect them this afternoon when I found the message in my pocket." A muscle ticked at the edge of Flint's mouth. "I don't know how it got there."

I saw the flash of something unsettled move, shadow-swift, across Flint's face. He wasn't the sort of man to have his pocket picked without realizing what was happening. Whoever had planted the message on him was extremely skilled at moving covertly.

"There was a note," Flint said. "Gave me your description. Pretty girl, dark hair, in the chorus at the Savoy. Said if I didn't want every business I owned burned to the ground, I'd grab you off the street on your way to the theater tonight." He swallowed. "Want to know what the note was wrapped around? A human finger."

"McHale's?"

"How do I know? He didn't keep his name tattooed on his fingers. Could have been his, could have been someone else's."

I liked this less and less. So far our adversary had managed to kill General Pettigrew by means that we still hadn't discovered, manufacture a ghost, plant a bomb that nearly killed me, my father, and everyone else at 221 Baker Street—and, not least of all, had managed to rattle a man like Flint Bayles.

"Can you tell me anything else?" I asked.

Flint eyed me warily, but said, "No. That's all."

There was always the chance he might be lying, but I didn't think that he was. Another advantage of being an actress was that it gave me a fairly good idea of when someone was trying to spin a convincing untruth.

"Thank you, Mr. Flint." I stepped back, dropped the glass vial into a carpet bag, and swept the array of knives and scalpels in after it. "I believe we may consider this interview finished, then."

I nodded to Uncle John, who opened the door for me. I started to walk out.

"Wait a bloody minute!" Flint's voice rose as he struggled against the ropes again. The wooden slats of the chair creaked, but held firm. "Where are you going? You can't just leave me here!"

"Oh, but I can, Mr. Flint. Don't worry, though. I promise to send the police along to collect you soon. They'll be quite grateful, I imagine, to find you all nicely trussed up for them like a Christmas turkey."

Flint's face was choked, suffused with rage, the look in his eyes enough to raise all the fine hairs on the back of my neck. Though I managed to keep from shivering until Watson and I were out of the room, with the door firmly shut behind us.

"Well done, Lucy, my dear," Uncle John said.

We picked our way carefully across the empty factory, hulking machines crouching like bizarre metal beasts in the darkness all around.

"You were absolutely terrifying in there."

"Thank you."

Suddenly I was exhausted, weary all the way down to my bones. We reached the outer door to the factory and stepped out into the chill, pre-dawn air. Morning was only a few hours away.

We walked in silence for a time. The street lamps made the wet pavement shine almost silvery in the darkness. Here and there, we passed by sailors and dockworkers, already hurrying towards their day's labor at the docks and shipyards.

"What do you think of what Flint told us?" I asked at last.

"What do I think?" The gas lamps lighting the street showed the lines of Uncle John's face as grave beneath the makeup, his eyes somber. "I think that there is hatred behind this."

"Hatred." I hadn't thought of it that way. "You mean the threats and the mutilations and the missing fingers. Do you think we are dealing with some kind of political zealot? Someone determined to undermine the strength of our armies, and through that, the British Empire?"

I felt as though I had already dealt with enough madmen of that particular type for several lifetimes.

Uncle John, though, shook his head. His voice was thoughtful. "No, I should not have said that. A political idealist—some might say zealot—may commit heinous crimes in the name of what he sees as the greater good. But that is not the feeling I get from Flint's account. There is hatred there—intense, personal hatred. As though whoever has committed these crimes is nursing some injury, some sense of having been wronged, and is lashing out in revenge."

"You could be right." I fought not to feel chilled.

We paused on a street corner, waiting as a big delivery van drawn by a team of four draft horses rumbled past.

"Was it really poison you threatened Flint with?" Watson asked.

"No. Just some muddy water from the gutter. Although given the general filth on London streets, it might be as harmful to the eyes as poison for all I know."

The street ahead of us was clear to cross. Watson offered me his arm, and I rested my hand on the crook of his elbow. "You know, I always thought that having a family, people you cared about, made you weaker because you had something or someone to lose. But it's almost frightening to realize how far you'd be willing to go to protect the people you love."

"It is indeed, my dear." Uncle John covered my hand with his. "It is indeed."

CHAPTER 28

I woke to darkness and the patter of rain drumming against the windows. For a disoriented moment, I lay staring up at the shadowed ceiling of the bedroom, trying to recall where I was and what had woken me. Then I heard it: a faint, surreptitious rustle of noise from the outer sitting room.

Sitting up, I saw that the trundle bed Becky had been sleeping on when I went to bed was empty, the covers pushed back. I got up, my breath quickening, and went to open the bedroom door.

A ghostly apparition hung suspended in the middle of the darkened sitting room, trailing white robes glowing with an unearthly light.

I clamped down on a shriek, though I couldn't quite stop myself from jolting an instinctive step backwards.

The apparition giggled.

Holmes's voice spoke from the darkness to my left. "Ah, Lucy. Good morning. Miss Kelly and I were just conducting an experiment in the manufacture of ghostly manifestations."

The drawing room lights came on, revealing Becky standing on a chair in the middle of the room and draped in what looked like one of Mrs. Hudson's white linen tablecloths.

My heart started beating again. "Was that one of Mr. Maskelyne's suggestions?"

"Yes. Apparently this arrangement is frequently used by spirit mediums to cause the spirits to appear under convenient cover of darkness." Holmes eyed the figure Becky made critically. "It is difficult to believe that such parlor tricks are actually capable of deceiving anyone. But then, the majority of the populace have remarkably lazy minds, willing to ascribe a supernatural explanation to any problem without an immediately obvious solution."

"The unearthly glow is right," I said. "But no one was standing on a chair in General Pettigrew's rooms. If there had been, there wasn't nearly time enough for them to vanish so quickly."

"Indeed," Holmes said. "We shall have to continue our experimentation. The glow is caused by phosphorescent paint, by the way. Quite effective."

I suspected that Mrs. Hudson would have something to say about the ruin of her tablecloth, but Holmes would doubtless find that out for himself.

Becky jumped down off the chair, and I helped to unwind the fabric from around her.

"I talked to Jack!" she said.

"You ... what?"

A glance at the clock showed me that, despite the dark skies outside from the rain, it was actually nearly nine o'clock in the morning. I had fallen into bed somewhere around three o'clock, which meant that I had been asleep for almost six hours. But apparently it hadn't been enough to clear the general haze of fatigue that felt as though it wrapped me like cotton wool.

"*Jack!*" Becky hopped from one foot to the other, beaming. "He called on the telephone while you were still sleeping, and I talked to him!"

My heart instantly lurched, beating harder. "What did he say?"

"He couldn't talk for very long. But I told him all about seeing Mr. Maskelyne's magic show. And he said that he was doing all right and he hoped he'd see me soon."

I drew a breath of relief. If Jack had used the telephone, it meant he was back in their St. Giles rooms. More importantly, it meant that he hadn't been arrested—or killed—the night before.

"Quite right," Holmes said. "And now, Miss Kelly, do you think you might ask Mrs. Hudson whether she could have breakfast served to us upstairs? I am quite famished."

The only time Holmes took an interest in food was when he was either *not* engaged on a case or was half-dead from starvation. It was an excuse only, a reason to get Becky out of the room, but Becky skipped out happily, and a moment later, I heard her footsteps clattering towards the kitchen.

"What happened last night?" I asked Holmes.

He hadn't yet returned to Baker Street when Uncle John and I came home. Now, despite the fact that he must have had even less sleep than I had—if in fact he had even gone to bed at all—he looked entirely rested, his morning coat immaculately brushed, his jaw shaved, his gray eyes alert.

"We may, I believe, count the night's endeavors a cautious success. Flint Bayles was discovered and arrested, along with the men in his employ whom we took captive. Due to the weapons found on the premises of the coffee house owned by Mr. Bayles, all three will be charged with theft of Her Majesty's property. There is even talk of charges of treason being brought against them, since the weapons were intended for military use. Barring anything unforeseen occurring, Flint Bayles' view will be limited to the inside of prison cell for quite some time to come."

I exhaled slowly. Becky was safe. Jack was free of the threat of Flint's revenge. It seemed almost too good to be true.

"I also spoke with Constable Kelly for a few moments," Holmes said. "There was not time for a lengthy discussion before Miss Kelly, having heard the ring of the telephone, joined me, but I was at least able to inform him of the arrests. I asked if he wished to speak with you, but he said you ought not to be disturbed."

Of course he did. Still, if Jack now knew that Flint had been locked up, that was something.

"Was Mr. Bayles able to give you any information on the man who hired him?" Holmes asked.

"Nothing conclusive."

I repeated everything that Flint had told me the night before.

Holmes listened with pursed lips and half-lidded eyes. "Suggestive, but as you say, ultimately inconclusive. Certainly not enough to make me feel more sanguine about the prospect of the ball at Lansdowne House tonight."

"Lord Lansdowne is going ahead with the ball? Even after the bomb incident yesterday?"

"Lord Lansdowne has arranged for his house to be heavily policed by Lestrade's constables. He believes that the police presence will be enough to ensure the event's safety."

"And you?" I asked.

"I believe that allowing Lestrade—much as I respect him, as policemen go—to be in sole charge of any event's security is a version of a Vaudeville production involving custard pies in the face and ludicrously oversized shoes," Holmes said. "However, allowing the event to proceed may be to our advantage. I have it on Lord Lansdowne's authority that Mr. Dimitrios will be there, as will Lord Armstrong and Sir Andrew."

Cold crawled through me. "You mean that anyone who wished to kill one or all of them before may use the opportunity presented by the ball to make another attempt?" I asked.

"As you say. I have already directed Lestrade's men to keep watch on the storage facility where Mr. Bayles had stashed the stolen weapons."

"Why?" I frowned, then answered my own question. "Oh, of course. Whoever hired Flint set up the police raid, hoping for Flint's arrest. That means that whoever it was must already know where Flint had the weapons stored. He must have followed Flint or one of his men."

"Or extracted the information from the man McHale, also known as the waiter Royce," Holmes said. "Assuming that the finger was his and that he is now a captive of Flint's nameless employer."

There was a kind of abstracted tension in Holmes's voice, as though he were talking to me, but at the same time recalling something else.

"Was anything missing from the cache of weapons?" I asked. "Anything to show whether Flint's buyer had already started to access the guns?"

I saw in my father's face that my guess had been right. "Only two items." His lips compressed. "A large crate, containing some fifty pounds of gunpowder. And a Maxim machine gun."

My mouth dropped open, but no words came out. Last summer, Uncle John had witnessed demonstrations of the kind of destruction a machine gun could unleash.

Holmes's expression was still tight. "As you are about to observe, such weapons being in the wrong hands is—"

"Every kind of bad," I finished for him.

"Another Americanism?" Holmes asked. "I shall have to remember that one. It is quite expressive."

I fought through the feeling of having my lungs crushed by an invisible hand. "Do you think whoever took it will try to detonate an explosion at Lansdowne House tonight? Or fire the Maxim into the crowd?"

"Possible, but I believe unlikely. The grounds of Lansdowne House are well policed and guarded, thanks to his position in the government, and transporting fifty pounds of explosives is not something that can be accomplished in a subtle manner. Neither is a Maxim a weapon of stealth; it requires a tripod mount and boxes of ammunition, neither of which will be easy to smuggle into a ball, especially given the security measures that will be in effect. What I am more concerned about is the chance of a sniper's—"

The sitting room door flew open, and both Holmes and I cut off speaking as Becky came back in.

"Have you shown her?" Becky demanded of Holmes. "Have you shown her the letter yet?"

"What letter?" I asked.

"The final letter General Pettigrew ever wrote was tracked down to the Diogenes Club outgoing mailbag and retrieved by some of Inspector Lestrade's men. He passed it on to me, and Miss Kelly and I have been going over it, hoping for some clue as to how he died."

"I'll fetch it so that Lucy can see, can I?" Without waiting for Holmes's response, Becky ducked out again, and I heard her tripping lightly up the stairs to 221B.

"Clues?" I raised an eyebrow at Holmes. *I would dearly like to concentrate on writing this letter, but unfortunately some annoying personage whose name I shall divulge shortly insists on waving a canister of cyanide gas under my nose?*"

Holmes twitched one shoulder. "It has served to keep the child occupied and to keep her mind diverted from her brother's absence, which was my primary—"

He stopped again as Becky came back, letter in hand. "Here it is!"

The letter was addressed in a spidery, cramped hand. A few crumbs of red sealing wax still clung to the back of the envelope. I took the letter out, unfolded it, and read the few short paragraphs.

"So his final letter wasn't to the editor of the *Times*, after all, but to the membership committee of the Diogenes," I said. I scanned the general's words. "*Must protest in the strongest terms the lax standards for admission ... new arrivals who do not at all uphold the high standards set by our revered founders ... indeed, I had recent cause to suspect rank deceit, or at least fraud ...*"

I stopped reading, looking up to find Holmes's gaze on me.

"I trust that if you come to feel that the object of the general's rancor has anything to do with the case in hand, you will inform me?" Holmes asked.

Of course Holmes could tell just by watching me that I suspected I knew the unnamed subject of General Pettigrew's letter. I shouldn't have been even mildly surprised.

"I will."

I had scanned the rest of the letter, and it mentioned no specific names. But still, the fraud General Pettigrew had spoken of almost had to be Susan—otherwise known as Suzette—Teale.

"At the moment, I don't think it has any bearing at all on our missing weapons. But if there is some link, I promise I won't hold anything back."

"Very well, then." Holmes made Becky a gallant bow. "Miss Kelly, would you do me the honor of accompanying me upstairs to breakfast?"

Becky took his arm.

"While we eat, we may discuss our plans for tonight," Holmes said. As his gaze met mine over the top of Becky's head, his expression turned grave. "For I believe that our best chance at averting disaster lies in keeping our eyes open and our attention vigilant at tonight's ball."

CHAPTER 29

"Oh dear, did I tread on your foot *again*, Mr. Dimitrios?" I opened my eyes wide. "I am so terribly sorry. How clumsy of me."

Mr. Dimitrios gave me a bleary look, swaying slightly—as well he might, considering the number of glasses of champagne he had drunk.

"Quite all right, my dear Miss James. No need to appol-appol—there is no need to be sorry." His heavy accent, combined with the slurring of his words, made his speech very close to unintelligible. "A beautiful girl such as yourself—"

He started to sidle closer, and I suppressed a sigh, preparing myself to stamp on his foot yet again—this would make the third time—if he tried to snake an arm around my waist.

All around us, the Lansdowne House ballroom was aglow with the light of candles and gas chandeliers. Potted palm trees and hothouse orchids and lilies lined the walls, and at the head of the room, a musical quartet played while couples in evening dress circled the mirror-polished dance floor.

Other guests were circling the room, admiring the famous Roman marble sculptures that had been set into the walls.

A podium had been set up in front of one of the marble friezes, where later on I presumed that Lord Lansdowne would give the speech or presentation he intended to make tonight.

Always assuming that our adversary didn't murder him first.

I had come over to speak with Mr. Dimitrios nearly half an hour ago in hopes that I might learn more about whoever had planted the bomb. So far, though, all I had succeeded in learning was that Mr. Dimitrios was far too fond of speaking about himself and of female company, particularly when he was intoxicated.

Although there was some slight consolation in that fending off Mr. Dimitrios' unwanted attentions had left me with very little time to worry about my own memories or waking nightmares coming back.

Now his eyes nearly crossed as he made an effort to focus on my face. "Where was I? Ah, yes, I was telling you about the development of the recoil-operated firing systems—"

A voice spoke behind me. "Miss James, might you do me the honor of allowing me this dance?"

I turned to find Edward Barton holding out one gloved hand. He wore a black tie and white waistcoat, and his russet-colored hair was combed straight back from his face.

I hesitated. But I couldn't honestly think that further conversation with Mr. Dimitrios would achieve anything but the increased risk of my sooner or later breaking one of the arms dealer's toes.

I put my hand into Mr. Barton's. "Thank you. I would be delighted."

The back of my neck prickled as we made our way out onto the dance floor, although it was difficult to tell whether that was my own nerves or simple awareness that something could happen at any time. I had seen the blue-uniformed police constables fairly crawling over the grounds outside and checking invitations one by one before the guests were admitted to the house.

So far, there had been no sign of any danger, but I couldn't shake the weight of Holmes's prediction that there would be trouble tonight. My father wasn't entirely infallible, but his predictions had a habit of generally coming true.

The strains of a waltz began playing, and I rested my hand on the top of Mr. Barton's shoulder. "I never got the chance to thank you, Mr. Barton, for getting Becky and Mrs. Hudson out of the house so quickly the other morning."

Mr. Barton smiled at me as we started to move with the other couples across the dance floor. "Edward, please. I believe the experience of nearly being exploded by a bomb together ought to obligate you to use my given name."

"Edward, then. And I do thank you."

"You're very welcome. Have there been any new discoveries in the case?"

"None to speak of. Were you put in charge of the added security measures for tonight?"

"In part," Edward said. "It was something of a scramble to arrange everything on such short notice."

Uniformed police officers stood just outside the windows that lined the ballroom walls and opened out onto a narrow paved terrace that circled the house.

Maybe that was what was making my skin crawl with the sense of being watched.

I looked around the room again, searching for Holmes, but couldn't find him. He was—for a wonder—not in disguise and was mingling amongst the various members of Parliament and government officials who were here.

We passed by one of the large mirrors on the ballroom wall, and I caught sight of our reflection. I was wearing the gown that Becky had selected as the prettiest in my wardrobe back at home: a pale green satin with short puffed sleeves and a belt of deeper green. Pearl clasps—also Becky's choice—held back my hair.

Even a brief glance showed that I looked pale, though.

I tried to drag my attention back to the dance.

Edward was a good dancer, polished and sure and good at leading. We spun around the floor in silence for a few moments and then he said, "I hope I didn't misinterpret your expression of glazed boredom just now, Miss James. But I thought it looked as though you would be glad of an excuse to leave our friend Mr. Dimitrios behind."

"Have you met Mr. Dimitrios before?"

"He has had dealings with the War Office, from time to time. He's a weasel, will try to twist and turn any contract to his advantage. And I wouldn't trust his word if he told me that the sky was blue."

The strains of the waltz were fading. Edward brought us to a halt, and I held up one hand. "Wait a moment. I believe you're trying to give me a subtle hint as to what you really think of him."

Edward laughed. "I'm sorry. My opinion was rather more than blunt. But I have little patience with these merchants of death—leeches who grow fat off the business of war."

His amiable face darkened.

"That's rather an odd point of view for someone who works for the War Office," I said.

"Well, I did tell you that I had hoped to run away to sea and lead a life of adventure." He smiled, his expression lightening. But then he shook his head. "Modern theory holds that to be at war is a part of man's natural state. That might will make right and that we, the lights of civilization in a dark world, must ensure that we have enough might to conquer the uncivilized savages of the world or be overrun. But I cannot help wondering whether all our efforts to build better guns and stronger naval ships and more deadly mortar shells would be better directed towards working for peace."

I couldn't disagree, though it would probably give half the men Edward Barton worked with an apoplectic fit to hear him voice such a terribly un-British opinion.

The orchestra struck up the strains of another waltz. Edward bowed. "Another dance, Miss James?"

I knew that I *should* stay here in the ballroom. I should dance and mingle and try to keep a watchful eye, as Holmes had said.

But I felt sick to my stomach, and my heart was racing so that it was hard to draw breath. The noise and lights and bright dresses of the ballroom were tilting around me, threatening to coalesce into a sickening, spinning whirl.

I forced a smile. "Thank you, but no. Do you think you might see whether you can fetch us anything to drink? It's quite warm in here."

"Of course, Miss James. Your wish is my command."

He departed, weaving his way slowly but confidently through the throngs of people. I waited until he was just out of sight before turning in the opposite direction, towards the entrance to the ballroom.

If Edward Barton wasn't a murderer—like other seemingly pleasant men I had known—it was somewhat unkind of me to be slipping away from him this way.

If he wasn't what he appeared, though, I couldn't tell him the truth. And if he *was* the perfectly nice young man he seemed to be, then he would probably out of gallantry insist on accompanying me.

I didn't want company, any more than I wanted the drink I had sent him to fetch. What I wanted was to confront my memories, stare the nightmares in the face, and lay them to rest once and for all.

* * *

Three police constables stopped me as I made my way away from Lansdowne House towards a small grove of trees at the back. They let me go, though, as soon as I mentioned mine and my father's names. Not the first time I had been aware of the benefits of being associated with Sherlock Holmes.

There was bright moonlight tonight and no fog. With the lights of the house behind me, it wasn't hard to find my way.

I ducked through the trees and then stopped, staring at the small building that had been the focus of my nightmares for the past six months.

The ice house looked exactly the same as it had the night of the Jubilee Ball: square, squat, and completely innocuous, a small brick place designed to keep ice chilled through the summer months.

I couldn't see any police on patrol out here. Their efforts were all concentrated closer to the house.

My heart hammered hard enough to make me almost dizzy. *Stop.*

I wasn't being marched inside at gunpoint this time. No murderers or madmen lurked inside. There was absolutely nothing to be afraid of. That was the whole point of my coming here, to prove to myself that I didn't have to be afraid.

The door was locked, but it was a simple one, there not being much market for stolen ice, particularly in the middle of autumn's rainy chill. A moment with one of the pins from my hair and I felt the lock click open.

I swung the door open and was struck by the smell of damp and the straw used to pack the ice. I shut my eyes for a second and, for the first time in six months, instead of trying to lock the memories away, I let them come, practically daring them to come back.

You want me to remember you? Fine. Let's see how frightening you really are.

The inside of the ice house was dark, shadowed, but I could see that the chair I had been tied to was gone, and of course no trace remained of the ropes that had bound Mycroft's ankles and hands.

"Lucy?"

The voice behind me made my heart jolt to a stop, stealing my breath. I spun, slipped on a patch of damp ground, and would have fallen if Jack hadn't moved instantly out of the shadows to catch me.

"Are you all right?"

I nodded, unable to draw breath enough to speak. Just for a moment, it was hard to believe that Jack was *real*. His appearance almost seemed as though it had to be part of another waking dream. Except that Jack was never the one to arrive at the ice house in the nightmares.

I'm sorry, Lucy, but he's gone. In the past three months, I had heard Uncle John say those words in my dreams more times than I could even count.

"What are you doing here?" I finally managed to ask.

Jack was wearing his policeman's uniform, the dark blue almost blending in with the surrounding shadows. The silvery moonlight overhead patched his lean face with shadow and silvered his dark lashes.

"Your father told me about the ball tonight and the patrols Lord Lansdowne had ordered. I didn't think anyone would notice one more police constable around."

They almost certainly wouldn't, he was right.

"I saw you leave the ballroom," Jack said.

I could hear the implied question in his voice, but for the moment I couldn't answer. I still felt as though I were somehow trapped, caught in the state between dreaming and awake—or possibly between present and past.

Jack was silent a moment, and then he said, "Becky told me what happened here, the night of the Jubilee Ball."

I went motionless, my heart tightening. It hadn't occurred to me that Becky would have recounted the story to Jack, though it should have. She wasn't exactly known for her ability to keep secrets, and she had played a starring role in the events at the ice house.

"It was lucky for me that she was here," I said.

Jack's hands were still on my upper arms, from where he'd caught me from falling. The touch of his fingers was a small point of warmth in the chill all around.

"I'm sorry I wasn't here too," he said.

"You'd been shot and nearly killed. I will grant that as a reasonably good excuse for missing the excitement of that particular escapade."

I tried to speak lightly, but my voice shook a little on the last words. I could remember so vividly the blood on the steps of St. Paul's cathedral, soaking Jack's uniform, staining my hands. Jack's face, white against the sheets covering the operating table in Uncle John's surgery.

None of that was a nightmare, it was simple fact, a reminder of just how close he'd come to dying. I shivered involuntarily.

"I came out here tonight because I was hoping that if I went back—if I faced being here again—the memories would go away and stop haunting me so much," I said.

"That'd be nice." Jack's voice was still quiet. "But I don't think it's ever that simple."

I was still shivering. Jack shifted position, and I braced myself for him to let go and step away from me. But instead, slowly, almost carefully, he drew me in, pulling me close against him.

"Life just doesn't work that way." His words were a breath of warmth, stirring my hair.

"I know."

I leaned against him, feeling the iron-hard strength of his arms around me, the steady thump of his heart beneath the rough material of his uniform.

After a moment, he straightened, starting to move back. "Sorry, I shouldn't have—"

Of course, he would have to go back to treating me as though I were poisoned.

I shut my eyes for a quick second, cutting him off. "Could you just not move for one more moment?"

Jack looked down at my hand, curled around his arm. "I'm not sure that's such a good—"

I interrupted him again, hating the way my voice wavered, but unable to stop it. My throat hurt and my eyes burned.

"Even if you blame me for what happened at the Jubilee, even if you've changed your mind about how you feel about me, even if you never want to touch me again, could you just let me have five minutes to *pretend* that you do?"

I felt a jolt, as of surprise, go through him, and he stared at me.

"If I blame *you*?" Jack's eyes were colored with shock in the moonlight. "That's crazy. You didn't pull the trigger on the gun that shot me. And as for not wanting—" He shook his head. "God, I've been going out of my mind trying *not* to—" He stopped, the words seeming to catch.

We stood face to face, so close that I could feel the tension that vibrated almost like an electric current through his muscles.

"Not to what?" I couldn't seem to speak above a whisper.

Jack's gaze met mine. From back at the house, I could hear the strains of orchestra music, but they seemed to come from a long way off, as though the rest of the world had retreated away from us. The air between us felt suddenly warmer and almost charged, like the atmosphere before a thunderstorm.

Then, instead of answering, Jack leaned forward, lowering his head until his lips brushed mine, just lightly at first, then more urgently.

The touch spread all through me, like the feeling of coming home to warmth and firelight on a dark winter day.

I felt Jack's breath go out in what I would have sworn was relief, as though he really had been fighting not to let himself draw so close to me, and was happy beyond words to give up the struggle. His hand cupped my face, his thumb gently brushing across my cheek.

But then he pulled back, so suddenly that I felt him almost stumble as his weight shifted to his bad leg. "You shouldn't be here with me like this."

"What?" I had barely managed to recover from the shock of the kiss, as if I had been spun around and hadn't yet found my footing either.

Jack let go of me, stepping away. I could see a fine tremor moving through his body, but his voice was firm, if uneven. "The two of us together ... I'm not right for you."

"Why not?"

Jack gave a humorless half-laugh, disbelief etched across his face. "You're joking, right? I knew from the first day we met I didn't stand a chance with a girl like you." He waved a hand towards the noise and lights of the house. "You think all those people inside the ballroom back there, the ones you were talking to just now, would so much as let me in the door? The second I opened my mouth, they'd know I was an East-ender they might hire to polish their shoes or guard their valuables, but that's as far as they'd go. I used to be part of a criminal gang, I only just earn enough to keep a roof over Becky's and my heads, it takes me half an hour to read a newspaper article, and I could barely write you a *letter*, much less a poem or whatever you're supposed to do to court a girl of your station."

I stared at him. "A *poem*?"

Jack kept going as though I hadn't even spoken.

"And as if all that's not enough, now I can't even do my job because I'm crippled, maybe for good. And you ask why I'm not *right* for you?"

"Because it's not true." I folded my hands tightly together. "None of that is true. Or maybe it is, but it isn't what matters to me."

"Right." Jack's voice was all at once hard, tinged with bitterness. "Because you just can't say no to a hard-luck case, can you?"

I jerked back. "What is *that* supposed to mean?"

Jack raked a hand distractedly through his hair. "Let's see. You wind up owning a chicken because you can't stand the thought of killing it, you won't tell old Mr. Griggs that he can't cook, you'll risk your own safety tracking down a blackmailer who's threatened your friend ... I don't want you out here with me out of pity or because you think you owe me something for saving your dad's life—"

Something hot ignited in my chest, racing through my veins. "That's a horrible thing to say!"

In the silvery light of the moon, Jack didn't look angry, just suddenly tired, which was somehow worse.

He gestured again back towards the lights of the main house, twinkling golden through the bare-branched trees all around us. "Lucy, you have a life—in there, where you belong, with people like you. Forget about me and go live it."

Anger sparked through me, like fire along a detonation cord. "I somehow missed the vote when *you* were put in charge of deciding where I do and don't belong!"

Footsteps—running footsteps—suddenly echoed through our small clearing.

The breath snagged in my throat, and Jack instantly whirled around. A man's figure staggered and stumbled at an uneven run through the trees towards us, crashing into branches without even seeming to realize they were there.

Mr. Dimitrios. A ray of moonlight slanted across him, and I recognized the broad lines of his face and the peak of his dark hair on his forehead. He was breathing hard, his breath audibly sawing in and out.

And he was carrying a long sword of some sort in one hand and a heavy revolver in the other.

My heart slammed painfully into my ribs, but Jack didn't hesitate. He stepped into Dimitrios' path.

"Stop."

Mr. Dimitrios lurched to a halt—more from the shock of Jack's appearance, I thought, than because he actually meant to obey. His face was ghastly in the moonlight, blanched yellowish white and sweating, his teeth bared, his eyes wild and staring.

"Get … get out of my way." He was still drunk. Possibly even more drunk than he had been in the ballroom. His words slurred. But that only made him more dangerous, not less. He gripped the revolver tightly, one finger on the trigger as he waved it threateningly.

One involuntary twitch of his fingers and he could let the gun discharge, whether he meant to or not. His other hand gripped the sword, which I now saw with a fresh lurch, was covered with something that looked wet and glistening dark in the moonlight.

Jack didn't move. His posture was easy, his voice calm. "You don't want to do that. Just put the gun down."

"No!" Mr. Dimitrios shook his head, seeming to speak almost to himself more than Jack, slurring the words under his breath. "No. Got to get out of here. He's dead." Then suddenly his head snapped up and he gave a sudden lurch forward, slashing furiously with the sword.

"Dead, I tell you!"

Jack ducked out of the way of the flashing blade, but only just.

I stepped out of the shadows. "Mr. Dimitrios!" My heart was pounding crazily against my ribs, but I kept my tone light, friendly.

Mr. Dimitrios clearly hadn't noticed my presence until this moment. Now his gaze swiveled in my direction, confused, as he tried to make sense of who I was and how I had come to be here.

That's right. Look at me, not Jack.

I summoned up a bright smile. "Mr. Dimitrios, I am *so* glad that I found you again! We were interrupted just before you could tell me those very interesting details you were sharing about recoil-operated firing systems."

Mr. Dimitrios shook his head as though trying to clear his thoughts, wiping his forehead with the back of the hand that held the revolver.

I tried hard not to flinch, expecting a shot to go off.

"I … what?" His words were still so blurred together they were scarcely intelligible.

"You were telling me all about your gun factory. Don't you remember?" I said.

I didn't dare look at Jack directly, but out of the corner of my eye, I could see him edging forward, step by slow step, circling around to Dimitrios' side.

Don't die, I ordered him silently. *Please don't get killed tonight.*

I willed myself to keep smiling, to keep talking. "It was so very interesting!"

Unfortunately I was running out of things to say about recoil-operated firing systems, about which I knew absolutely nothing.

Jack had reached a point to the right and just behind Mr. Dimitrios, in line with the other man's shoulder.

"Maybe you could tell me more—" I began.

Jack moved so fast he was almost a blur of motion, knocking Dimitrios' gun hand up with a short, sharp blow and at the same time tackling him so that they both went crashing to the ground.

The gun flew out of the arms dealer's hands, and I saw the sword drop to the ground too. By the time I had managed to find the revolver and pick it up, Jack had wrestled the other man face down and twisted one arm behind his back.

Mr. Dimitrios struggled for a brief second, but then lay still.

Jack raised his head to look at me, breathing hard. "You could have gotten yourself killed, confronting him like that."

I glared back at him. "Aphorisms about pots and kettles spring to mind!"

I crouched down, examining the blade of the sword without touching it, sickness twisting through me as I realized I'd been right. The blade was wet with something that would probably appear rusty red if there were better light.

"Is that—"

"Blood," Jack said. He sounded grim. "It's all over his hands too." He was holding on to Mr. Dimitrios' wrist and drew back so that I could see the sticky smears that marked the Greek man's fingers and palms.

"He's dead." All the fight seemed to have gone out of Mr. Dimitrios. He sagged on the ground, his voice breaking on a drunken half-sob. "He's *dead*, I tell you."

Still keeping firm hold of Mr. Dimitrios' arms, Jack dragged the older man to his feet. "Come on. You'd better show us."

CHAPTER 30

"There," Mr. Dimitrios said. Jack still had his hands pinned behind him, so the arms dealer made a vague, exhausted gesture with his head.

His directions had led us around to the back of the house, where bright lights and the sounds of laughter and raised voices were spilling from the ballroom windows.

Outlined in the billiard room windows, I could see the gentlemen who had escaped from the noise and dancing of the ballroom playing pool.

"Through the trees over there," Mr. Dimitrios said.

I had picked up the revolver and was keeping it trained on him, our present safety outweighing any concern I had about destroying fingermarks. But so far he had only stumbled drunkenly on in what seemed almost a hopeless trance.

Jack moved forward, pushing Mr. Dimitrios ahead of him in the direction he'd indicated. Then he stopped short.

As I moved up to join him, I saw the man's body sprawled on the ground at our feet, hands flung out, head tipped back, legs bent at an odd angle.

I drew in a sharp breath. The man's face was one I'd never seen before: close on thirty, square-jawed, with curling dark hair. But I suspected I might be able to put a name to him nonetheless. One of the outflung hands was heavily bandaged, and I suspected that if the bandages were to be unwrapped, we would find him missing a finger.

"Is that—"

Jack answered without my even having to finish the question. "Yes."

McHale, our missing waiter. I didn't need to check whether he was dead. There was light enough to see the torn, bloodied mess where his throat should have been, the blood pooled on the ground beneath him, and the way his eyes stared glassily and sightlessly up at the night sky.

Mr. Dimitrios gave a hoarse cry. "Dead. Told you." He staggered, stumbling forward in Jack's grasp.

For a second, I thought he was trying to attack again, and I got as far as flicking the safety catch off the revolver.

But instead, Mr. Dimitrios' eyes rolled up in his head, his knees buckled, and he collapsed onto the ground. Jack bent, pulling up one of the arms dealer's eyelids, then shook his head.

"He's not shamming."

"Drunk?"

"Probably." Jack looked up at me. "I'll stay on guard here with the body. You go and tell your father and Lord Lansdowne what's happened."

* * *

"Your name and rank, constable?" Lord Lansdowne asked.

We were in his private study on the second floor of Lansdowne House, one of the few rooms not crowded by ball guests. The room was more like a library than an office, with comfortable chairs, a large oak mantel, and shelves of leather-bound books lining the walls.

Jack stood straight, projecting the air of relaxed and yet disciplined competence that made him so good at his job.

"Kelly, sir. Detective constable."

Lord Lansdowne nodded. Fortunately, he didn't seem aware that Jack hadn't officially been assigned to duty here, and Lestrade wasn't here to tell him.

Lestrade and the rest of the men he had brought were outside, ranging over the crime scene and combing the grounds for any signs of further intrusion.

My father and I sat in matching chairs on either side of the hearth, Uncle John was next to my father, and Edward Barton sat beside Lord Lansdowne.

"Very well, constable, you may proceed," Lord Lansdowne went on. "You were telling us of apprehending the suspect as he attempted to escape the grounds."

"That's right, sir."

Lord Lansdowne shot a quick glance at Uncle John. "Dr. Watson, our suspect has not awakened yet?"

Watson shook his head. "I would estimate that it will be several hours before he is in any coherent state to answer questions. To be blunt, he has in my considered medical opinion imbibed enough liquor to pickle his insides."

At the moment, Mr. Dimitrios was unconscious in one of the upstairs bedrooms, handcuffed to the bed and under guard of two police officers.

Lord Lansdowne asked Jack, "He was armed with both this sword and this revolver?"

He gestured to the weapons that currently lay atop Lord Lansdowne's desk, a sheet of newspaper spread out beneath them to protect the desk's surface. Just as I had thought, the sword blade was clotted and sticky with blood.

"He was," Jack said.

Holmes had been silent until now. As both the owner of the house and the highest ranking official in the room, it was perhaps within Lord Lansdowne's rights to ask all of the questions. Although since my father typically cared absolutely not one iota for rank, I suspected some other reason for his allowing Lord Lansdowne to take the lead.

Now, though, he abruptly shifted position slightly and said, "Not just a sword. I believe the article in question is a *shashka*. A traditional Russian sabre."

I glanced from the weapon to my father, scrutinizing his face. "You believe that is significant?"

Holmes lapsed back in his chair, his fingers twitching in the brief, dismissive gesture that could mean anything from *it is a capital mistake to theorize in advance of data* to *I simply don't feel like telling you right now.*

"Mr. Dimitrios is, I believe, of Russian heritage."

"Quite so," Lord Lansdowne agreed. He returned his gaze to Jack.

"You heard nothing before Mr. Dimitrios' sudden appearance? No fight, no outcry or sounds of a struggle?"

For the first time since we had all entered the room, Jack's gaze flicked just for a brief moment to me. But then he refocused on Lord Lansdowne.

"No, sir. I heard nothing of that kind."

I tried to think back, remembering those few minutes by the ice house. I could recall the noise of the party, the sounds of music, the wind creaking through the tree branches ... nothing else.

Would either Jack or I have heard a struggle if there had been one? I would hope so, but I couldn't be entirely sure.

"You knew right away, though, that something was amiss?" Lord Lansdowne asked.

"Yes, sir. Apart from the weapons, Mr. Dimitrios' hands were stained with blood. Following his directions, we searched around the back of the house and found the body."

Lord Lansdowne looked at Jack sharply. "Mr. Dimitrios actually led you back to the body?"

"Yes, sir."

"Did he seem guilty to you?"

"He was ... frightened. Confused. Other than that, I can't say."

Lord Lansdowne glanced at me. "Miss James, you concur?"

"Yes. He was badly frightened—shocked—as well as intoxicated. I'm not sure he fully realized what he was doing."

Edward Barton leaned forward, speaking to Jack for the first time. "You allowed Miss James to accompany you to find a dead body?" he asked, his voice incredulous. "That did not seem to you like reckless endangerment of Miss James' safety?"

I clamped my mouth shut to keep from interrupting. Interrupting would make it look as though I didn't think Jack could answer the question on his own.

I had glossed over the reason for my having been outside, saying only that I had gone out of the ballroom for a breath of air when—coincidentally, at the same time as Jack—I had happened to see Mr. Dimitrios.

But otherwise I had kept silent while Jack was recounting what had taken place out on the house grounds. We hadn't had a chance to make sure our stories lined up, and I didn't want to accidentally contradict anything he might say.

With the exception of Uncle John and my father, I didn't particularly care what anyone at Lansdowne House thought of me. But I was aware that Lord Lansdowne, as Secretary of War, could probably cause Jack to lose his job with a single telephone call or a word in the right ear.

Lord Lansdowne couldn't find out that Jack had known the dead man personally.

Not to mention, if it were known that at the presumed time of the murder Jack had been standing in the grove of trees by the ice house, kissing me, the questions put to him would be significantly more awkward than the ones he was answering right now.

I willed myself not to flush at the memory, which I was trying to keep locked away. I wasn't sure what I would do if I let myself think about it for too long. Although crossing the room and smacking Jack hard enough to rattle his teeth was a distinct possibility.

"Reckless," Jack repeated. His voice was neutral.

"It means—" Edward began.

Jack's jaw tightened fractionally, the expression so brief and slight I could have blinked and missed it. But his voice stayed perfectly level and calm. "I'm familiar with what the word means. No, I wasn't concerned."

His gaze just barely touched me again.

Three months ago—at least if we'd been alone—I would have expected a joke about the fact that I'd been the one holding the gun at that point, and he wasn't crazy enough to suggest I stay out of danger for fear of getting himself shot.

Now I couldn't at all tell what he was thinking.

"The suspect had been caught and disarmed, and I had no reason to think there might be further danger," Jack finished.

Lord Lansdowne studied Jack. "You were unarmed, Constable Kelly, and yet you tackled a man wielding both a loaded revolver and a sword?"

"Miss James had distracted him."

"Even still, the odds were surely not in your favor."

"My job is to apprehend criminals, sir," Jack said. "There was nothing in the oath I took about getting to pick only the fights I know I'm going to win."

"Yes, well, it was very well done, Constable," Lord Lansdowne said. "Your actions were commendable. Unless Mr. Holmes has any further questions, you may return to your duties now."

"Yes, sir."

Jack's dark brown gaze met mine for another brief second before he left the room. I still couldn't tell for certain what he was thinking, although if I had to guess, it would be somewhere in the neighborhood of a grim *I told you so*.

The worst part was that he wasn't wrong.

Lord Lansdowne had spoken politely—cordially, even. But polite or not, everything about his manner had practically dripped with an inherent sense of superiority, his words an order, given to a subordinate.

And there was absolutely nothing I could say right now that wouldn't make it worse.

Jack was right about one thing, if nothing else he'd said tonight. Men like Lord Lansdowne—*even* men like Lord Lansdowne, who was fundamentally a good and honorable gentleman—wouldn't accept Jack as an equal just because Lucy James said so.

After Jack had gone out, Lord Lansdowne turned to my father. "Since our murderer has already been apprehended—and since as far as we know, the man he killed was never even inside the house—do you see any objections, Holmes, to allowing the rest of the evening to proceed as planned?"

As Lord Lansdowne said, the man McHale had never been inside or, if he had, he had managed to escape the notice of every police officer on duty here. The vast majority of the ball guests did not even know that anything untoward had happened.

"Objections?" My father repeated. His eyes had the unfocused look that meant the vast majority of his brain was engaged elsewhere.

"The charitable presentation, Holmes," Watson said. Long experience with my father made him speak patiently. "The endowment of the pensioners' home." He looked at Lord Lansdowne. "For myself, I see no reason why your presentation may not proceed as planned. I believe you had hoped to give a speech about the need for the project, in hopes that those in attendance here tonight might feel moved to make donations."

"Thank you, Doctor Watson." Lord Lansdowne looked at my father, his brows creeping together in a frown. "Mr. Holmes? May I take it that you are in agreement?"

Holmes's gaze was fixed on the bloodied sword, and I suspected that he hadn't heard a single word either Lansdowne or Uncle John had said.

"Mr. Holmes?" Lord Lansdowne repeated.

My father stood up in a sudden explosion of movement. "The body—to where was the body brought?"

Lord Lansdowne blinked once. "I believe Lestrade has summoned a police wagon, to convey it to the city morgue—"

"*Tcha!*" Holmes gave an exclamation of either frustration or disgust and strode from the room.

Edward was the first to speak, turning to Uncle John with a faint smile. "Dr. Watson, I believe that I begin to understand what you once wrote about there being madness in his method."

CHAPTER 31

"Ladies and gentlemen." Edward Barton raised his voice to be heard over the noise of the crowd.

He stood at the podium I had seen earlier, his hand lifted to attract attention.

"Our host tonight, Lord Lansdowne, wishes to say a few words."

There were a few murmurs, and then the noise of the ballroom died down. Lord Lansdowne, slim and straight in his black evening jacket and white tie, approached the podium. I could still see the faint lines of strain gathered about his eyes, but he smiled as he faced the room.

"Ladies and gentlemen, thank you for being here."

Uncle John and I stood a little off to one side, Holmes having still not returned from viewing McHale's body. Despite the fact that, with Mr. Dimitrios in custody, the danger ought to be over, my skin was prickling with uneasiness, and all my nerves were stretched tight.

If the Greek arms dealer really were our killer, I would at least have the satisfaction of my earlier suspicions proving justified. But I couldn't convince myself that the threat had actually passed.

Lord Lansdowne was still speaking, saying something about the proposed pensioners' home. I listened with half an ear, letting my gaze travel around the ballroom.

Some of the guests looked mildly bored, others attentive, but I couldn't pick out anyone who looked as though they were biding their time, waiting for a chance to attack.

I couldn't find Jack in the crowd at all, not even among the constables guarding the windows and doorways.

I shook my head—an unsatisfying substitute for being able to yank Jack Kelly physically out of my thoughts—and refocused on Lord Lansdowne.

There was a magic lantern projector on the podium in front of him, the sort that projected an image or photograph onto a larger screen. The screen in this case had been hung from the ceiling directly behind Lord Lansdowne, the lower edge just clearing the top of his head.

There was something odd about the magic lantern itself, though. I had seen them before, and this one didn't look quite right. The case that ought to hold the slides seemed not quite to fit—

"And now if you will bear with me a moment, I can show you some photographs detailing the good and noble work your charitable contributions …" Lord Lansdowne began.

The rest of what he was saying was lost to me, turning into a jumbled roar in my ears as I saw his hand reach for the switch that would turn the lantern projector on.

"No!" I threw myself forward, trying to stop him—and did manage to crash into him, knocking him aside.

But in the same instant, I heard a click, then a hiss. A smell of bitter almonds filled the air.

My head swam, my vision darkening and my lungs burning. Then everything seemed to fold together, like the pages of a book slamming shut.

Darkness swallowed me whole.

* * *

"Uncle John, I'm all right," I said. "I really am all right."

We were back home in Baker Street, in the sitting room of 221A. Becky was sound asleep on the trundle bed in the bedroom, so Uncle John had set me down on the couch after insisting on carrying me inside from the carriage we had taken home.

Now he scowled at me, the edges of his mustache pulling down.

"I beg your pardon, I was making the mistake of thinking that I was the only licensed physician in this room. Oh." He gave an exaggerated start of surprise. "Wait just a moment. I *am* in fact the only doctor in the room. And as such, perhaps you will do me the honor of allowing me to assess whether the effect of the poison you inhaled is severe."

He took out his pocket watch, reaching with his other hand for the pulse in my wrist. I leaned back, letting him count off the beats of my heart.

In fact, I did feel somewhat ill, with a lingering headache and a sick, dizzy feeling making the room waver slightly. Though the effects were nowhere near as severe as they could have been.

Uncle John finished taking my pulse, then exhaled. "Very well. I believe I may be cautiously optimistic that you will suffer no permanent effects. However, you are to rest quietly for the next several days. I am about to send a letter to Mr. Harris at the Savoy, explaining that you will of medical necessity be absent from performances for the next few nights. Do you understand? You are to remain here, quietly, and not set foot on stage or do anything more strenuous than lift a teacup."

From his expression, arguing would be a wasted effort, and I didn't have the energy in any case. "Thank you." I squeezed his hand. "I'm sorry I frightened you, Uncle John."

My memories of our departure from Lansdowne House were something of a haze: a confused jumble of someone shouting for a doctor, and Uncle John saying that he *was* one ...

"Is Lord Lansdowne all right?" I asked.

I had still been drifting in and out of consciousness on our carriage ride here, unable to ask.

The door to the sitting room opened, admitting Holmes in time to hear my question.

"He is practically recovered already. You knocked him aside, such that he inhaled even less of the cyanide gas than you."

"The cyanide was inside the magic lantern?"

Holmes looked down at me. His face was less fierce than Watson's, but I still had the feeling from his expression that I had frightened him as much as I had Uncle John.

"The device was rigged such that a press of the switch released the valve on a pressurized canister of cyanide gas. A bold plan, if a somewhat fallible one. In a room as large as the Lansdowne House ballroom, the gas would dissipate too quickly to be fatal. Unless, of course, it was received directly in the face. As would have been the case with Lord Lansdowne, had you not intervened."

I let myself lean back against the sofa cushions, relief making my muscles feel weak. *Weaker*.

"Will she be all right?" I heard Holmes ask Uncle John.

"I have difficulty enough in keeping just you alive." Watson's gruff voice seemed to come from a long way off. "The strain of keeping two of you from running headlong into danger and certain death may possibly drive me into an early grave. But yes, with a night's rest, I believe she will be perfectly fine."

I wanted to open my eyes and tell them that I *was* fine. But I couldn't seem to find the energy. Distantly, I was aware of someone pulling a blanket over me and turning out the lights, though whether it was Watson or my father, I couldn't be sure.

* * *

"Lucy? Lucy, are you all right?"

The ragged shreds of the ice house and Arkwright's sneering face melted away, leaving me gasping and staring up at the sitting room ceiling.

Becky was sitting perched on the edge of the couch beside me, her blue eyes concerned. "Were you having a bad dream?"

"I—" I managed to get my breath back and sit up. "Yes, I suppose I was."

So much for banishing the nightmares with my visit to the ice house. The dream-memory had been every bit as vivid and stomach-twisting as before.

The room was dark, but I could see pale gray light filtering around the edges of the curtains. It must be early morning.

Becky crawled under the blanket to curl up next to me. "I thought so." We were both quiet a second, and then Becky twisted her head to look up at me. "Did you see Jack last night?"

The effects of the cyanide gas seemed nearly gone; all that was left was a faint, lingering trace of a headache. But I still couldn't seem to gather my thoughts for any kind of coherent response. I just stared at her, no words coming out.

"I know he's not really in Bath," Becky said. Her small, freckled face was pale, her hands balled up into fists on top of the blanket. "He's here in London, doing something dangerous, something he doesn't want me to know about. But I *do* know. You're both not *lying* to me, but you're not telling me the whole truth either. I can tell."

I sighed and rested my cheek on top of her head. "I'm sorry. We should have told you the truth. There was someone— someone who would have hurt you, if he could, and Jack too. Jack didn't want you to be in danger or frightened. But you're an intelligent, strong girl, and maybe you deserved to know."

I was thinking of my nightmare and the memories of that night in the icehouse. Becky had quite possibly saved my life and Mycroft's. If not for her, I might not even be here.

"I suppose sometimes we like to think that we know what's best for other people," I said. "Especially people who we ... who we care about. But we're often wrong."

I blinked, trying to clear away the memory of Jack standing in the moonlit grove of trees and telling me to go back to where I belonged.

Becky sat quiet for a moment. "Did you catch him? The man who wanted to hurt me and Jack?"

"Yes. He's in prison now. And likely to stay there."

"And Jack is all right?" Becky's gaze searched my face, intent. "You'd tell me if anything had happened to him?"

"Yes, I would tell you. And yes, he's all right."

At least in Becky's terms he was. Jack's being criminally stubborn and blind-sighted probably wasn't what she was worried about.

"Good." Becky let out her breath and leaned against me for another moment. "Sometimes I have bad dreams too."

I smoothed her flyaway blond hair. "What are your dreams about?"

"My mother, sometimes." Becky rested her head against my shoulder. "Sometimes I dream about when she was dying. Or sometimes I dream about the night of the Jubilee Ball. You know, about that man who caught me."

I went still, guilt sliding through me like a hot knife. Becky had been caught by one of our opponents that night, tied up, and used as a bargaining chip to try and force our surrender. At the time, she had been more outraged by the ordeal than frightened, and I had never heard her speak of it until now.

But it was still my fault—my fault that she had been at the ball in the first place.

"I would *never* have let him hurt you," I said.

I might not dream about it, but I had still replayed that part of the night in my imagination a hundred times, all the what-if's and the might-have's crowding into my mind. I was ninety-eight percent sure that no matter *how* hard Griffin had tried, I could have stopped him from harming Becky, even if it meant dying myself.

"I know. You *saved* me. But sometimes I dream that I'm back there, tied up again," Becky said in a soft voice.

I hugged her more tightly. "Have you told Jack?"

Becky shook her head. "No. I didn't want him to worry."

"Well, you can always talk to me, if you want to. *Always.*"

Becky was silent for a second. "I still remember it," she said finally. I felt her muscles quiver, her small frame taut. "The way he made Mr. Holmes put his gun down in exchange for letting me go. That's why you didn't want to tell me about the man you had arrested, wasn't it? You were afraid I might get caught and almost make a mess of things again."

"What?" I stared at her, shocked. "Becky, no! I mean, yes, I didn't want you to be hurt. But your being captured that night was *not* your fault."

I could see in Becky's face that she didn't entirely believe me. "Becky, listen to me." I put my hands on her shoulders, looking directly into her eyes. "You were so, so brave that night. You were quick-witted and clever and courageous, and you did everything exactly right. If anyone is to blame for what happened, it's me. If you hadn't been worried about me, you would never have even been at Lansdowne House that night."

"But I don't blame *you*." Becky's eyes widened, and then she flung her arms around my neck. "Apart from Jack, I love you more than anyone!"

I hugged her tightly. I still wasn't sure I was free from blame. But then, Holmes and I *had* gotten Flint arrested last night, thus neutralizing a threat to her and Jack that would have existed even if Becky had never met me at all.

Sooner or later, even without the newspaper attention of the Jubilee, a man like Flint would have found a way to come after Jack and Becky both.

Did that make the scales even out?

"Life is a complicated affair," I said.

Becky pulled back to look at me, her face confused. "What does that mean?"

I hugged her again. "It means that I love you too, and I am *very* glad that you're safe."

"So am I." Becky settled back beside me.

Outside in the street, I could hear the rumble of the milk wagon's wheels, making the morning deliveries.

"I suppose you can't marry two men at the same time, can you?" Becky asked.

I looked at her blankly. "What?"

I was by now accustomed to conversations with Becky bouncing from topic to topic like an India-rubber ball. But in this case she had lost me.

"Two men," Becky repeated, her voice patient. "Could you marry them both at once?"

"It's generally frowned on. Why? Which two men were you thinking of marrying?"

Becky giggled. "Not *me*, of course. You. Mr. Barton sent you flowers a little while ago. Mrs. Hudson brought them in while you were still sleeping."

She gestured towards the small consul table by the sitting room door, where I now realized a large floral arrangement of pink and yellow roses rested in a white wicker basket.

Mr. Barton must have practically dragged a florist out of bed to have the bouquet delivered so early in the morning.

"He was nice the other day, when he was here," Becky went on. "I liked him. And my mother once told me that a gentleman only sends flowers to a lady he admires." She looked up at me. "So do you want to marry him?"

I looked at the flowers. Maybe Edward Barton was the sort of man I should think of marrying—or at the least encouraging.

Assuming he hadn't tried to murder his employer with cyanide gas last night, he *was* nice, as Becky said, and intelligent—

I sighed. "No, I don't want to marry him. Not even a little bit."

"Oh. Good." Becky looked relieved. "That's what I thought, actually—that if you married Mr. Barton, it would mean you couldn't marry Jack."

I sat up with a jolt. "What?" The word came out slightly uneven, and I stopped, swallowing and trying to find my normal voice. "Who said anything about me marrying Jack?"

"I did," Becky said. She spoke matter-of-factly, seemingly oblivious to my staring at her. "It was yesterday, when I talked to Jack on the telephone."

Her bare feet had started to poke out the bottom of the blanket, and she rearranged the covers, tucking them under her before going on.

"I told Jack that I missed him, but that I love living here with you too. And I said, *Wouldn't it be nice if we could all live together, the three of us?* But Jack said that wouldn't be considered proper, not unless the two of you were married. So I asked him why he couldn't just marry you then, because I would *love* to have you for a sister." Becky looked up at me. "I said, *Don't you think Lucy is very pretty?* And Jack said, *Of course I do, Beck, she's beautiful, but*—oh!"

Becky cut off speaking abruptly, clamping both her hands over her mouth. Above the tips of her fingers, her blue eyes were huge. "Oh *no!*"

"What's wrong?" I asked her.

Becky shook her head. "Jack asked me not to tell you about any of that. He made me *promise*, and I gave him my faithful word I wouldn't breathe a single syllable of it to you." She looked at me, her expression almost comically guilty and hopeful in equal parts. "I don't suppose you could just forget that I ever said anything about it?"

That was somewhat less likely than Holmes giving up detection and deciding to pen romantic novels for a living.

But I gave Becky an overdone look of confusion, wrinkling up my brows. "Forget what? I haven't the slightest memory of what you're talking about."

Becky giggled again, nestling closer against my shoulder. "Thank you."

I sat quiet, listening to the quiet sounds of London waking up outside, the rattle of pots and pans as Mrs. Hudson started bacon and sausage frying in the kitchen.

I might wish that Becky had remembered her promise to Jack just a few moments later, so that she could have told me what he had said. But I couldn't in good conscience ask her to break her word, much as I would have liked to know how he had finished that sentence.

"You could still be my sister if you'd like, though," I said instead.

"Really?" Becky looked up at me, her delighted smile bright and wide enough to show the gap of her missing front teeth.

"Most definitely." I hugged her again. "I've always wanted one."

CHAPTER 32

I reached the top of the stairs and the door to 221B, then paused, my hand on the knob. The room inside was in darkness, without any light filtering out around the edges of the door or through the keyhole.

I leaned forward. "Am I going to find myself suddenly haunted if I open this door?" I asked through the panel.

Becky had scampered off to join Holmes and Watson for breakfast upstairs, after which I had bathed and gotten dressed. The last shreds of the headache had melted away, but I still wasn't sure I felt up to coming upon any more ghostly apparitions unexpectedly.

"Ah, Lucy." My father's voice answered me. "Your timing is excellent. If you could wait perhaps another fifteen seconds before opening the door while we make the final arrangements? I believe we will then be ready to offer you a demonstration of our latest apparatus."

I could hear rustling coming from inside. I counted to fifteen inside my head, then opened the door.

Heavy curtains shrouded the windows, leaving the room in darkness. A ghostly, glowing face, the features weirdly distorted, bobbed for a moment in the shadows by the mantel, then vanished with a sharp *crack*.

I stared. "That's it," I said. "That looks very close to what we saw in the Diogenes. How did you manage it?"

The lights came on, revealing Becky—once again standing on a chair, but this time shrouded in dark fabric that looked like one of Watson's overcoats. She also held what I recognized as Uncle John's fishing pole, purchased for his holiday to Scotland two years earlier, to which was attached a tattered scrap of fabric or … rubber?

I looked at Holmes, who I now realized was sitting in his chair beside the mantel. "A child's toy balloon? *That* was what we saw?"

"Sometimes the simplest explanations prove correct." Holmes eyed the fishing-pole arrangement with appreciation. "That was one of the newer models of balloon, of the type that employs vulcanized rubber in the manufacture. At my direction, Miss Kelly and Mrs. Hudson sallied out to purchase it from a toy shop in Bond Street while we were at the ball last evening. The effect is quite striking, is it not? A human face, painted on the inflated toy balloon, and then the whole thing coated with phosphorous. It would not, of course, stand up under close scrutiny. But in low light, and as an illusion designed to last a mere few seconds, it is quite effective."

"So the crack and the flash of light we saw at the Diogenes was designed to cover the balloon's being burst?" I said slowly.

"And the whole apparatus being drawn through the crack at the top of the slightly opened window," Holmes said. "Once the balloon was deflated, a scant inch of space would be all that was required."

Becky hopped down from the chair. "Mr. Holmes? Could I do an experiment with your chemistry things?" she asked.

Holmes studied her appraisingly, then nodded. "Yes, I believe we have sufficiently covered the basics that you may be trusted to experiment on your own. With the stipulation that you refrain from exterminating us by means of either explosion or poisoned gas. Dr. Watson's nerves have been tested enough already these past days."

Becky bobbed her head. "Yes, Mr. Holmes."

She moved to Holmes's worktable and began assembling test tubes and beakers, her mouth twisted in concentration.

I looked around the sitting room. "Where is Uncle John this morning?"

"He had patients to see at his surgery."

"And Mr. Dimitrios? Has he been able to give a statement?"

"Lestrade sent his notes on the interview over by first post. Mr. Dimitrios avows that he is innocent of committing murder. According to him, he received an anonymous note asking him for a meeting on the grounds of Lansdowne House."

I felt my eyebrows climb. "And he didn't suspect anything suspicious about such a message?"

"Mr. Dimitrios was unwilling to admit as much, but I rather imagine he was anticipating an offer of intelligence from someone inside a rival armaments firm—an offer either to spy or to sell trade secrets."

"Ah. And you think he is telling the truth?"

Holmes made a gesture that I took to mean *still undecided*.

"I would also not be entirely shocked to learn that the sabotage both firms have reported in the last months could, in fact, be laid at Dimitrios' door. He could easily have sabotaged one or two of his own weapons as a blind or simply falsified the reports from the weapons' testing."

"Did he say how he came to be in possession of the murder weapon and the gun?"

"He cannot recall. He believes he might have picked them up at the scene of the murder or that someone gave them to him. But his memories range from hazy to nonexistent. Or so he claims."

"*Gave* them to him?" I frowned. "Do you think, if he is in fact innocent, that he might have been not just drunk last night, but also drugged somehow? Given something to make him dazed and easily led?"

"I believe in the future, a fruitful branch of medical research will be the development of a test that might detect evidence of drugging in the human system. For now, we must simply enter the possibility under the category of *conditionally likely*."

I thought back to the night before, the lights and music and crowds of the ballroom. "One of the wait staff could have given Dimitrios a doctored drink. He was swilling champagne; I doubt he would have noticed if one of the glasses tasted slightly off. And I know Lestrade had police constables on guard, checking everyone who came in. But they were primarily looking for bombs or weapons, not poison, and they were mostly focused on guarding Lord Lansdowne. If someone disguised himself as a waiter, with a vial of laudanum or veronal or some other opiate in his pocket, it's possible he could have slipped in. Though that doesn't account for how he managed to get a sword and a revolver past security."

"I rather imagine that the dead man—Royce, as we know him—brought those himself. He must have been either bribed or intimidated into entering the Lansdowne House grounds, probably believing that he was assisting in a murder plot. What he did not imagine was that the murder was to be his own."

I shivered and picked up a small scrap of the popped balloon from the carpet. "So whoever created the illusion must have been ... in the room next door to the one where the general's body was laid out?"

"Most probably leaning out the adjacent window to control the pole or whatever was used to propel the balloon into the general's room."

"Why, though? Why go to all the trouble?"

"I imagine the first appearance of the supposed ghost was a diversion, created to allow someone a chance to look through Lord Lansdowne's papers and discover the location of the weapons shortly to be shipped out to the Sudan." Holmes steepled his fingers, leaning back in his chair. "The second sighting, just after General Pettigrew's murder, would have been another diversion, created to give McHale, alias Royce, the chance to escape."

"So Royce must have had some confederate working with him, someone who was actually on the club premises that morning," I said.

"Indeed."

"Do you think Royce was the one responsible for the general's death? Or was it our mysterious unknown?"

Holmes's muscles gave a brief twitch of frustration. "Until we can identify the means by which General Pettigrew met his end—"

Becky looked up from whatever she was mixing in a beaker and interrupted. "It was the sealing wax!"

Holmes and I both turned to stare at her.

"The sealing wax on the general's letter," Becky went on. "There was just a little bit left on the envelope, so I tested it for cyanide, and look, it's positive."

She held up the beaker, which I saw contained a dark blue pigment. She stood up very straight and recited, clearly repeating something she'd memorized from one of Holmes's lessons, "Iron sulfate is added to a solution suspected of containing cyanide. The resulting mixture is acidified with mineral acid. The formation of Prussian blue is a positive result for cyanide."

It was not often that I saw Holmes even mildly surprised, much less completely dumfounded. But in this case, he continued to stare at Becky, his expression of astonishment a mirror to mine.

"I was thinking about the Sign of Four," Becky added. "You know: *if you eliminate the impossible, whatever remains, however improbable, must be the solution.* The poison had to be in something that General Pettigrew touched, and we knew it wasn't in his coffee ..."

Holmes remained motionless and open-mouthed a moment more, then abruptly leaped up, took the beaker from Becky's hand, and held it up to the light, staring at the blue liquid inside.

He finally spoke. "Miss Kelly, at some future time, I will personally escort you back to the Egyptian Hall, and we will watch Mr. Maskelyne's magic show until we both understand and can reproduce every single trick in his repertoire."

His eyes unfocused as he kept speaking, half to himself now. "A pocket of hydrogen cyanide, or prussic acid, hidden and sealed off within the stick of wax. When the general used his candle to melt the wax, it would cause the cyanide to boil, releasing it as a gas. In an open chamber, the effect might not prove fatal, but the general was closed off within one of the small writing cubicles at the Diogenes. The letter was then removed from the general's desk, I imagine by Mr. Royce, with the intent of seeing it destroyed. But he must have been surprised in the act and dropped the letter into the outgoing mailbag instead. It was still a reasonably safe hiding place. Even if found, there was nothing to point the way back to our killer."

"Who, though? Who hired Royce? I ... wait." I scrutinized my father's face. "You're thinking about Reginald Carey, aren't you? General Pettigrew's nephew. He's a gambler, we know that already. You said you were wondering whether he preferred dice or cards. Did you mean you were wondering whether Reginald might have at some point frequented Flint's illegal gambling den?"

"That is precisely the question which currently occupies my attention. If Mr. Carey did strike up an acquaintance with Flint and his subordinates—"

Holmes broke off as Mrs. Hudson appeared in the doorway. "What?" he barked.

Mrs. Hudson startled back, looking slightly alarmed, and Holmes gentled his tone. "I beg your pardon, Mrs. Hudson. Was there something you required?"

"There's a young woman here to see Miss Lucy," Mrs. Hudson said. "Mrs. Teale, she said her name was." She turned to me. "I told her that you'd been ill and were still recovering, but she seemed terribly upset—"

"It's all right, Mrs. Hudson. Of course I'll see her. I feel perfectly all right." I could only think of one reason for Susan to have come: She must have heard from the blackmailer again. "Is it all right if Mrs. Hudson brings her up here?" I asked Holmes.

Holmes's brows were drawn together in a fierce frown of concentration, his attention still fixed on the beaker of Prussian blue. But he waved one hand in a gesture that I took to mean *go ahead*.

Given Holmes's current preoccupation, it was unlikely he would be willing to listen to Susan with his full attention. But even still, there might be something he could deduce from her story, something that I had missed.

I heard Susan's footsteps on the stairs a few moments later, and then she came in. Under her fur-lined capelet, she wore another ruffled and beribboned dress, along with an enormous hat that was trimmed with enough silk roses to look like a flower vendor's stall.

A lace demi-veil partially covered the upper part of her face, but I could see that she still looked pale, her lips pinched tight with worry and her eyes reddened, as though she had been crying.

"Lucy, thank you for seeing me." Her voice was ragged as she came to catch hold of both of my hands. "I didn't know what to do. All I could think of was to come here. Neville isn't at home, so I couldn't even tell him—"

"It's all right." I squeezed Susan's hands. "But come and sit down and tell me everything from the beginning, all right?"

Becky had settled herself on the hearth rug to work on the trick of palming a sovereign coin. Susan's gaze passed over her without really noticing, though her attention snagged on Holmes, and she startled.

"Wait a moment. Is that—"

Holmes didn't look up, so I said, "Sherlock Holmes." There was no point in trying to hide it, not now. "He will be happy to see whether he can do anything to help you too."

He would, even if I had to strong-arm him into it.

"Thank you." Susan collapsed onto the sofa, drawing a shaky breath.

I sat down beside her. "What has happened? Did you receive another blackmailing letter?"

"Yes." Susan's voice wobbled, and she wiped her eyes with her gloved fingertips. "Yes, it came this morning, and this one"— she gulped—"Lucy, this one asked for *five thousand pounds*."

I blinked. It was a huge sum. But perhaps not terribly surprising that the blackmailer—Fred Miller, if that was who we were dealing with—had decided to increase his demands. Susan had already shown that she was willing to pay to have her secret remain hidden. He must have decided that he could do better than demand a paltry fifty pounds every month or two.

Susan's hands shook as she clasped them together in her lap, her words tumbling out faster. "I don't have that amount of money. I couldn't possibly come up with that sort of sum, not even if I sell the jewelry Mrs. Teale gave me. Besides, she'd be sure to notice. And Neville isn't even at home for him to withdraw it from the bank. He's traveled to a sale of some collection of rare books in York. I don't know what to do! The note said that the money has to be paid *tomorrow,* no later than three o'clock—"

Her voice broke.

Telling her not to worry would be pointless, so I said, "I promise we'll think of some solution. Do you have the letter?"

Susan gulped again, then nodded, opening her reticule. "Yes, I brought it. I have it here."

She extracted an envelope and handed it to me. I turned it over. The name and address on the outside was printed in rough black capitals with cheap ink. No identifying marks about the envelope; it was of the inexpensive type that could be purchased from dozens of London stationers.

I drew out the single sheet of paper inside. Like the other letters Susan had described, this one was made up of individual letters, cut from newspapers and pasted onto the paper to form words.

"Five thousand pounds at the foot of the William III statue in St. James Square," I read out loud. *"Or else you know what will happen."*

The letters had been cut from copies of the *Sentinel* and the *Times*—I recognized the fonts—and pasted down by someone who was right handed. But neither of those two facts seemed likely in any way to be of help.

Susan had started to cry again. She dug through her reticule, clearly searching for the handkerchief that she seemed once more to have forgotten.

"Here." Becky appeared beside her. "You can have mine."

Susan jumped a little at the sight of Becky holding out the yellow silk handkerchief she had been using for one of her magic tricks.

"Thank you, sweetheart. That is very nice of you."

She took the handkerchief and mopped her eyes. Becky watched her, her expression at once sympathetic and concerned.

"Would you like to see a magic trick?" she asked. "I know Lucy and Mr. Holmes will help you with whatever your trouble is. But I could show you how to cut a rope in half and then join up the pieces, if you think it would cheer you up?"

Susan hiccupped a small laugh, blowing her nose. "That is *very* kind of you. I would love to see your trick." She smiled at Becky. "It's a pity that my husband isn't here. I know he would love to see a magic show too. He once worked as a magician's assistant himself."

I sat up, almost dropping the envelope and letter.

I would have sworn that Holmes had been paying absolutely no attention to our conversation. But he, too, straightened, set down the chemistry beaker, and crossed the room in practically a single stride.

"*What* did you just say?"

Susan looked at Holmes, wide-eyed and a little intimidated by the strange man suddenly looming over her. "I … I just said that my husband … Neville, is his name … once worked as a magician's assistant. That was how we met. I was on stage at the Savoy and had some friends who performed in the same revue where Neville was in the magician's act. That was how Neville supported himself—one of the ways—when his father had cut him off. The Great Berlini, that was the magician's name." She smiled slightly. "He was famous for his supposedly haunted cabinet. He would have the cabinet brought on stage and show everyone that it was empty, then lock the doors. And when he opened them again, there would be a ghostly face, hovering inside. Neville wasn't supposed to tell anyone how the trick was done, but he once let it slip to me that—"

She happened to glance at me as she spoke, and her voice faltered as she caught sight of my expression. "Lucy, what is it? Is something wrong?"

"Susan, when—" I stopped, trying to think how to put the question. A cold feeling was spreading through me, making me think I knew the answer already. But I didn't have any other choice but to ask. "Susan, was Neville at home last night?"

"No." She shook her head. "No, the sale of books was to start very early this morning, in York, so he took the train up yesterday."

"You actually saw him get on the train?"

"No, he left the house in a cab that was to take him to the station ..." Susan's gaze searched mine. "Lucy, what is all this about? What's wrong?"

Holmes was leaning against the mantel, looking down at Susan. For all his earlier talk of being ill-equipped to lend sympathy to the bereaved, his face was oddly gentle as he studied her.

Then he turned to me. "Mr. Teale asked to use the telephone that morning at the Diogenes."

"You're right." I remembered Neville asking whether he might leave the cloakroom to telephone to Susan.

He could have used the opportunity to create the illusion of the ghost upstairs.

"Means and opportunity do not alone make up proof of guilt," Holmes said quietly. "There would need to be a motive."

"I know." My thoughts were already racing, running through everything we knew, everything we had surmised, everything that I had said to Holmes and that Holmes had said—

My thoughts snagged, like fabric catching on an exposed nail as the memory of what Uncle John had said suddenly came back to me.

There is hatred behind this. Hatred and a thirst to cause hurt, perhaps in revenge.

I turned back to Susan. "Where was it Neville was stationed during the short while he spent in the army? His mother spoke of fearing that she would lose him in a foreign war. Was he somewhere overseas?"

"India, I think," Susan faltered. "He scarcely ever talks of it though."

A sick, sinking feeling filled me. "Was it—" I tried to remember the name of the place that Mr. Carey had mentioned. "Was it Manipur?"

"Maybe. I don't know. That might be the place, it sounds familiar." Susan shook her head, her eyes wide and frightened now, as she looked from me to Holmes, one hand spread over the curve of her middle, as though she were trying to protect the unborn baby inside. "Lucy, what *is* all of this? Motive for what? What are you talking about?"

I drew in a breath, still feeling sick. There was absolutely no good way to say this.

Holmes surprised me again, coming forward to take Susan's hand. "Mrs. Teale, you know already of the murder committed on the premises of your husband's club. You are too intelligent not to draw the obvious conclusion as to the reasoning behind the questions we have just asked."

"You think that *Neville*—" Susan drew in a sharp breath, covering her mouth with one hand. "But that's—"

I thought she was going to argue or say that such a thing was impossible. But instead she stopped and sat completely motionless, her gaze fixed on Holmes's face. "How sure are you?" she asked at last. Her voice was almost a whisper.

"Sure enough to be causing you the distress of speaking my conclusions out loud—a decision I do not undertake lightly," Holmes said.

Susan had turned so pale I was afraid she might faint. I took her hand, though I doubted she even felt it or noticed.

"Mrs. Teale." Holmes's tone was still gentle, but grave. "Have you any idea where your husband might be now?"

Susan shook her head, one hand at her throat. "No … I … there is his club, of course. But he wouldn't—" She stopped, shutting her eyes. "I must go home. I must speak with his mother. If what you way is true, she ought to know. She ought to be prepared."

I wasn't sure what was worse: telling Neville's mother of our unproven suspicions or letting her continue in happy ignorance until he was caught.

If he was caught.

"Would you like me to come with you?" I asked.

Susan shook her head. "No. Thank you, Lucy. But I would rather be alone. I had our carriage driver bring me here and then wait. He's just in the street outside. I shall be quite all right."

She rose, turning to Becky and trying to smile, though it was shaky. "Thank you again for the loan of your handkerchief, it was very kind. Perhaps you may show me your magic tricks"— her voice trembled—"another day."

CHAPTER 33

"If we are correct, Lestrade is never going to let me hear the last of this," Holmes said.

It was true, and in other circumstances, it might have almost been funny. For once, Lestrade might have identified the murder culprit on the very first try.

"Do you think she'll be safe?" I asked.

I was at the window, watching Susan's coachman help her climb into the waiting carriage.

"I believe so," Holmes said. "Her husband has no reason to wish her harm. And if we are correct in our conclusions, his attentions are presently directed elsewhere."

I felt a chill prickle across my skin.

"Of course. You don't think he's done, do you?"

"Hardly." Holmes paced from one end of the sitting room to the other, his hands clasped behind his back. "We are hypothesizing a personal connection, are we not? A series of crimes carried out in revenge for some grievance that occurred during the Indian uprising in Manipur in—"

Holmes cut off speaking and, in an explosion of movement, strode to a cabinet, seized hold of a leather-bound volume, and began flipping the pages.

Becky watched him, wide-eyed.

"Ah, 1891!" Holmes cried at last. He slammed the book closed, holding it in one hand. "Lord Lansdowne was viceroy of India at that time and, as we know, personally helped deal with putting down the rebellion. General Pettigrew also had a role to play." He frowned. "It hangs together." Holmes dropped into a chair and leaned back, lost in thought, his face alert, his expression keen. No one who saw him could doubt that it was in such moments as these that my father came most alive.

He sat forward abruptly, refocusing on me. "Do we know the nature of Mr. Teale's service in India?"

"Only that he supposedly had some trouble with his commanding officer and was discharged. His mother might know more."

"She might. However, a trip to interview her would cost valuable time—time in which Mr. Teale might choose to strike. He has tried already to murder Lord Lansdowne twice: once by the bomb sent to these premises and once at the ball. We also know that he has in his possession a considerable quantity of gunpowder, as well as a machine gun. I do not believe he will hesitate to use both for destructive purposes. The question is *where* and *when* he will make his next strike."

"There's Lansdowne House, of course," I said. "If Neville snuck in the night of the ball to set up the slide projector and frame Dimitrios for murder, maybe could he have also smuggled in the gunpowder to create a bomb?"

Holmes shook his head. "If that were the case, why not set it off the night of the ball?"

Holmes was right. We were missing something.

"Lucy?" Becky had come to stand beside me. "What about the ghost?"

"What about it?"

"You told me that the charwoman said her supply cupboard was haunted. But why a closet? Why make the ghost appear in there? Why not a bedroom or somewhere, I don't know, more eerie?" She wrinkled her nose in disapproval. "A broom closet isn't very frightening."

"It would make a terrible title for a gothic horror story," I agreed. *The mystery of the haunted mops and brooms*. But then, I suppose a closet would be dark and easy to make the ghost look—" I stopped, looking at Becky and shaking my head slowly. "No. No, you're right. That is *twice* today that you've proven you're a genius."

"Really?"

I pressed my fingers to my temples, trying to think.

I could hear Mrs. Mudge, swearing she would no longer go anywhere near her upstairs cleaning cupboard. Something else was nagging at my memory too. Something connected to the club or to Neville—

I looked up at Holmes. "Guy Fawkes."

Holmes looked at me with raised eyebrows.

"When I saw him, Neville was reading a book about the reign of King James I. My knowledge of seventeenth-century history is hazy, but what I do remember about his reign is that—"

"—Guy Fawkes famously attempted to blow up the House of Lords." Holmes finished for me. He looked grim. "Gunpowder, treason, and plot. With an emphasis on the gunpowder."

We stared at each other for a beat. "Parliament?" I said. "Do you think he's going to try to replicate the Guy Fawkes gunpowder plot?"

Holmes shook his head slowly. "No. Not Parliament. Working backwards, Parliament might have been indirectly responsible for the political climate in India which led to the Manipur rebellion. But Mr. Teale's anger is more likely to be directed at—"

Holmes cut off speaking abruptly and strode to the door.

"We must go." He was already shrugging into his overcoat, unwinding a scarf from the hat stand.

I crouched down by Becky, looking into her face. "I'm not just trying to protect you by saying that you can't come along right now. I need you to do something for me, something very important. First, I need you to telephone Dr. Watson at his clinic. Then telephone to Lestrade at Scotland Yard. Mrs. Hudson has both the numbers. Tell them both to come to the Diogenes Club. Can you do that?"

Becky's lower lip trembled, then firmed. "Yes. I'll do it." She hugged me. "Just, please be careful, Lucy. Don't die out there."

CHAPTER 34

"Nothing!" Holmes made a sharp sound of disgust as he stared at the interior of the second-floor broom cupboard.

It wasn't actually empty; there were the expected assortment of mops, buckets, and brooms. But there was nothing to give us any indication—

"Wait a moment." I leaned forward, crouching down to examine the faint marks on the floor that had just caught my attention. "Does it look to you as though—"

"—a rectangular object was stored here," Holmes finished for me. His hands marked off the space indicated by the lines of dust on the floor. "Unless I am much mistaken, a wooden box matching the precise dimensions of the case used for shipping a Maxim machine gun and its mount."

Tension knotted my insides. "The question is, though, where is it now?"

All around us, Lestrade and his officers were making an exhaustive search of the Diogenes Club, though they had already gone room to room and found no sign either of Neville Teale or a bomb.

As a precaution, the club members had already been evacuated and, save for low murmurs and the occasional tramp of police feet, the place had an eerily deserted feel that felt almost tomb-like.

There was a small, narrow window at the end of the hallway beside the cupboard. I went over, drumming my fingers against the windowpane as I looked down into the heavy street and pedestrian traffic of Pall Mall below.

Carriages, lady shoppers in wide hats and elegant fur muffs, businessmen in overcoats and dark suits …

A tall man in a black frock coat and top hat approached the club entrance, swinging his cane as he strode along. I tensed, but he passed by, heading in the direction of Carleton House.

Not Neville Teale.

I could see the War Office building outside the club window now: a stately, rectangular brick building, without any of the neoclassical touches that graced most of the clubs and buildings on Pall Mall.

The War Office was also being quietly evacuated, while teams of Lestrade's police officers went through the building, starting from the basement up, in search of any gunpowder or bombs.

But so far—as far as we had heard—they had found nothing at all.

I thought Holmes was handling the strain of waiting better than I was, until he said, in a voice tense with concentration, "We are assuming that Teale's target will be the War Office. Lord Lansdowne was viceroy of India during Neville Teale's time there and, in addition, he now serves as Secretary of War."

I couldn't find flaw in any of our reasoning. But all the same, my skin was still crawling with the feeling that we could be doing more ... or that there was some clue we had overlooked—

At least Becky had actually kept her word about staying home with Mrs. Hudson. I telephoned back to Baker Street on our arrival here, and Mrs. Hudson had promised me that Becky was with her and safe. For once, I didn't have to be worried about her and Jack—

My thought broke and snapped off, my heart lurching at the sight of a figure in the street below: dark hair, straight shoulders, lean, hard-muscled frame.

No. No, no, no.

Jack shouldn't be anywhere *near* here.

He was, though. Even if I hadn't known his face as well as I knew my own, I would have recognized the slight unevenness of his gate as he walked down the street.

He was directly in front of the War Office. *Right* where he would be in the line of fire if Neville Teale set off an explosion or fired a weapon or—

I gasped. Jack had stopped walking and was frowning up at one of the lampposts that lined the street.

I could almost feel a tangible snap as the missing pieces rose to the surface inside my mind, and then realization—the same realization that must have struck Jack—hit me with the force of an oncoming train.

"Pall Mall. That's *Pall Mall* out there!"

Holmes looked at me, brows raised. "Are we stating the obvious? Because if so, we are also in London. The earth, as Watson kindly informs me, orbits the sun, and—"

I interrupted. "There was a notice in the papers the other day. An announcement that the gas lighting on Pall Mall was to be shut down for the next week for supposedly routine repairs. Except what if they *weren't*?"

My memory served up the echo of Jack's words from days ago. *Not the kind of thing you'd say if everything actually is just normal routine.*

"What if there was sabotage of some kind, and the lighting company just didn't want to admit it—"

A mother leading a small boy of about four or five by the hand was just passing by the spot where Jack was standing.

My breathing hitched.

Even if I opened our window and shouted, I was too far away to be heard over the noise of the traffic.

"I have to go out there!"

I spun from the window, ready to run downstairs.

A burst of gunfire split the air, followed a second later by the roar of an explosion.

I whipped around and was just in time to see Jack dragging the mother and child with him as he dove behind the cover of a carriage parked at the side of the road.

The gas light he'd been studying was on fire, shattered glass and twisted metal fallen all around.

People were running in all directions, screaming, chunks of broken pavement were torn up, and at least three people were lying on the ground, bleeding—

"The gunpowder is inside the gas lights," I gasped. Threads of fear pulled inside me, tight to the point of snapping. "He's firing the machine gun at them, setting off the explosions. We need to get out there and—"

"And accomplish nothing but to add our own bodies to the other casualties?" Holmes said. He sounded calm— infuriatingly so—but he had a point. "The gunpowder did not explode on its own. He must have some sort of trigger- ing device—flint or metal that makes a spark when it's struck with a bullet—"

Another burst of gunfire interrupted him.

"The roof!" My pulse was drumming crazily, blood beating all the way out to the tips of my fingers.

Down in the street below, people were still screaming, horses were rearing as terrified pedestrians dove in front of them in the street.

I couldn't see Jack anymore. *Please still be alive.*

"Did Lestrade's men search the Diogenes roof?" I demanded.

Another sharp crack rent the air, followed by another explo- sion. I fought the urge to press my face against the window and scan for casualties.

Holmes was already in motion, moving towards the door. "There is a trapdoor in the upstairs attic, with a ladder—"

The rest of what he said was lost as his long strides carried him out of the room.

I raced to catch up with him, taking the stairs two at a time and arriving out of breath in a dimly lit, low-ceilinged attic.

Dust covers shrouded lumpy shapes of furniture all around. The air smelled of must and mothballs.

"There." Holmes pointed to a trapdoor in the ceiling just above our heads, with a ladder built into the wall leading up to the opening.

The door was closed, and I couldn't hear any sounds from up above, though that could have been because my heart was hammering too loudly for me to hear anything else.

Holmes set his hands against the sides of the ladder, but I stopped him.

"No. I should go up first."

Holmes turned to face me with his most ferocious glare. "Why? Because nearly dying once in a twenty-four-hour period is not quite achievement enough for you?"

"No. Because Neville is less likely to view me as an enemy or as an immediate threat. He obviously has a gun up there with him. If you try to go up or if we summon Lestrade's men to go up there after him, he could shoot you the moment you climb through the trapdoor. Or he could set off more of the gunpowder. People out there in the street will die."

More people.

I was forcing myself not to think about Jack or the fact that I had no idea whether he could have been hurt—or worse. But there had to be casualties already out there.

The noise from outside was fainter where we were, but I could still hear shouting and the sharp blasts of police whistles. Lestrade's men must be working to get the street cleared.

"And you believe you stand a better chance of persuading Teale to abandon his murderous intentions?"

"Maybe not. But I *do* think I stand a chance of getting him to talk to me."

Holmes frowned. "Why?"

He was asking the question honestly, I realized. He didn't like any part of the thought of sending me up there, but he had locked that emotional response down to consider the problem logically. He was genuinely asking for my opinion, ready to listen to what I would say.

It was encouraging and also utterly terrifying.

I spoke in a rapid undertone. "Everyone, even scoundrels and murderers, are heroes in their own minds, the starring performers in the story of their own lives. Neville has kept his secrets from everyone—his mother, his wife. He's effectively trapped himself up there on the roof, which means that I don't think he's planning on surviving this. But I think that will make him all the more eager to tell *someone* his side of the story."

My father's face was unreadable. "You are proposing to risk your life on the assumption that a deranged killer will not want to miss his chance at delivering the stirring Act III monologue."

I forced a smile. "As Shakespeare said, *all the world's a stage.*" I set my foot on the lowest rung of the ladder, then turned. "I'll distract him, try to turn his attention away from this trapdoor, if I can."

"At which point I will climb up and disarm him," Holmes finished for me.

He might not like the plan, but he was quick-witted enough to understand without my having to spell it out.

"Do you still have the gun you were carrying the other night?" I asked.

Holmes let his overcoat swing open, revealing the weapon in an inner pocket. "It evens the playing field somewhat. However, to get off an accurate shot, I will still need his attention diverted."

Otherwise, Neville could shoot Holmes before my father had the chance to aim his own weapon.

"I can do that."

We looked at each other a moment. I still couldn't read Holmes's expression, but if our minds really were anything alike, he was imagining all the ways in which this could go wrong.

"I shall never become accustomed to this," Holmes said at last. "Go, now. Before I am tempted to change my mind."

I gripped the rungs of the ladder.

For a moment, I wondered whether I should give Holmes some message for Jack—and Becky too. Just in case. But I couldn't think of what I would say, and with every second that ticked past, there was a greater chance of Neville setting off the rest of his bombs.

I started to climb.

CHAPTER 35

I reached the top of the ladder and set my hands against the surface of the trapdoor. It was hinged to swing outwards, which meant that I would have to be at least partly exposed to push it up and open.

The back of my neck crawled with awareness of how easy it would be for Neville to swing the Maxim around and shoot me the moment my head appeared.

The longer I waited, the greater chance that innocents would die.

I steadied myself with one hand on the uppermost rung of the ladder and shoved, sending the trapdoor flying open with a sharp bang as it hit the roof.

"Stop!"

I had ducked back down and couldn't see Neville, but his ragged shout came instantly. "Stop right there. Don't come up or I swear I'll shoot!"

"Neville?" My heart was beating hard enough to blur my vision, but I tried to speak calmly. "Neville, it's Lucy James. You remember, Susan's friend. Please, may I come up? I just want to talk to you."

Neville was still outside my line of sight, but I heard him moving—pacing, it sounded like. Then nothing. Silence.

"Neville?"

More silence. I counted to twenty, then levered myself up through the trapdoor.

The roof of the Diogenes was flat, surrounded by a low parapet. Neville was crouched at one end, his back against the parapet and the Maxim rifle mounted on its tripod beside him.

His face had been buried in his hands, but at my appearance, he jerked upright, instantly seizing hold of the machine gun and starting to pivot it towards me.

"Stay there!" he barked.

At least he was no longer aiming down at the street below.

I held my hands up. "I'm not armed. I told you, I just want to talk."

"Why should you want to talk to me?"

Neville's face was pale and twitching, his eyes ringed by dark circles and his hair wet with perspiration.

I drew in a breath. "I want to understand."

He hadn't yet shot me, which made me think perhaps I'd been right, and he did want to talk. "How did you come to hire Flint Bayles to steal weapons?"

"I had a friend who gambled away his fortune in one of Bayles' clubs." Neville's mouth twisted. "He shot himself when he couldn't afford to pay Bayles what he owned. Not in fear of a scandal, but in fear of what that man would do to him."

Having met Flint, I could believe it.

"Is that why you're doing all of this? To avenge your friend?"

Neville laughed, the sound ragged. "That was more of a side benefit." He glanced at the War Office. From up here, I could see that several windows at the front were broken, with chunks of bricks missing from the facade. If the building hadn't been evacuated, people inside would be hurt right now.

A scowl crossed Neville's face. "Why are they not running outside? I was going to wait until they ran outside, until *Lansdowne* ran outside, and then I was going to shoot him and watch him bleed to death in the street."

My pulse was jumping, cold fear traveling inch by inch down my spine. But I took a step closer to him. "I know you're a decent man, a good husband, a dutiful son. You wouldn't commit an act like this without reason."

Another police whistle sounded in the street below. Neville started to turn towards the noise.

All or nothing.

"Is it because of Manipur?" I asked.

Neville's head snapped around, his face going momentarily slack with shock. "How—"

I had to keep his attention. More than that, I had to both keep his attention *and* get him to turn so that he was no longer facing towards the trapdoor.

I edged slightly sideways, willing myself to make the movement look unstudied.

I felt as though I were balanced on a knife's edge, trying to walk across a pit of fire.

"How do you know about that?" Neville choked out.

"Your mother told me about your military record. She said that you had had trouble with your commanding officer. And that you were never meant to be a soldier. Was that the trouble?"

I took another half-step sideways. "That you aren't a killer by nature, but the army tried to make you into one?"

That was the way I had written the story inside my head. I could see the gentle, sensitive, bookish boy Mrs. Teale had spoken of suddenly snapping under threat of violence.

Neville, though, threw back his head and laughed—a grating, ugly sound. "My mother? My mother knows *nothing*."

"From what she said, it sounded as though your father was very hard on you."

"*Hard*?" Neville's hands shook on the butt of the rifle. "Hard? My father was heartless. Forever shouting at me, telling me that I was too soft, too weak. He swore he would make a man of me."

Neville's face darkened, his voice shaking with remembered rage. But at least he was no longer looking out at the street.

"He forced me into the army. Said that he would disown me if I refused." Neville dragged in a ragged breath. "He purchased my commission for me, and I became Captain Teale. I was shipped out to India. And then I met John."

Neville's chest was rising and falling so quickly he might have been running.

Oh. The story was completely different from the one I had mentally written.

"John?" I asked softly.

"Colonel Boynton. He was the commanding officer of my regiment. He was—" Neville's face twisted, his voice cutting off on a broken sound that was almost a sob.

He still had a grip on the Maxim, but raised one arm, dashing at his eyes with the heel of his free hand. "We were very careful, discreet. No one could know about the two of us. But somehow the general found out. Maybe one of the native serving boys saw something and thought he could make a few rupees by turning informant."

I stared at him, almost forgetting to keep edging my way towards the wall. "Do you mean General Pettigrew?" I asked.

"He was a monster!" Neville's voice rose to almost a shout. "A monster. I would have been court-martialed, but no one wanted the scandal. *Degenerates*. That was what Pettigrew called us. He said there was no place for a pair of degenerates in the Queen's army. So I was dismissed, discharged. And John—" Neville's voice broke again, then steadied, turning ragged with fury. "The general sent him off to die in Manipur. The *Senapati*, the local leader and the head of the rebellion, invited a few British officers into the palace, supposedly to negotiate. It was a trap. Everyone knew it was a trap. But General Pettigrew ordered John to go in there regardless. He was killed—murdered—just for having fallen in love."

I was nearly at the edge of the roof now. To keep speaking with me, Neville had pivoted slightly. But I didn't doubt that he would still see Holmes out of the corner of his eye if my father dared to climb up now.

Wait.

Disbelieving would be far too mild a word to describe my father's views on telepathy. But I tried to send him the silent message all the same while keeping my eyes on Neville.

"That's horrible," I said.

It was. It was a horrible, tragic story.

Neville's whole body was shaking now. "I came back to England, and I waited, biding my time, swearing that when the moment came, I would punish them—all of them, from Lord Lansdowne on down—for what happened to John. I researched firms of armaments and pretended to be an employee of the Venezuelan government and a potential buyer."

He laughed shortly, his teeth bared. There was cruelty in his face now, the kind of bitter cruelty that springs from the cruelest kind of loss. "No one actually knows what the official seals of Venezuela look like. I got information about their shipments and hired Flint to steal the weapons. And now I'm *ready*. Ready to take my revenge."

His gaze moved towards the street again. My heart contracted hard.

"It was a terrible injustice," I said, still trying to inject a measure of calm into my voice. "But all those people in the street down there? They had no part in it. They never wronged you or Colonel Boynton. Besides." I took another step towards Neville. "Colonel Boynton—John—loved you. Is this really what he would have wanted? For you to waste your life in plotting and executing revenge? Letting your heart grow so full of hatred and bitterness that you close yourself off to even the possibility of love?"

"*Love*?" A spasm twisted Neville's face, and he almost spat the word. "I don't want love! You know what love does? It crushes you, rips your heart to shreds, and then leaves you, broken and bleeding. Hatred is—"

A shot rang out, then another. Neville's body jerked. He cried out, and then crumpled to the ground, a pool of blood spreading across the ground under him.

Holmes finished climbing up through the trapdoor in the roof and came to stand next to me.

I let out a shaky breath, looking down at the fallen man. "Is he …"

"Certainly not." Holmes's breathing was slightly more rapid than normal, but he looked far more composed than I felt. "I try never to end lives unnecessarily, even those of insane murderers. I shot him in both arms, that is all."

On the ground, Neville gave a low groan.

Holmes's mouth tightened. "He will live to be tried for his crimes."

* * *

Pall Mall was still in an uproar when I emerged from the Diogenes back out on to the street. Police were working at clearing up the broken bricks and glass from the explosions, calming the hysterical, and assisting the injured.

Somewhere above me, police were also taking Neville into custody, after which he would be taken to the hospital wing of Holloway Prison. But at the moment—except to be thankful the danger was over—I hardly cared.

A greengrocer's stall had been turned into a temporary medical station, where those requiring treatment could receive care. I recognized one of the doctors working at bandaging cuts and checking patients for broken bones.

"Uncle John!" He must have received Becky's message and come to Pall Mall just in time to witness Neville setting off his bombs.

A wave of almost dizzying thankfulness swept through me that he hadn't been hurt.

Watson looked up from bandaging a cut on a young girl's arm. "Lucy! The officers on duty outside the Diogenes told me that you and Holmes were uninjured and were, in fact, the heroes of the day. As such"—he gave me a stern look—"I will overlook the fact that you are ignoring my prescription for several days of quiet rest."

I smiled slightly. "You know you never really expected me to heed that advice. Sound though it undoubtedly was."

Watson huffed into his mustache. "At any rate, you and Holmes appeared not to need me, so I thought I would make myself useful here."

He gestured around to the wounded being bandaged. Some who had already been treated were being helped into carriages to be driven away. Others, who clearly needed more extensive care, were lying on the ground, their heads pillowed on coats and cloaks, sacks of apples from the greengrocer's stall, and whatever else came to hand.

"Was anyone killed?" I asked.

Uncle John shook his head. "By the grace of God, no. We have several gunshot wounds, a few head injuries, cuts and abrasions, and a few broken bones, mostly suffered by people who were trampled in the panic. But no deaths."

I took what felt like my first full breath in the past half hour. "That is good news."

Uncle John wasn't the only doctor working amongst the wounded. Two more men, one elderly and grizzled, one fair-haired and younger, were treating the injured as well.

Uncle John followed my gaze. "They happened to be passing by and offered their medical expertise. It is heartening, is it not, how times like these bring out the best and finest side to human nature?"

I smiled at him. If I wasn't able to go quite as far as Uncle John's view, it was at least good to be reminded that human nature *had* a better side.

Then I stopped, my attention caught by a woman and child a short distance away. It was the same mother and small son Jack had dragged out of the way of the first blast, I was certain of it.

The boy's once white sailor suit was dusty and torn, and the mother had a few cuts and scrapes on her face and hands, but otherwise they seemed unharmed. I walked over to them.

"Excuse me."

The mother raised startled, slightly dazed eyes to my face. "Yes?"

The little boy was resting his head against his mother's shoulder and, at sight of me, his face quivered, as though he were trying to decide whether the situation called for tears.

"Hello." I smiled at him. "I just came over to see whether there were any *extremely* brave boys here who would like a badge for their courage?"

I had tied my hair back with a blue ribbon that morning. I pulled it free and knotted it loosely around the boy's chubby wrist. "There. That marks you as a hero."

The boy examined the ribbon seriously. "Like a soldier's medal?"

"Exactly like."

"Thank you." The mother gave me a tremulous smile.

"Do you need help getting home?" I asked.

"No." She shook her head, shifting the boy's weight in her arms. "A policeman came by a short while ago and said that transport was being organized. That's what we're waiting for."

I hesitated, then asked, "There was a young man with you earlier. When the first explosion struck?"

"Oh—oh yes." The woman tightened her grip on her son. "He stayed with us long enough to make sure that we were all right. But then he left to go and help others." She looked up and down the street. "I don't see him now, though." Her voice shook a little. "I would have liked to thank him again. If it hadn't been for him—" She stopped, her face paling, her eyes swimming with sudden tears.

"Are you asking about Constable Kelly?"

I looked up and realized that Uncle John had finished treating his patient and come to stand beside me.

"We owe him a great debt," Watson went on. "Apparently, at the same time that you were sending a message to Lestrade, he was speaking with the police commissioner himself. That is why the police forces were able to mobilize so quickly. They were already on their way here." Uncle John glanced at me. "Your minds must have been working along precisely the same lines. It is quite extraordinary, the way the two of you arrived at the identical conclusion, independently, and yet almost at the same time."

"Extraordinary," I echoed. Even I heard the hollowness in my tone.

Uncle John gave me a worried look. "Jack stayed to make sure that you were all right. I was with him when the news came down that you and Holmes were safe. But then Police Commissioner Bradford asked that Jack accompany him to make an official report as to what happened here. He could hardly refuse the request."

"No, he hardly could." I shut my eyes for a brief second, but then turned back to Uncle John. "You have other patients to treat, clearly. So tell me what I can do to help both you and them."

CHAPTER 36

I sat in the Baker Street sitting room, scowling at the patch of bright golden sunlight that was slanting through the window and onto the floor.

The one day in London when the weather was actually gloriously sunny and fine and, in my current frame of mind, I would have vastly preferred storm clouds, hail, and freezing rain.

The danger was over, I had given my statement to the police, and thanks to Uncle John, I wasn't even allowed on stage at the Savoy for the rest of the week. Mr. Harris had called in an understudy. Which left me with nowhere to go and nothing that I needed to do.

I heard the door to the street open, and a moment later Becky's footsteps clattering towards the kitchen. The door to the kitchen banged as it burst open, and then Becky's excited, piping voice reached me.

"Mrs. Hudson, it was *wonderful*! Mr. Holmes and I worked out exactly how Mr. Maskelyne made his assistant levitate—"

I hadn't spoken to Jack yet, but Mrs. Hudson had yesterday, briefly, while Uncle John and I were still helping in the aftermath of the explosions on Pall Mall. Jack was to be trapped in meetings with the police commissioner, the War Office, and probably every government official in between for most of today, at least, and had asked that we keep Becky with us for one more day.

Holmes had taken the opportunity to fulfill his promise of taking Becky back to the Egyptian Hall.

I heard his slower footsteps a moment later, but instead of going up the stairs to 221B, he paused outside my door, then knocked lightly.

"Come in."

Holmes opened the door and crossed to join me, taking the seat opposite mine without speaking.

One of the best things about my father's character was his complete disregard for social convention. No silence was ever awkward with him because it would never have crossed his mind to find it so, nor would it occur to him to fill such a silence with inane small talk.

"Did Neville somehow sabotage the gas lights on Pall Mall?" I asked at last.

"Indeed. Apparently the gas lines on the street were repeatedly damaged these last months. But the lighting company believed it would reflect badly on them if they reported the sabotage, so they kept the whole affair quiet. Mycroft is currently engaged in making various heads in their administration roll."

"And he planted the bomb in Mr. Dimitrios' attaché case?"

"We shall perhaps never know the truth. But I believe that we may assume so. I imagine he was the gardening enthusiast who sat next to Mr. Dimitrios on the train. He could have planted the bomb while Mr. Dimitrios slept."

We sat quiet for another few moments. Then Holmes shifted, crossing one leg over the other.

"From the fact that you are currently trying to incinerate that patch of sunlight with the sheer force of your glare, I deduce that you are less pleased than one might expect, considering you just captured a brutal killer and saved perhaps hundreds of lives."

I watched the dustman's cart roll by in the street outside the window, mops and chimney brushes rattling in their holders. "How much of Neville Teale's story did you overhear up there on the roof?"

"Nearly all of it. I was just below the trapdoor, and his voice carried quite clearly." I wasn't looking at him, but I could feel Holmes's gaze resting on me. "You are wondering to what extent Mr. Teale may be held accountable for his actions, given the father—and the society—that did what might be considered their sovereign best to break him."

"Something like that."

I didn't typically look to half-crazed murderers for romantic advice, but I could still hear the echo of Neville's voice. *Love leaves you broken and bleeding ...*

"Mr. Teale suffered both cruelty and injustice, of that there is no question." Holmes's voice was quiet, with the measured, precise calm that was so much a part of him. "However, other men suffer equal or still greater tragedies, live out similar stories, but they do not attempt to commit mass murder. At some point, we all must stand responsible for the choices we make."

For once I was grateful for Holmes's ability to cut past all emotion and personal bias and see straight to the heart of a matter. "True."

I could feel Holmes studying me again, and then he asked, "Did something of which I am as yet unaware occur at the Lansdowne House ball?"

I might have known Holmes would make that deduction.

"I think inhaling cyanide gas might be the part of the evening I remember most fondly."

"Descriptive, certainly," Holmes murmured, "but ultimately uninformative."

I finally turned away from the window to face him.

"Jack thinks that I view him as some sort of charity case, that I only want to be with him out of duty, or pity, or gratitude for his having saved your life."

My father pursed his lips. "I see."

My fingertips curled into my palms at the memory of Jack's words.

"As though—" I began.

Holmes held up one hand. "I do not for a moment believe Constable Kelly's assessment, so before you burst into a fiery and entirely unnecessary denial, will you allow me to say something?"

I could hear Becky and Mrs. Hudson talking in the kitchen. We probably had another few minutes before Becky came in to regale me with her account of the magic show too.

"Go ahead," I told Holmes.

Holmes leaned back in his chair. "Constable Kelly is self-disciplined to a fault and does not appear to me to have much experience in allowing others to share the burdens he carries. What he *does* possess, however, is a wealth of experience in having others abandon him in times of need. His father, whom he never even knew. His mother, who abandoned him to a childhood of fending for himself on the London streets." Holmes ticked the points off on his fingers. "Even the police force he has served with such courage and distinction was quick enough to believe him guilty of murder when he was framed for the crime last year."

My father paused, gray eyes regarding me steadily.

"So far, the life your young man has led would give him small reason to hope for loyalty—still less for unconditional love—from anyone he cares for."

I stared back at Holmes.

Usually, as Holmes himself sometimes said, he dealt in hard evidence, leaving the study of the human spirit and heart to Uncle John. But in this case—

"You're right," I said. "You're *completely* right. What do you think I ought to do?"

"As to that, I cannot say." Holmes smiled faintly. "Though based on my own experience, I should estimate that you are uniquely adept at crashing through an individual's defensive barriers." He was silent again, then leaned forward, covering my hand with his own just for a moment. "I can wish you the best of luck, however. And say with some authority that if you succeed in breaking through Constable Kelly's defenses, then he is a lucky man."

Tears clogged my throat and stung my eyes, making Holmes's familiar sharp features blur.

"I love you, Father."

I'd never called Holmes *father* before—not once since we first met. But now the words came out as naturally as though I'd been saying them my whole life.

"I—" Holmes coughed. "Yes, well, I ... feel the same."

In another man, the words might have been stiff and cold. In Sherlock Holmes, they were nothing short of miraculous.

"I will go and see Jack," I said.

Probably. *Maybe.* Despite everything, a twist of nervousness still went through me at the thought.

I looked at the clock over the mantel, then stood up. "First, though, I have to go and help Susan Teale deal with a blackmailer."

CHAPTER 37

I lifted the knocker of 33 Saint James Square and rapped on the door. Behind me, bright sunlight shone on the William III statue and gilded the last of the autumn leaves, turning the trees in St. James Park to fiery bursts of orange and gold.

The door opened, and I almost startled at the sight of Mrs. Teale instead of the stately butler from my last visit.

Susan appeared at the older woman's side. "I've told Mrs. Teale everything," she said. "The full truth."

Both women looked exhausted, as though they had hardly slept last night. Mrs. Teale's eyes were red and puffy-looking, her face drawn with sadness. But there was also an odd look of almost peace about her as well, as though the worst had happened and she no longer had anything to fear.

"I should have known," she said. "I am too old to believe in miracles." She wiped her eyes. "I blame myself. I tried to stand up to Neville's father, to protect Neville from him as much as I could. But I must have failed him so dreadfully."

"You didn't fail." Susan turned to her mother-in-law. "You did everything you could. And I believe that Neville loved you, in his way."

"Thank you, my dear." Mrs. Teale's smile was still terribly sad, but she straightened. "I have already been in touch with our family solicitor. Neville shall have the best legal counsel that can be found. And now, are we ready to depart?"

I glanced at Susan. We had exchanged messages this morning, making plans for this meeting, but none of them had included Mrs. Teale's presence.

"Are you sure that's wise—" I began.

"Certainly." Mrs. Teale squared her shoulders, her mild, gentle face unaccustomedly set with determination. "I should like a word with this man, and I intend to have it."

I couldn't argue with her, not after everything she had suffered in the past twenty-four hours.

Besides, I had spent a significant fraction of my life in places most people told me a lady had no business to be.

"Let's go, then."

* * *

We circled around the park, approaching the William III statue from the rear, and stopped just behind a clump of bushes that partially screened us from view.

The bell of St. James Church had just tolled three o'clock and, through a gap in the branches before us, I could see a man's figure crouching at the base of the statue and appearing to hunt for something in the dead leaves and dirt.

"Hello, Fred."

Susan stepped out into the open.

The man jolted upright, whirling to face her with an audible gasp of surprise.

Fred Miller was as Susan had described him: a man of something under average height, slim, and with dark hair and eyes. His eyes were a little too closely set together, his mouth slightly too full and red for a man's. But he might have been considered on the handsome side, if not for the ugly look that twisted his face at sight of Susan.

"Where's the money?" he demanded. "You know what I'll do—"

Mrs. Teale stepped forward to join Susan and interrupted, holding herself very straight.

"My daughter-in-law will not be paying you a single penny more than the money you have shamefully extracted from her already."

Fred's face tightened with brief shock at the sight of the older woman, but then his lips drew back in a sneer. "You're willing to face a scandal—"

Mrs. Teale interrupted again, speaking with brisk authority. "Young man, any scandal which you may stir up quite frankly pales in comparison to the one which we are about to face. Nor do I care a single jot for what my friends, neighbors, or society at large may say. My daughter-in-law was married to my son quite legally which, in the eyes of the law, makes her son or daughter my grandchild, and I intend to see that the child is born and raised as such."

Susan was staring at Mrs. Teale, open-mouthed, her expression nearly as astonished as Fred Miller's.

Mrs. Teale went on. "I intend to provide my son with the best legal defense possible and see him through his trial." A flash of pain crossed her face, but then was banished as she squared her jaw with determination once again. "Then provided Susan agrees, we shall close the house here and travel, somewhere our names have never been heard of. I have always had a fancy to see Canada. What do you think, Susan?"

"I think …" Susan still looked nearly too stunned to speak, but she managed to say, unsteadily, "I think I would love that."

Fred Miller's face twisted with fury, and with a sudden cry he lunged at Susan, something glinting in his hand.

A knife.

Even as the horrified realization flashed through me, I was already moving, darting to knock Susan out of the way of the blade, blocking Miller's strike with an upraised arm.

A red-hot burst of pain slashed across my palm, but I scarcely felt it.

I kicked Miller's leg out from under him, then spun, elbowing him hard in the stomach. He doubled over, and I hit him across the back of the neck, sending him to the ground.

He collapsed, groaning and shaking his head, dazed. "What—"

I drew the service revolver I had borrowed from Uncle John and leveled it at Miller, aiming between his eyes.

"That's enough." Blood was trickling down my wrist, but I ignored it and flicked the safety catch off, focusing on Miller. "You are going to turn around right now, walk away, and never bother either of these two women again. Otherwise I will make it my personal mission to make life very, *very* unpleasant for you. Is that clear?"

Miller blinked, and I could see the flash of anger brightening his eyes. But then his gaze focused on the revolver, and his face blanched.

He scrambled to his feet and ran, crashing away through the bushes.

"Lucy, your hand—" Susan began.

"It's not too bad." I hadn't yet examined the damage, but I didn't want to worry either Susan or Mrs. Teale. "I'll ask Mr. Holmes to organize someone to keep watch outside your house for the next few days, just in case Fred comes back. But I doubt you'll see him again."

Like most bullies, Fred Miller struck me as fundamentally a coward. Once he realized he could no longer terrorize his victims, he wouldn't contact them again.

Susan stepped forward and hugged me. "Thank you, Lucy."

"You don't have to thank me. I'm so sorry, Susan."

Susan shook her head, though. "If you mean you're sorry about Neville, you shouldn't be. You didn't make his choices for him. Besides, I would rather know the truth. That's always better than living a lie." She looked pale and shaken, but she looked at Mrs. Teale and smiled just a little. "We can still have a family: the baby and Mrs. Teale and I. That was always the best part about being married to Neville, really."

I hugged her again. "Then I'm glad for you, Susan. I wish the three of you the absolute best of everything."

CHAPTER 38

I stood at the door of Jack's lodgings while all around me early evening fog crawled across St. Giles, shrouding the crowded tenements, the garish advertisements plastered on the sides of buildings, the vendors' carts, and the barefoot children playing in the street.

I hadn't entirely planned on coming here tonight, directly after leaving Susan and Mrs. Teale, but fate had apparently decided the matter for me. The knife cut running across my palm was deeper than I had first thought. My glove was a total loss; I had already discarded it in a trash heap on the way here, and the handkerchief I'd wrapped across the wound was nearly saturated.

My hand was throbbing, my stomach was twisting with nerves—and also I was going to start dripping blood all over Jack's front doorstep if I didn't just get it over with and knock.

I raised my left hand and rapped on the door.

Jack opened it a moment later. "Lucy—" he began. Then he stopped, shock crossing his gaze at sight of the bloodied makeshift bandage around my hand. "What happened?"

He must have just recently gotten back from his meetings with the police commissioner and other officials. His dark hair was more neatly combed than usual, and he still wore his dark blue uniform trousers, though he'd taken off the blue coat and wore only a plain cotton shirt.

My heart was beating too hard and too fast. I worked at not letting my voice shake as I answered.

"Do you mind if I come in? I can't go back to Baker Street like this. I'd frighten Becky for one thing and, for another, I'll give Uncle John heart failure if I turn up covered in blood. He still hasn't recovered from my accidentally breathing in cyanide gas the night of the ball."

"Of course."

Jack stepped partly aside, though he glanced up and down the street as I moved past him into the front room. "Are we expecting any visitors?"

"No, there's no danger anymore."

I sat down at the Kellys' rickety wooden table and unwrapped the handkerchief. I'd been hurt in the course of investigations before, but I still had to fight against wincing at sight of the deep gash that ran from my smallest finger all the way to the base of my thumb.

I started to wipe away the blood with a clean patch on the handkerchief, awkward with my left hand.

"Here, let me." Jack took down a clean cloth and a jug of water from the kitchen shelf and carefully swabbed at the cut. "I don't think you need to have it stitched," he said after a moment. "But it's going to hurt for a few days, no question. How'd this happen?"

At the time, I hadn't really been frightened. Men like Fred Miller weren't worth being afraid of. But now a slight shiver of reaction went through me.

"I was helping Susan Teale face down her blackmailer. It seemed like the least I could do, considering I'd just gotten her husband arrested for murder. Unfortunately, the encounter didn't go entirely as planned. Well, we frightened Miller off successfully, I just wasn't expecting him to have a knife."

Jack was still holding my hand in both of his. His expression darkened. "I'm sorry. I should have been there."

"Yes, well." I took the folded square of cotton from him and pressed it over the gash. "You have quite a number of things to be sorry for, including nearly getting yourself killed on Pall Mall yesterday. Although since at least two people probably owe you their lives, I suppose I can overlook that. My getting hurt, though, is not your fault. If you think I view you as a hard-luck charity case, then *you're* not allowed to see my safety as some sort of responsibility of yours."

"Lucy—" Jack started.

My pulse was still beating hectically. I drew in a breath and looked up at him. "Have you ever wished that I would stop speaking with an American accent? Or that I would stop performing at the Savoy? Or not take part in my father's investigations? Or, I don't know, have blond hair instead of brown?"

Confusion crossed Jack's face. "Of course not. I've never wanted you to change."

"But it's inconceivable that I might not wish anything were different about you?"

It *was* inconceivable to him. I could see it in Jack's expression: He couldn't even imagine my feeling that way.

The knowledge made my heart twist up inside me, tight to the point of breaking for him. But I kept speaking. *Uniquely adept at breaking down defensive walls*, Holmes had said.

"My whole life I've been on my own. When I was Becky's age, I used to dress up as a boy and sneak out to fight clubs because I wanted to be strong enough to take care of myself. No one else was going to do it for me. I used to tell myself that it was an adventure, being alone in the world. That I was lucky not to have a family to disapprove of anything I did and that I could just be free, without having to answer to anyone else. That's true, in a way. But it's also ... lonely. You have to know that as well as I do."

I stopped. Jack had a fire burning in the grate, and it crackled in the momentary stillness.

"What I really wanted more than anything was just to ... to *belong*," I said. "To have someone I fit with, someone who saw me and understood me, just the way I am. I sing on stage, and I love it, but that's not the whole of my life, and I can't ever be completely honest with the people I know from the theater, not really, because they only see that part of me. And my father ... I've more or less strong-armed my way into his life, and I do believe he's glad now to have me. Maybe he's even the better for it. But he's Sherlock Holmes. He never *needed* me. It's not as though there was some Lucy James-shaped hole in his existence that he was just waiting for me to come and fill. I—" I stopped again. "Do you remember last spring? When we took Becky to the zoo for her birthday?"

It had been a Saturday in early April, when Jack had a rare day off duty and I hadn't needed to be at any performances at the Savoy. We'd wandered around the zoological gardens in

Regent's Park all afternoon, eating roasted peanuts and watching Becky's eyes get big and round at the sight of the lions and camels and elephants.

"I remember—" My throat hurt with the effort not to let my voice waver. "I remember looking around, not at the animals, but at all the other families there, and thinking that for the first time in my entire life, I had people *I* belonged with too. I wasn't just Lucy James, making my way alone in the world. I had a family. At least, it felt that way."

Tears pricked behind my eyes, but I blinked hard and kept going. "I'm not sorry to have joined in my father's investigations, but ever since I started working with him, I've realized how many people lie or cheat or are dishonest in at least some area of their lives. I sometimes feel as though I can't trust anyone, and it's as though I'm going through life just … just constantly holding my breath."

I'd been staring down at the gash across my palm as I spoke, but I forced myself to raise my head and look at Jack. "I never feel that way with you, though, because I *know* that I can trust you. You're honest and courageous and honorable and you understand the way I think. And you always do the right thing, even when it costs you—"

The firelight ran golden across the lean, hard planes of Jack's face. I couldn't read his expression, but he opened his mouth as though he were going to say something.

"No." I shook my head fiercely. I'd been in mortal danger twice—three times, if you counted Fred Miller—in the last two days. I wasn't going to wait to say this anymore.

Besides, telling Jack how I felt couldn't possibly be any worse than looking out the Diogenes windows and watching as he was nearly killed by a machine gun.

"No. I'm going to talk, and you just listen," I said. "I don't care. I don't care what you've done in the past before you joined the police force. I don't care whether you talk like an East-end Londoner or earn a constable's salary for the rest of your life. I don't care whether you walk with a limp or—what was the other thing? Oh yes, poetry. Do you honestly think I want anyone to rhyme *love* and *stars above* or compare my eyes to woodland pools? Because if so, you really need to choose another line of work."

I stopped, the breath painful in my chest.

"Do you know what I keep having nightmares about? Yes, it's being trapped in the ice house at Lansdowne House, but it's more than that. That night, when I came up with the plan to use myself as bait, I thought you might be dying. You'd been shot, and you'd lost so much blood, and Uncle John didn't even know whether you would ever wake up—" I swallowed hard. "It wasn't that I *wanted* to die too, but a part of me wasn't sure I cared whether I kept living if you were gone."

Even the memory dragged a shiver through me.

"That's what I keep dreaming about. It changes. Sometimes in the dream Arkwright shoots me, and I know I'm dying. Sometimes Holmes and Uncle John arrive to save me, but then they tell me that you're dead. Either way, one of us dies, and I never get the chance to say—" My throat threatened to close off, but I kept going. I had almost lost the chance to say this. "To tell you that I love you."

I finally stopped speaking.

It would have been a perfect moment for Jack to say something. If we'd been on stage in a Gilbert and Sullivan operetta version of this conversation, he would say that he loved me too. But he was just staring at me, his expression hovering somewhere between shock and stunned disbelief.

I closed my eyes. "You're not wrong about one thing, though. There are people who would view you as an inferior, because of where you come from. *I* wouldn't care. But there would probably be people who were rude or condescending or unpleasant, whether consciously or otherwise. I'd hate it for you, but I wouldn't always be able to stop it."

I looked up at Jack, feeling the tears that had been threatening start to spill out all over again. "And I can't really give you any good reason why you should be willing to put up with that, except that you would be with me. But maybe that wouldn't be enough—"

Jack caught me up, pulling me against him as though he couldn't wait another single second, stopping my words as his lips found mine. I could feel his heart pounding crazily under my palms, his hands trembling a little as his fingers slid along my jaw to cup my face, tugging me closer still.

"I love you." He drew back just enough to look down at me, his voice husky, almost shaking. "God, I am so in love with you, Lucy James, you have no idea."

Epilogue

The Victoria Embankment was almost deserted at this early hour of the morning, gray curls of mist still rising from the river. Jack looked up at the imposing brick towers of New Scotland Yard, outlined against the city skyline and overlooking the Thames.

"I don't think I can do this."

In the pale morning light, his expression had a tense, set look I'd almost never seen in him before.

I took his arm. "So you'll jump in front of a loaded rifle, tackle a man armed with both a sword and a knife, and risk being exploded by a bomb or killed by machine-gun fire, but the idea of taking a written examination is ... terrifying?"

"Exactly."

I started walking again, pulling him with me. "Did I ever tell you about first time I had to perform on stage? I was absolutely terrified. It wasn't just ordinary stage fright, I thought I was literally going to die of sheer dread, except that it occurred to me that was a truly idiotic way to end one's life."

Jack raised an eyebrow at me. "You?"

"I know, it sounds nothing like me, does it? That's why it was so frightening. It completely surprised even me. And everyone says to picture the audience in their underwear before you go on stage, but you can take it from me that doesn't help at all. Because, really, who in their right mind feels *more* comfortable imagining themselves in a room with a lot of total strangers wearing nothing but their underclothing?"

Jack gave me a slightly wild look. "Is this supposed to be helping?"

I stopped in the shadow of one of the famous dolphin lamp-posts that lined the embankment. "What if I tried this?"

I tugged Jack's head down so that I could kiss him, long and lingering.

He was at least smiling when I drew back. "I'm not sure. Maybe you should try it again."

I laced my fingers with his. "You can do this, I know you can. And I want it for you because I know it's important to you. But apart from how you feel and what you want for your career, it doesn't matter to me whether you pass the sergeants' examination or not. You could decide to be an itinerant toothbrush salesman and it wouldn't make me love you any less or make any difference in how much I want to be with you."

Jack shook his head slowly, his dark eyes wondering. "I'll never understand why." He stopped, swallowing. "Lucy, there's something I need to say—or ask you—"

"Yes."

Jack gave a half-laugh. "I had to fall in love with Sherlock Holmes's daughter. How do you even know what I was going to say?"

I shrugged. "I could probably make something up about logical deductions. But really, I was just hoping—"

"Wait a second." Jack interrupted, looking at me as though he'd only just fully realized what I had said. "Did you actually just say—" He stopped his voice catching as though he'd just run out of air. "*Yes?*"

"I suppose that depends. Did *you* actually just ask me to marry you?"

Jack smiled, one-sided. "I thought I'd get all the terrifying hurdles over with in one day. Besides, if I don't ask you soon, Becky will probably lose all patience and ask you for me. She has a whole list of reasons why you should accept."

I laughed. "Is that what you made her promise not to talk to me about? I'll have to ask her to tell me the whole list sometime. I'd love to hear it."

"I think item number one was: Jack is very nice and also sometimes he brings home penny candy when he gets paid on Fridays."

Jack took my hand, his smile fading. "Lucy, you know how much I love you. I think I've loved you ever since you ordered me to say *moving* again."

"I did what?" For the moment, I had no idea what he was talking about.

"You'd just woken up on the side of the road, you'd been attacked and you couldn't even remember who you were. I said you had to be moving along, and straight off you were trying to work out the difference in our accents and deduce that you were American."

"I remember now. As I recall, you thought I was either drunk, crazy, or a street walker."

Jack shook his head. "I didn't. Not really. I kept trying to fit you into some sort of ordinary, familiar pattern, something I could easily identify. But at the same time, I knew there was something different about you, that I'd never met anyone like you before. You were so beautiful and fierce and smart." He touched my cheek, grazing my skin with the warmth of his fingers and making me shiver. "I had no idea who you were or whether I'd ever even see you again, and I'd already fallen in love with you."

"Really?"

"My forgetting to breathe every time I looked at you didn't give it away?" Jack looked down at me, pulling me a little closer. "Lucy, I'll never think I'm good enough for you, but I do swear that I'll love you with my whole heart and soul for the rest of my life." He took a breath. "Will you marry me?"

All around us, the city was coming to life: barges floating by on the great river, a hint of golden autumn sun beginning to break through the clouds.

My eyes were filling with tears, but happy ones. I smiled. "Does my earlier answer count?"

"I wouldn't mind hearing it again."

"Oh really? Well then." I stood on tiptoe, kissing him, then drawing back just enough that I could murmur the words against his lips. "Yes. Yes, I would love to marry you."

THE END

A NOTE OF THANKS TO OUR READERS, AND SOME NEWS

Thank you for reading this continuation of the *Sherlock Holmes and Lucy James Mystery Series*.

If you've enjoyed the story, we would very much appreciate your going to the page where you bought the book and uploading a quick review. As you probably know, reviews make a big difference!

The other five adventures in the series are currently available in e-book, paperback and audiobook formats: *The Last Moriarty*, *The Wilhelm Conspiracy*, *Remember, Remember*, *The Jubilee Problem* and the prequel to the series, *The Crown Jewel Mystery*.

In 2018, be sure to watch for *The Return of the Ripper*, and a collection of Sherlock and Lucy short stories!

About the Authors

 Anna Elliott is the author of the *Twilight of Avalon* trilogy, and *The Pride and Prejudice Chronicles*. She was delighted to lend a hand in giving the character of Lucy James her own voice, firstly because she loves Sherlock Holmes as much as her father, Charles Veley, and second because it almost never happens that someone with a dilemma shouts, "Quick, we need an author of historical fiction!" She lives in Maryland with her husband and three children.

 Charles Veley is the author of the first two books in this series of fresh Sherlock Holmes adventures. He is thrilled to be contributing to the series, and delighted beyond words to be collaborating with Anna Elliott.

Made in the USA
Las Vegas, NV
29 February 2024